My Sister's Keeper

By Mavis Applewater

I

ISBN 0-9744121-8-X
First Printing 2004
Cover art and design by
Linda Callahan
Author's photo taken by
A. J. Hoffman

Published by:
Dare to Dream Publishing
A Division of Limitless Corporation
Lexington, South Carolina 29073

Find us on the World Wide Web
http://www.limitlessd2d.net

Printed in the United States of America and the UK by

Lightning Source, Inc.

III

Acknowledgements

There are just so many people to thank and I always forget someone, so forgive me if I don't mention you. I would like to thank those nice folks at the Bards' Village, the Bards' Corner, the Royal Academy of Bards, the Athenaeum and the members of YoMavis for supporting my work the past few years. I would also like to thank Lisa Raymond, Joanne Forbes-Murphy, Sam and Anne, Toni Zulig, Theresa Nezwicki, Heather Stewart, David Bryson, Rae Haggerty, Chris Ewen and Allison Christiansen for their unwavering support. Also, I send a very special thank you to my family for putting up with my many quirks over the years. I especially thank my Mother who brought me into this world and Ma Bardsley who accepted me as her daughter-in-law.

<u>Dedication</u>

As always, this is for Heather.

CHAPTER ONE

Jenny Jacobs sat at the bar staring at the Amaretto Sour sitting in front of her. She ran her fingers through her long black hair as she contemplated just how she found herself in this situation once again. Was there some defect in her personality that led her lovers to betray her? From the first to the last, each one had brought her nothing but misery. "Officer," a cool Southern drawl greeted her. Her blue eyes blinked as she looked up at her friend Claire. Right now she didn't know if she needed to talk to Claire, her friend, or Claire, the bartender.

"Life is funny." Jenny sighed as she began to play with the cherry in her cocktail.

"It's a freaking' riot," Claire scoffed. "You going to tell me what you're doing here in the middle of the day?"

"What's your honest opinion of Wendy?" Jenny inquired absently as she continued to chase the elusive maraschino cherry with her drinking straw.

"Oh no," Claire groaned as she brushed her long curly auburn locks out of her gray eyes. "Jenny, you're a friend, but right now I'm going to give you some friendly advice from your bartender. Don't ask your friends what they really think about your girlfriend unless you're truly prepared for the answer."

"I guess that answers that," Jenny groaned as she pushed her drink aside. "I don't want that."

"What do you want?" Claire inquired seriously.

"Such an easy question." Jenny pondered it for a moment. "I

1

want to be in love."

"Aren't you?" Claire prodded as she removed the cocktail and wiped down the bar.

"No," Jenny confessed. It was not only the first time she admitted it to another person it was also the first time she'd admitted it to herself. "Why is it so hard to find the right person?"

Claire rolled her eyes in desperation as she placed a new cocktail down in front of Jenny. "Are you going to tell me what happened with Wendy?" the bartender persisted.

"What's this?" Jenny asked quizzically as she held the red concoction up.

"Something I think you need," Claire responded with a smirk. Jenny arched a single eyebrow before taking a sip.

"It's good," she responded, her body and heart still feeling the numbness from what had happened earlier. "What do I owe you?" she inquired.

"It's on me," Claire responded with a shrug.

"Isn't that illegal?" Jenny taunted her.

"Call a cop," Claire snorted in delight.

For the first time in hours the dark-haired policewoman found herself smiling. "So what is this? Another Claire original?" Jenny inquired in a vain attempt to avoid talking about why she was really there.

"Like I said, it's something that you need," Claire responded archly as she leaned seductively over the bar. "It's a Red-Headed Slut."

Jenny spit out the sip she'd just taken and started to choke. The tears rolled down her face as she laughed heartily. "Thanks. I needed that," Jenny sputtered as she wiped the tears from her crystal blue eyes.

"See?" Claire exclaimed in an innocent tone.

"How does your girlfriend put up with you?" Jenny chuckled.

"She puts up with me just fine," Claire teased. "It's my southern charm."

"Uh huh," Jenny scoffed as Claire cleaned up the mess she'd made.

"So?" Claire said with a determined look as she slapped the rag onto the bar.

Jenny sighed, knowing that she wasn't going to get off the hook very easily. She just gave in rather than fighting against it. After all, she knew deep down one of the reasons she'd wandered into the Comet that afternoon was to tell someone how her life had just collapsed around her. "I was working a detail this morning. You know, directing traffic around some roadwork."

"That must have sucked in this weather," Claire said in concern.

Jenny's body still ached from standing out in the heavy rain all morning. "Yeah, it did. But the money for those jobs is so good and Wendy's always pointing out that I don't make enough money," Jenny explained.

"I've noticed," Claire spat out bitterly. "I've also noticed that she never picks up the check."

"No, she doesn't," Jenny, replied thoughtfully. "Well, the construction crew finally gave up on the weather breaking, and I thought 'great'. Instead of directing traffic around a big hole in the ground I could spend my day off snuggling with my girlfriend. I even stopped and bought her flowers. I noticed the white Lexus out in front of building but didn't really think anything about it."

"Oh no," Claire groaned. Jenny simply nodded.

"She didn't even seem bothered when I walked in on the two of them," Jenny spat out through clenched teeth. She took a calming breath and another sip of her drink. Then she took another breath and another sip before she felt the effects of the alcohol. She was fighting against the image of her lover wrapped up in another woman's arms. *'In our bed!'* her mind hissed. "Do you know the girl she's been seeing?" Jenny finally worked up her courage to ask.

"I've heard rumors," Claire admitted reluctantly.

"And you didn't tell me?" Jenny squeaked out in surprise.

"Jenny, I'm your friend," Claire said firmly. "If you really want to know what your friends think about Wendy, I'll tell you." Jenny nodded mutely as she braced herself for what she was about to hear. "We don't like her. She's loud, obnoxious, and always trying to pry information out of people. Basically, for the past three years we all thought that the bleached blonde was just using you for your paycheck."

"Don't hold back," Jenny choked.

3

"I won't," Claire stated firmly. "Now I'd heard rumors about her and some rich lawyer. But for all I knew, that's what they were - rumors. I didn't feel comfortable stirring up trouble between the two of you, even if I think she is a money grubbing whore."

"So she's moving up the food chain," Jenny groaned.

"Jenny girl, she was going to leave you whether or not you caught her in the act," Claire explained calmly. "She probably just would have lied about there being someone else." Jenny sat there allowing the truth in her friend's words to sink into her mind. "Which brings us back to what I asked you earlier," Claire continued. "What do you want?"

Jenny pondered the thought for a moment. Her answer was still the same. "I want to be in love," she responded honestly. "But there's a catch. I want to be deeply in love with someone who is just as deeply in love with me."

"Sounds easy, doesn't it?" Claire said thoughtfully as she patted Jenny's hand.

"It isn't," Jenny grumbled as she stared at her empty glass, wondering when she'd drunk the contents. "For now I'll just have to settle for another Red-Headed Slut."

Jenny continued to drink, knowing that it wouldn't solve anything. The alcohol would only succeed in temporarily numbing her pain. She talked Claire's ear off about how she'd had to check into a motel and buy some clothing so she could go out. It was illegal for a cop to wear their uniform in an establishment that sold alcohol if she wasn't there on business. So with only her uniform stored back at the fleabag motel, the clothing on her back, and her almost-maxed-out credit cards, she found herself wallowing in misery with only her friend and several Red-Headed Sluts to keep her company.

As evening approached Claire made a call to Jenny's partner, Nuru. The tall ebony beauty joined her sometime later in the evening to commiserate. "You didn't like her either, did you?" Jenny inquired at one point in a drunken slur.

"Wendy?" Nuru inquired. "Nope, I thought she was an obnoxious wench."

"Why didn't anyone tell me?" Jenny whined.

"Because you kept ranting about how in love you were," Nuru

pointed out. "Not that any of us believed you."

Jenny blinked her crystal blue eyes as she tried to focus on her partner and friend. She was always telling the woman that she was a dead ringer for Lisa Leslie, the star player for the LA Sparks. "I really did love Lizzie," Jenny muttered in defense.

"Who?" Claire and Nuru inquired in confusion.

"She's a mess," a strong voice said from behind her. Jenny spun around to see Kate standing there. Kate was also on the force and one of the girls, but not just any girl. Jenny was always a little uncomfortable talking about her love life around Kate. Not because Kate was straight, but because she had known the tall Sergeant since she was a kid. Jenny weaved slightly on her barstool, trying to recall what she'd just said.

"Who's Lizzie?" Claire demanded curiously as Kate took a seat at the bar.

"My kid sister," Kate responded in confusion. "She and Jacobs were best friends growing up."

"Oh!" Nuru and Claire choked out in unison.

"I need another drink," Jenny hiccupped. Her mind was reeling. *Tell me I didn't say anything about Lizzie. Please not now. And not with Kate sitting right here. Why does it always come back to her? It's the damn rain. She always comes back to me when it's raining.* Jenny's mind was spinning as her body began to protest against the unfamiliar invasion of alcohol.

"So where's your sister now?" Claire pried as Jenny flashed her a pleading look. "Married?"

"Kind of." Kate laughed.

Please don't, Jenny silently pleaded as Nuru and Claire stared at Kate. "What do you mean 'kind of'?" Nuru pushed as Jenny's inner voice begged for this moment to end.

"She's a nun," Kate responded flatly.

"Kill me now," Jenny muttered softly as she watched Claire and Nuru's jaws drop. She knew that they had put two and two together. *Yup, that's right, girls. The great love of my life is a nun,* her inner voice tormented her.

"You sure know how to pick them," Nuru muttered softly so only Jenny could hear her.

"Claire, another Red-Headed Slut," Jenny demanded as Claire

flashed her a stern look.

"Maybe you need to switch to coffee," Claire suggested.

"I think she's right," Kate said firmly. "Speaking of red-headed sluts, what happened with Wendy that's driven you to drink Jagermeister?"

"Jagermeister?" Jenny choked out. "You've been giving me Jagermeister? I don't drink Jagermeister. It is disgusting."

"You don't normally drink," Claire pointed out.

"Fine. Give me a designer water and you two can fill the Sarge in on my pathetic life," Jenny conceded.

Jenny settled back as her friends filled Kate in on what the gold digging whore (their words, not hers) had done. Jenny sipped her five-dollar bottle of water, stared out the window of the bar, and watched the rain. *It's always the rain. And it always brings back Lizzie, my first love. She was my first kiss; in fact, she's been my first everything. Why does she still haunt me? She was my first, and at the time I had no doubt that she would be my last. But what does a teenager know? The beginning of our end, that's the problem. Neither of us was the cause; it was the damn rain.*

The memories suddenly flooded Jenny as she stared out the window, allowing them to overcome her. Jenny could still recall every detail like it was yesterday. The way they'd rushed into the Carrington's kitchen. How their clothing was dripping wet after being caught in the sudden downpour. Of course they hadn't noticed the sudden change in weather at first. They'd been too busy making out in Jenny's little Datsun. It was the sudden clap of thunder that had jolted them out of one another's arms. They'd rushed through the rain and into the kitchen.

Jenny could still recall the taste of Lizzie's lips as she kissed her gently. *'Why didn't we stop with just one kiss?'* she wondered. *'Because we were seventeen and in love,'* her inner voice responded. One kiss was never enough for them. Their tongues and hands began to explore one another as Lizzie backed her up against the refrigerator.

Warmth suffused Jenny's body as the sensations of that long ago evening filled her entire being. No longer aware of her surroundings, Jenny simply allowed the memory to replay as it had so many times before.

Hungrily Lizzie kissed her neck and then playfully tugged on her earlobe with her teeth. Jenny's body pulsated as Lizzie's hips moved up against her thigh. "You know what the rain does to me," Lizzie whispered in that voice that drove Jenny over the edge.

"How could I forget?" Jenny moaned in response. She could feel her body shaking with desire as Lizzie began to unbutton her blouse. Without hesitation the petite blonde unhooked her bra. Lizzie looked up lovingly as she cupped Jenny's full breasts.

"I love it when you wear a bra that hooks in the front," Lizzie said in a breathy tone.

"That's why I wear them," Jenny moaned as the palms of Lizzie's hands brushed against her aching nipples.

Lizzie smiled up at her. There was no mistaking the look of desire in that smoky green haze. The blonde leaned in and captured one of Jenny's breasts in her mouth. Her tongue moved slowly at first as her other hand continued to play with her other breast. A gasp escaped from Jenny's lips as Lizzie began to suckle her nipple eagerly.

Another clap of thunder jolted Jenny back to the reality of their situation. Lizzie wasn't fazed as her hand drifted from Jenny's breast and down her body. Lizzie quickly freed the button of Jenny's blue jeans. "Wait . . . your parents," Jenny protested as she captured her lover's wandering hand.

Lizzie looked up at her with a mischievous grin. "Bingo night," she said softly. "They won't be back for hours." Jenny could only smile as she released her lover's hand. Lizzie sank to her knees and turned her attention to the zipper of Jenny's Levis. Jenny inhaled deeply as she placed her hands on her lover's shoulders. Lizzie slowly lowered the zipper. Jenny's heart raced as her lover's breath caressed her stomach. Lizzie tugged urgently on the wet denim until she had pulled it down to Jenny's ankles. Lizzie slid her hands up Jenny's calves and thighs, placing gentle kisses along the way. Having worked her way up Jenny's long legs, Lizzie then lowered Jenny's panties.

Jenny stood there, leaning against the refrigerator with her pants and underwear pooled around her ankles. Her wanting exposed to Lizzie's wanting. She opened herself to her lover, sighing deeply as Lizzie took her into her mouth.

Far too caught up in the moment, they failed to hear the front door opening and closing. Jenny's eyes fluttered shut as her lover feasted upon her. She reeled as her lover's tongue entered her. Her heart pounded so loudly that she never heard the heavy footsteps of Lizzie's mother approaching the kitchen. They did however hear her high-pitched scream. Jenny had never seen anyone that angry before in her life.

"Mary Elizabeth Frances Carrington! What in the name of God are you doing?" Jenny panicked as she saw the veins bulging in Mrs. Carrington's neck.

Lizzie jumped to her feet, placing herself between her mother and her lover. Jenny thought it was strange that the small girl was protecting her as she quickly pulled up her pants and underwear. "Sinners!" Mrs. Carrington screamed as she struck Lizzie across the face. Jenny tried to move to stop her, but Lizzie continued to block her. The small blonde managed to hold her back as her mother continued to scream.

"Filthy whores," Mrs. Carrington growled as she grabbed Lizzie by her long blonde hair and yanked her away from Jenny. The small angry woman struck Lizzie soundly in the head before Jenny could stop her. The blow was so severe that Lizzie fell to the floor, bleeding. Jenny rushed to Lizzie's side and wrapped her frightened lover up in her arms. Mrs. Carrington continued her assault as she began to kick the fallen girl.

"You're insane," Jenny screamed as she tried to push the crazed woman away from her lover. "Stop it!" she screamed as she shielded Lizzie's body with her own.

Mrs. Carrington was like a rabid dog as she tried to beat both girls. Jenny kept screaming for her to stop as she tried to lift Lizzie to her feet. "Get out of my house," Mrs. Carrington bellowed in a tone that frightened Jenny to her core. The tall girl tried desperately to pull Lizzie up. She had to get her lover out of there. Somehow she had to get her to safety. "Get out! Get out!" Mrs. Carrington screamed as the veins in her neck bulged, looking as if they might burst at any moment.

"Get out of this house, you filthy slut," Mrs. Carrington continued as Jenny somehow managed to get Lizzie to her feet. The *physical assault had ended but Jenny knew that Mrs. Carrington was still volatile as she kept screaming for Jenny to leave. Both she and Lizzie were crying as Jenny held her tightly against her body.*

"Go. I'll take care of this," Lizzie pleaded with her.

"No," Jenny fumed. "Come with me."

"I can fix this," Lizzie pleaded. "If you stay, she'll only get angrier. Please, Jenny, you have to leave." Lizzie pushed her away. Jenny was confused by the frightened pleading look Lizzie gave her. "It will be okay," Lizzie promised her.

At that moment Jenny made the worst decision in her life - she trusted Lizzie. She left her lover behind as Mrs. Carrington's screams burned in her ears. Jenny was just about ready to run back when she heard Lizzie yelling back at her mother, "Shut up! I love her." Somehow hearing Lizzie defend their love gave Jenny the confidence to trust that Lizzie knew what she was doing.

A clap of thunder stirred Jenny out of her painful memories. *'I never should have left you, Lizzie,'* Jenny thought bitterly at the memory of the last time she'd spoken to her first love. She had had enough for one day. Between the harsh memories and Wendy's betrayal she just wanted to go to bed and forget about everything. Jenny stumbled as she tried to stand. The rush of alcohol she'd consumed hit her hard.

"Hold on there," Nuru said as she reached out to steady her. "Where do you think you're going?"

"Tired," Jenny muttered as the room began to spin.

That was Jenny's last conscious thought before she woke up the next morning. If she could find the guy with the jackhammer that was pounding on her head, she was going to shoot the little bastard and then she would really hurt him. Her blue eyes opened slowly as the wave of nausea hit her. She couldn't for the life of her understand where she was. The day before seeped slowly back to her. *'This isn't the hotel,'* she said silently. She looked around the strange living room as best she could without lifting her head. She did notice that she was lying on a futon. She peeked under the blankets that were covering her to discover that she was completely naked.

As she contemplated her surroundings she wondered why her

mouth felt like a wad of cotton. "Damn Red-Headed Sluts," she grumbled as her head pounded.

"Most people say good morning," a hauntingly familiar voice, offered lightly.

Jenny lifted her head and was greeted by a sharp pain. She sat up, allowing the blanket to fall just below her breasts. She couldn't believe what she was seeing. Or rather, whom she saw. She was sitting in an oversized chair underneath a window. It was still raining outside. Somehow that made the image of her seems more like one of her dreams. She had her legs draped over an arm of the chair and a book in her lap. She was dressed in a faded pair of jeans and a sleeveless white shirt. She looked the same and yet different. Older and her hair was blonder. The long locks were gone, replaced by a short cut that fell neatly on her tanned neck.

Nevertheless, those blue green eyes that always reminded Jenny of the ocean were still the same. Jenny blushed as she pulled the blanket up to cover her half-naked body. "Lizzie?" she stammered in disbelief.

CHAPTER TWO

The normally stoic policewoman felt like the walls of reality were crashing down around her. The blonde that was watching her seemed to be amused by her strife. Jenny rubbed her aching temples. "Lizzie?" she repeated in disbelief. There was no mistaking those emerald eyes. Jenny just couldn't clear her muddled mind enough to understand why she was sitting in front of her.

Jenny rubbed her eyes and then blinked several times in hopes that the vision of her former lover would simply vanish. "Hello, Jenny," the blonde finally offered in a flat even tone.

"Oh my God," Jenny muttered in agony.

"No, just on the payroll," the nun quipped. Jenny growled as the blonde shrugged. "How are you feeling?" Lizzie inquired nonchalantly.

"Oh, just peachy," Jenny moaned in agony. "Other than the feeling someone is tap dancing on my head, and I'm naked in a strange apartment. How did I get naked by the way?" Jenny arched one eyebrow as she stared at the nun.

"I helped you to bed," the blonde explained calmly. Lizzie's casual attitude was really starting to annoy the hung over brunette. There was something else that was eating away at her; it was a familiar sensation pulsating through her body. "Kate brought you home," Lizzie explained as if it was an everyday occurrence. "She said something about the place where you were staying not being fit for the rats living there. She grabbed your stuff. It's over there." Lizzie pointed to a corner of the tiny living room where Jenny's few meager belongings were laying.

"And you're here because . . ." Jenny choked out, fighting against the wave of nausea that was swelling up inside her.

"I'm visiting my sister," she responded flatly.

Jenny was fighting with the physical and emotional hell that was suddenly thrust upon her. Kate entered the living room dressed in her uniform. "Lizzie?" Kate called to her sibling brightly. Lizzie put her book down, seemingly unaware that her sister was speaking to her. Her emerald eyes flashed in sudden recognition.

"Sorry, I'm not used to being called that," she apologized.

"Oh yeah, what are you called these days?" Jenny grumbled from the futon. *'Why do I care what's she's called? I just need to get out of here,'* Jenny fumed internally.

Lizzie smiled at her and Jenny's heart skipped a beat. Jenny shifted uncomfortably as her childhood friend smiled at her with a sweet innocence. Jenny struggled to turn onto her side without losing any of the blankets. "Sister Rachel," she explained finally.

"I am so not calling you that," Jenny griped bitterly.

"It's alive," Kate shouted at Jenny. The blonde covered her mouth quickly with her hand. Jenny knew she was fighting to stop the laughter from escaping. They both knew that Kate was intentionally torturing Jenny. Unable to withstand the pounding in her head, Jenny buried her head in her lap as she groaned once again.

Kate was laughing boisterously, sending sharp pains throughout Jenny's body. "Please stop," Jenny begged. She felt the bile rising steadily. She lifted her head, which somehow opened the floodgates. She tried to stand but her long legs refused to cooperate. "Oh no," Lizzie gasped. Out of the corner of her eye Jenny saw the petite blonde jump up and move quickly towards her. Before she knew what was happening she was assisted to her feet and led quickly into another room. Somewhere in the fog that had settled around her mind, she was aware that she was in a bathroom.

She heard the lid and seat being lifted with a loud clank. Then gently but rapidly she was placed on her knees in front of the toilet. As she lost what little there was in her stomach, she felt Lizzie pull her hair back. She released the poison from her system while she silently vowed never to drink again. She could feel Lizzie rubbing her back gently. The blonde's breath caressed her ear. "Ssh. It's going to be all right," Lizzie reassured her.

"I've heard that before," Jenny spat out. She could feel Lizzie's body tense behind her. The blonde took a deep breath before she stood and began to run some water in the sink. As Jenny leaned back, Lizzie offered her a cool damp washcloth.

She wiped her face, enjoying the feel of the cool cloth on her skin. Lizzie settled down behind her once again and wrapped a comforting arm around her. Jenny was too tired and emotionally spent to pull away. Jenny glanced down at the tanned muscular arm that held her steady. She ran her fingers along the simple gold band on Lizzie's ring finger. "What's this?" she inquired absently.

"Bride of Christ," Lizzie responded simply. Jenny snatched her hand away as if it had been burned.

"You have got to be kidding me!" Jenny snapped as she tried to stand. For some unexplainable reason the thought irritated Jenny.

"Not yet," Lizzie said softly as she held her in place. Jenny wanted to run. "You might get sick again," Lizzie explained. Jenny didn't know if Lizzie had grown stronger over the years or if she was as helpless as she felt.

Jenny gave into the feeling of Lizzie holding her as her head pounded and her stomach churned. Her body was a mess and her mind muddled as she relaxed into the feel of Lizzie's arms wrapped around her body. Neither of them spoke as Jenny's eyes fluttered shut and Lizzie rubbed her back in a soothing manner.

"Did you ever tell Kate what happened?" Jenny finally managed to ask. Kate had pestered Jenny over the years to tell her what had happened that night.

"No," Lizzie said flatly. "I . . . couldn't," Lizzie stammered slightly. Jenny wondered if Lizzie was now ashamed of the love that they had once shared. "The only explanation I've offered to her over the years was that I got caught."

'I guess that answers that question,' Jenny thought bitterly as they remained kneeling in the cramped little bathroom. The awkward silence hanging around them became unbearable for Jenny to endure. "I need to get up," she stated gruffly. Lizzie's hands moved to her hips.

Jenny jerked away, wrapping the blanket around her more

tightly. Lizzie stepped back without a word and allowed Jenny to walk out of the bathroom on her own. Jenny staggered as she made her way over to the corner where her clothes were piled. "And just what do you think you're doing?" Kate's voice inquired harshly.

"I have to get ready for my shift," Jenny mumbled as her legs trembled.

"I've already called you in," Kate explained.

Jenny turned to see her superior's body tense as she glared at the brunette. "You're grounded," Kate stated firmly. Jenny opened her mouth to speak and then snapped it shut quickly. Kate Carrington was not someone you wanted angry with you.

"Yes, ma'am," Jenny responded dutifully.

"Stop being such a bully, Kate," Lizzie chastised her older sibling as she entered the room. "But she is right, Jenny. You really should rest today." Jenny looked at the two of them standing side by side. In many ways the siblings were very similar and yet quite different. The hair and eyes were the same; the height was the first thing that set them apart. Kate stood about five foot seven while Lizzie was a good four inches shorter. Of course Lizzie would insist that it was only two inches.

Despite the same powerful bodies, their personalities were as different as night and day. Kate was straight forward and no nonsense. Lizzie, at least the Lizzie Jenny remembered, never thought things through and just seemed to bounce through life, somehow always managing to land on her feet. That was until that rainy night so long ago when both of their lives changed forever.

"I'm not being a bully," Kate protested as she glared down at her sister. Lizzie snorted indignantly as she swatted Kate playfully. "Brat," Kate retorted. "Look, I have to get going. Why don't the two of you spend the day getting reacquainted? Jenny, I'll leave you the keys to my truck just in case you feel well enough to get some belongings from your old place."

"Sarge, I . . . Uhm," Jenny stammered as the realization that her life with Wendy was over.

"I'm sorry," Kate apologized softly. "I just assumed that you would end things with her."

Jenny didn't miss the surprised expression on Lizzie's face. This isn't the way she'd wanted the two of them to meet again. She had hoped that they would both be happy and healthy. She never expected Lizzie to reenter her life at its lowest point with her looking and feeling like something the cat dragged in from the rain. "I am," Jenny stated confidently.

"Then I suggest you go get what's yours before Wendy changes the locks," Kate stated with conviction. "I don't trust her."

"Now there's an understatement," Jenny grumbled as she flopped down on the sofa.

"The truck is parked on the next block," Kate explained quickly. "Lizzie can help you out; just don't let her drive."

"Why not?" Lizzie whined.

"You don't have a driver's license," Kate snapped.

"And?" Lizzie teased as Kate growled.

"I have to go," Kate said as she hugged her sister. "Jenny, you're welcome to crash here as long as you need to. And don't let her drive," she added sternly. "And you call Dad to let him know that you're back in the country."

"I need his number," Lizzie said softly. "And I'll call Mom as well."

"Screw Mom," Kate spat out. "Dad's number is in my address book on the dresser in my bedroom."

"Kate, you really should try and make peace with Mom," Lizzie offered in a compassionate tone.

Jenny's mind was reeling. *'How could you defend that woman?'* she screamed internally.

"Maybe I would if I knew what really happened," Kate argued. "I bet you know," Kate said, turning to Jenny.

"I need to take a shower," Jenny muttered in discomfort. She turned and made her way unsteadily back to the bathroom.

"Coward," Kate called after her.

Jenny could hear the two women arguing even after she closed the bathroom door tightly. Jenny tried to block out the sound as she turned on the water full blast. She stepped into the shower and allowed the water to fully encompass her. As the hot water caressed her body, Jenny allowed her mind to wander. Kate was right and wrong about what Jenny knew. Jenny knew that Lizzie had been sent away the day after Mrs. Carrington had caught them making love. It had taken her weeks to find out that small piece of information. She also knew deep in her heart that she should never have left without Lizzie that night.

Lizzie had asked her to leave with the reassurance that everything would be all right. In the end nothing was ever the same. Lizzie was sent away a few days before the two of them were scheduled to begin their senior year of high school. Lizzie, as Jenny would discover in the lonely weeks that passed, had been unceremoniously shipped off to a convent school in Minnesota. She had to hand it to Mrs. Carrington; the woman certainly took care of things quickly.

Jenny's first love had been literally ripped from her arms, yet the devastating event wasn't what finally destroyed their love for one another. No, Jenny's first heartbreak came later.

For weeks after their separation all Jenny could do, when she wasn't crying uncontrollably, was to mope around. Jenny couldn't help herself; it was as if a part of her had died. She managed to find out the name of the school Lizzie had been sent to. She wrote to her lover every day. All of her letters were returned unopened with the words 'Return To Sender' boldly stamped across them. She knew that it was the nuns that were keeping her heartfelt words from her lover. Perhaps that's why she still had a chip on her shoulder where the clergy was concerned.

Jenny kept writing in the desperate hope that Christian charity would kick in or just that somebody would simply get careless. It never happened. Jenny's parents were at a loss as what to do with their desperately unhappy child. Since they were clueless as to just why Jenny was so depressed, they tried everything to cheer her up. Finally, in an attempt to shake her out of her funk, they forced her to attend the school's annual Halloween dance.

Jenny now understood the logic behind what they had done. But when she was seventeen she was convinced that her parents were the meanest people on earth. Her mother tried to explain that perhaps being around her friends would help her deal with her best friend moving away.

An added thorn in Jenny's side was that her parents insisted that she attend the dance with Robby Ventnor. Robby had lived directly across the street from Jenny her entire life. Her parents thought he was a nice young man. Jenny thought he was an arrogant blockhead. Robby wasn't a bad guy; he was just Robby. Eventually the Jacobs wore down their stubborn daughter's resistance and she agreed to go.

All and all, attending the dance was a huge mistake. Jenny had bounced out of her depression to find herself completely miserable. It became very clear that Robby viewed himself as her escort for the evening. To Jenny, Robby was nothing more than a friend with a car. For the life of her she couldn't fathom how he thought it was a date. He asked her to go, and she refused. Then when her parents insisted she attend the dance, she asked if she could catch a ride with him.

Jenny never understood the mind of a teenaged boy. How did 'can I catch a ride with you' translate into 'I like you'? Robby kept trying to get her to dance and to put his arm around her in a possessive manner. The last straw came when Robby asked if she would pose with him for a picture. Just as one of his jock friends snapped the picture, he planted a sloppy kiss on her lips.

Enraged and somewhat grossed out, Jenny stormed out of the high school gym. As she walked the three miles back to her house, she cursed Robby and herself. She was angry with herself for not seeing Robby's attitude coming; he had been chasing her since puberty. Now Lizzie was no longer around to act as a well-needed buffer.

Robby stood about the same height as Jenny, and with his dark looks, was certainly a catch. Jenny never found him interesting. He and Lizzie mixed like oil and water from the very beginning. Robby was constantly trying to push Lizzie out of the way to get closer to Jenny. Lizzie to her credit pushed right back.

As time passed Jenny continued writing her unanswered letters to Lizzie. She lay awake at night, remembering each erotic encounter the two girls had shared during their all-to-brief courtship. When Lizzie failed to return home for Thanksgiving, Jenny felt herself sliding back into her depression. The only thing that kept her going was the knowledge that Lizzie would most certainly return for Christmas.

When Christmas came and went with no sign of Lizzie, Jenny was almost devastated. Somehow she gathered up enough courage to promise herself that she just needed to be patient and her lover would return to her. She would wait for Lizzie forever if need be. She didn't really think they would be apart for an eternity, just until the summer came. Then once they were out of high school they would be free to be together. Of course at seventeen, the time from December to June did seem like an eternity.

Valentine's Day was a sharp knife through her already fragile heart. The doorbell rang and Jenny was greeted by the delivery of a dozen roses. She assumed that they were from Lizzie. When she found Robby's name on the card, the pain overwhelmed her, and she threw the bouquet out the front door. Jenny rushed up the staircase to her bedroom and threw herself onto the bed, sobbing. She cried nonstop until it was time to return to school the following Monday. Her parents never asked about the flowers strewn across the front lawn.

The only bright spot during her dark days was that Jenny's grades soared for the first time in her life. Her parents were more than pleased with her new academic success until she remarked, 'No big deal. There's nothing to do but study.' The Jacobs' concern grew, and they started pushing Jenny to go out and socialize. She refused.

By the time spring had arrived in the little town of Haven, Jenny hadn't seen her lover in almost nine months. She couldn't endure the hell any longer. She saved her money and concocted what she considered to be the perfect plan that would finally reunite her with her lover. She told her loving parents that she was going on the class trip to the White Mountains. She even went so far as to have them sign a permission slip for the trip.

Her parents were ecstatic and happily signed the form, thankful that their brooding child was finally excited about something. On the day her classmates were on a bus heading north, Jenny drove to Logan Airport. She took the first flight out of Boston. She flew to St. Louis first. To this day she didn't understand why you needed to fly past your destination to get to where you are going. She endured a short stopover in Chicago. The roundabout journey only added to her excitement and nervousness.

Finally she arrived in the Twin Cities. From there she had to take a cab to the train station. It was an arduous journey that drained her energy and savings. But she was bolstered by the knowledge that at the end of the road Lizzie would be waiting for her - Lizzie with her strawberry blonde hair and emerald eyes that twinkled with tiny flecks of blue when she was excited about something. The thought of her lover was the only thing that kept Jenny going. Lizzie was worth the risk and the challenge. To Jenny, Lizzie was worth sacrificing everything.

While she rode on the train to Fairbanks she couldn't help but smile at how proud Lizzie would be. At the Fairbanks station she took yet another taxi since she had no idea how far the school was. She still recalled how the driver kept reassuring her that he would get her to St. Mathews before curfew.

Once Jenny arrived at the campus with the twenty-foot stone wall, she impressed herself with her detective skills. She found a far too perky nun and explained that she was Mary Catherine Carrington, Lizzie's sister and that she wanted to surprise her. She used Kate's name just to be on the safe side. The nun instructed Jenny on how to find Lizzie's dormitory.

Jenny waited outside the dorm, hiding in the shadows until she could slip in with a large group of girls. She scrunched down so not to be noticed by the nun sitting at the front desk. Between her height and lack of school uniform, she stood out. Fortunately the nun seemed to be close a century in age and failed to notice her. The seventeen-year-old roamed from floor to floor, searching for Lizzie's name on one of the doors. Finally she found it.

She stood there for a moment and ran her fingers across the nameplate - 'Mary Elizabeth Carrington'. Jenny's fingertips tingled from simply touching her lover's name. Unable to hold her excitement in any longer, she threw open the door. Nothing could have prepared her for what she discovered on the other side.

Both of them were naked as they sprung up from the bed. The faceless redhead that still haunted Jenny's dreams to this day wrapped her arm around Lizzie. 'How dare she touch my Lizzie?' her mind screamed as Lizzie just stared at her blankly. Jenny still didn't know if it was shock or guilt she saw in Lizzie's eyes. "Beth, do you know her?" the redhead asked in a jealous tone.

Jenny felt her heart shatter, and once again something deep inside of her died. She clenched her jaw defiantly before spinning *around. She stormed back down the hallway, leaving the door open in her wake. Somewhere behind her she heard the door slamming. 'Don't look back,' she told herself repeatedly as she walked out into the cool night air to face the long trek back to the train station.*

When Jenny returned to Massachusetts her parents were livid. With all of the transfers, she arrived home a day late. The Jacobs were normally kind tolerant parents. Yet discovering that their only child had hopped a plane for the Midwest instead of hiking with her classmates broke down their normally calm demeanor. Jenny was grounded for the rest of her natural life.

Of course she was sprung from her exile in time to attend the prom. Jenny already existed in a self-imposed exile. Being kept locked in the house seemed pointless. Even Jenny had to admit that she had to return to the land of the living. The Jacobs granted their permission for Jenny to attend the prom if she promised not to leave the state. To this day Jenny still smiled at her father's lighthearted consent. Jenny attended the prom with Robby.

Much to her surprise Jenny enjoyed the event and seeing all of her classmates dressed up. For the first time in a very long time she didn't feel like an outsider. Perhaps that is why she dated Robby for the rest of the summer. She even slept with him in a vain attempt to return to the straight and narrow. The effort failed to expel her demons. For her there seemed to be no cure. So when it came time for college, she ended the relationship.

Robby was brokenhearted and begged her for another chance. Jenny was firm and even tried to remain friends with him. But his constant visits and pleas for her to come back to him finally wore her down and she was forced to tell him to leave her alone. In the end they ended up being awkward acquaintances.

Jenny stepped out of the shower and began to dry herself off. Seventeen years had passed since she had last seen Lizzie Carrington and now she was forced to relive the pain. She emerged from the bathroom wrapped in only a towel. "I've put some coffee on," Lizzie said. Jenny turned to see the nun with her back to her, fumbling in the kitchen.

"Sorry I took so long," Jenny apologized as she looked through her meager pile of clothing. "The shower felt so good that I didn't want to get out."

"I know what you mean, "Lizzie said and then she squeaked.

Jenny turned to see Lizzie standing in the kitchen, which was just a small space off the living room. The blonde's eyes were bulging and her features had become flushed. "Are you all right?" Jenny inquired as she tried to understand what was wrong with Lizzie.

"Dandy," Lizzie choked out as she quickly turned away.

Jenny looked down at her appearance and realized that she was clad only in a very small towel. At first she assumed that Lizzie was embarrassed by her state of undress. Still there was something else lingering in the blonde's eyes and it wasn't embarrassment, to Jenny it looked more like desire. 'Interesting,' Jenny's mind processed.

"Kate said you could borrow some of her clothes," Lizzie explained while keeping her back to Jenny.

The policewoman entered the kitchen, noticing that the blonde was gripping the kitchen counter tightly. "You okay there, Sparky?" Jenny whispered in her ear.

"You're still a brat," Lizzie grumbled as she turned to Jenny with a smirk. "The coffee's done. Why don't I get you something to wear?" she suggested.

"Thanks, since my uniform and the clothes I wore last night are all I have," Jenny grumbled bitterly.

Lizzie left and returned a short while later. Jenny accepted the sweats and T-shirt and returned to the bathroom. She changed quickly, trying to decide if she should say anything about Lizzie's reaction to seeing her body. When she emerged from the bathroom she found Lizzie on the telephone. She helped herself to another cup of coffee while the blonde chatted away.

"No, tonight sounds good, Dad," Lizzie continued. "I'll check with Kate." Lizzie waved to Jenny who was adding more sugar to her coffee. "No, I haven't talked to her yet." Lizzie's face saddened as the conversation continued.

Jenny lingered in the kitchen, not wanting to intrude. It was a small apartment and she really didn't have anywhere to disappear to. Once she heard Lizzie end the conversation, she stepped back into the living room.

"How's your dad?" Jenny inquired as she sat down next

21

Lizzie on the still unfolded futon.

"Good," Lizzie responded absently as she stared blankly at the cordless phone. "He's happy that I'm home." Jenny simply stared at the blonde who seemed to be fighting an internal battle. "I should call my mother," Lizzie stated finally.

Jenny could tell that Lizzie really didn't want to speak to her mother. She had also figured out by Kate's comments earlier and the fact that Lizzie needed to call her parents separately that they were no longer together. "I didn't know that they'd split up," Jenny offered in a comforting tone. Lizzie simply nodded in response. "I'm sorry," Jenny added, hoping to comfort the unhappy woman sitting next to her.

"Dad moved out while I was at St. Matthews," Lizzie explained in a distant voice. "Mom still lives in the old house up in Haven. Dad lives here in town. They're not divorced because you know Mom's so religious."

"I've kind of noticed that about your mother," Jenny retorted bitterly.

Lizzie stared blankly at the telephone as they sat side by side. "Speaking of parents," Jenny finally broke the silence, "I really should give mine a call. I'm going to need to store my stuff up there until I find a new place." Lizzie handed Jenny the receiver.

Jenny dialed her mother and discovered that she was in court. She tried her father next. Both her parents were lawyers and sometimes it was difficult to track them down. "Hey, Dad." Jenny smiled into the telephone when she heard her father answer. Lizzie lay down beside Jenny and stared up at the ceiling.

"What's wrong?" her father inquired frantically.

"Nothing," Jenny reassured him. Both of her parents supported her career choice, yet they worried just the same. "Well, not what you're thinking," Jenny explained. "Wendy and I split up."

"Oh?" her father inquired carefully. "Is this permanent?"

"Yes," Jenny responded, firmly unaware that her hand was caressing Lizzie's stomach.

"Good," Jerome Jacobs said.

"So you didn't like her either?" Jenny grumbled.

"No," her father responded flatly. 'Do you want to talk about

22

what happened?"

"Not right now," Jenny sighed. "Look, can I store some of my stuff in the garage? I'm going to be staying with a friend until I relocate."

"Why is Wendy getting the apartment?" her father groused. "You lived there first."

"She can have it." Jenny groaned as she felt Lizzie's thumb brush the back of her hand. "I'm not ready to talk about this yet, Dad." She didn't have the heart to tell her father that she never wanted to set foot in her old apartment ever again after finding Wendy in their bed with another woman.

"Okay," he responded in a comforting tone. "Do you need any help moving?"

"No," Jenny said with a shy smile as she looked down at her and Lizzie's hands. "Kate Carrington is lending me her truck. In fact, I'll be staying with her for a couple of days."

"Good to know you'll be in safe hands," Jerome said with relief. "Kate was always a good kid. Maybe you can find out about Lizzie?"

"Funny that you should mention her." Jenny laughed as Lizzie lifted her head and smiled. Unconsciously their fingers became entwined. "You'll never guess who's helping me move."

"No?" her father gasped.

"Yes," Jenny teased.

"Are you okay seeing her again after everything that happened?" her father asked in concern.

"I . . . Uhm." Jenny hesitated, uncertain of just how she felt. A part of her was instantly relaxing into the familiarity of Lizzie's presence and another was screaming for her to run. "I don't know," Jenny finally responded honestly. Lizzie gave her hand a gentle squeeze, seeming to understand her confusion without knowing what she and her father were discussing. "Look, I'll be by today or tomorrow. I couldn't get hold of Mom. Could you tell her what's going on?"

"Sure, baby," Jerome reassured her.

"You can reach me on my cell," Jenny added. "I love you."

"I love you too," her father responded sincerely.

Jenny ended the phone call feeling much better than she had at the start of the day. Except that her head was still throbbing and she was curled up next to her ex-lover. "I've always liked your parents," Lizzie murmured.

"Yeah, they're okay," Jenny teased as she set the phone down next to the cup of coffee she'd abandoned earlier. Lizzie chuckled lightly at the comment.

Jenny lay down next to Lizzie, still holding her hand tightly, and sighed contentedly. Jenny studied her former lover's profile as Lizzie stared up at the ceiling. "When did you cut your hair?" she inquired thoughtfully.

"Years ago," Lizzie responded casually. "Actually I had to shave my head when I first entered the order."

"You what?" Jenny gasped.

"The order I entered is very conservative. No pride or vanity is permitted," Lizzie said with smile. "I looked quite ridiculous, but then so did everyone else. I think that's the point. After that I just kept it short. It's easier to deal with and more comfortable when I wear my habit. Plus in the places I've been living the heat is incredible."

"It looks great," Jenny said without thinking as she snuggled slightly closer to Lizzie.

"Thank you," Lizzie responded as she turned onto her side to face Jenny.

"So just where have you been living? You said you just got back into the country?" Jenny asked.

"For the last nine years I've been assigned to a lot of places," Lizzie explained thoughtfully. "El Salvador, Guatemala, Honduras, Nicaragua, and a few places I don't think exist on any map."

"Wow," Jenny responded in surprise. "What were you doing down there?" Lizzie smiled as she brushed a lock of hair out of Jenny's eyes.

"I'm a teacher," Lizzie explained with a shrug.

"Excuse me?" Jenny scoffed. "Miss 'hey Jenny let's skip class' is a teacher?"

"I know," Lizzie said as she crinkled her nose. "I love it."

Jenny hadn't realized that they'd moved closer together while they spoke. The familiarity of the situation was clouding her judgment as they stopped speaking and simply stared deeply into one another's eyes. Jenny's eyes drifted down to Lizzie's full lips. She hadn't realized what she was doing until their lips were almost touching. Jenny could feel Lizzie's breath on her skin. And suddenly it was gone. Lizzie pulled away and sat up as if nothing had happened.

CHAPTER THREE

Jenny was trying to understand what was going on in her still muddled mind. She'd just tried to kiss Lizzie! "I'm sorry," Jenny muttered as Lizzie busied herself in the kitchen. She didn't think that the blonde could hear her. "I must still be feeling the Jagermeister," she lied to herself.

"You should try to eat something," Lizzie said as she stepped out of the kitchen. "Do I want to know what Jagermeister is?"

Jenny's face paled at the mere thought of food. "I don't think so," the policewoman choked. Lizzie leaned against the doorframe with her arms folded across her chest staring out the living room window. Jenny leaned back against the wall and watched the rain falling. She didn't want to talk about the closeness the two women had just shared or about the past. Jenny felt numb and she didn't want to think about any of it. The constant patter of the rain wouldn't allow her the freedom to just shut out her memories. The rain had brought them together and had driven them apart.

Despite all of the turmoil she now had to face she would never regret that night. It had permanently etched a memory in her mind that she vowed to take to her grave. It had all begun that morning when they were barely sixteen. The two girls had just passed their learner's permit tests. They'd decided to celebrate with breakfast at Dante's, the local diner. Despite the fact that it still wasn't quite noon, the teenagers had passed on having the usual breakfast fare and had settled on hot fudge sundaes instead.

Being typical teenage girls they chatted endlessly about their future. They planned to save their money and buy a car together, not realizing that their parents would never go for the idea. All they could understand was that soon they would be able to drive. Haven was a small town where the only hot spot was Dante's. They couldn't wait to break the barriers and escape.

While they devoured their ice cream Jenny couldn't help but steal shy looks at her best friend. Lizzie and she had known one another since kindergarten. They'd met at the local park. Jenny had been sitting in the sandbox and Robby had been pouring sand over her head. The tiny dark-haired child was crying for her mother who was off with another parent. Suddenly a small blonde girl stomped over and punched Robby right in the face. Lizzie was her hero from that moment on.

Unfortunately her violent actions caused a flurry of activity from the other parents. Jenny managed to explain to her mother that the blonde had saved her from Robby's evil clutches. And the two girls had been joined at the hip from that moment on. They joined the brownies together, got caught smoking behind the gym, and almost every weekend of their short lives had slept at one or the other's home. They would spend all day at school together and then the moment they got off the school bus, they would rush to the telephone to call each other. Jenny could still hear her father asking what they could possibly have left to say to each other.

The only problem was that for Jenny things were beginning to change in the most confusing fashion. Somewhere around the time Jenny's height shot up, her body started reacting in the oddest way when she was around her best friend. Jenny didn't understand what was happening to her. Now when she would hug Lizzie her body felt a strange stirring inside of her.

They started holding hands like they'd done when they were little. Only now it felt different, and the teenagers were careful not to do it when anyone else was around. At the time Jenny couldn't understand what these strange new feelings meant. All she knew was that she was suddenly craving more. It was an unexplainable feeling that would suddenly overcome her. She couldn't understand just what else she desired from her friend, or why she would become jealous if Lizzie spent her time with anyone else.

28

Her emotions had been tearing her apart, and she came up with the idea of buying a car together. Somehow she felt the newfound freedom would give them more time together. Jenny could still recall how her stomach clenched as she watched Lizzie lick the ice cream from her spoon. It was one of those times when she felt the uncontrollable urge to kiss Lizzie. She never understood where the idea had come from. It was the same fiery emotion that would surge up from deep inside of her that made her want to touch Lizzie.

Being typical teenagers they spent the rest of their day just walking around and talking. They were so wrapped up in doing nothing that they lost track of the time. When night began to fall they headed to the Jacobs' home. When the rain started they didn't care. They began to push and shove one another as they splashed in the puddles. They were young and didn't have a care in the world. The only problem was that Jenny's body would tingle whenever Lizzie brushed against her.

By the time they entered Jenny's home, her body was trembling and it wasn't from the rain. "Where are the folks?" the small blonde inquired.

"They went to some kind of fund raiser; they won't be back for hours," Jenny answered as the two of them raced up the staircase to her bedroom. "We're drenched," Jenny remarked. "I may never be dry again," she teased as she felt the strange dampness gathering in her jeans.

"I know," Lizzie, answered brightly as she brushed back her long blonde hair. "We really should get out of these wet clothes and dry off."

Jenny had swallowed hard as she watched Lizzie pull her shirt over her head. She couldn't stop herself from watching Lizzie as she tossed the shirt onto a chair. It wasn't the first time they'd gotten undressed in front of one another; it was the strange pulsation coursing through Jenny's body that made this night different. Jenny's heart was racing as Lizzie stood there in her bra and jeans. The only light in the room came from the small table lamp sitting beside her bed. The sight of Lizzie's half-naked body sent Jenny into a panic. She was thankful for the darkness that hid her in the shadows, knowing that her face had turned a deep shade of crimson.

29

"I'll get some towels," she managed to stammer out.

Jenny's body failed to move as she watched Lizzie reach behind her back and unhook her bra. The site of her best friend's firm full breasts swaying slightly was too much for the tall brunette to withstand. Jenny forced herself out of the room and into the bathroom. Luckily for Jenny she had her own bathroom off her bedroom. As she braced herself against the wall, she wondered if Lizzie would simply leave if she cowered in there long enough.

"Fat chance," she muttered to herself. If only she could stop shaking. At the time she hadn't understood why she was acting like a coward. She only knew that she had to somehow gain control over herself. She wasn't certain of just what it was that she was afraid of. It wasn't Lizzie. She was frightening herself. She was terrified. If Lizzie found out what she was thinking, she would lose the blonde forever.

Finally Jenny regained a modicum of self-control, grabbed a handful of clean towels, and stepped bravely out of the bathroom. She found Lizzie bent over, wrestling with the wet laces of her sneakers. Jenny felt her legs shaking, and she was certain that she would simply collapse onto the floor. She fought to remain standing as she stared at Lizzie's breasts bathed in the moonlight. At least she thought it was the moonlight. More than likely it was the glow of the table lamp and not the moonlight. But in Jenny's memory it would always be the moonlight glistening across the youthful form of her love.

Lizzie finally freed herself of her sneakers and drenched socks and stood. She shook out her long blonde hair. The motion of Lizzie's breasts had mesmerized Jenny as they swayed gently. Jenny swallowed hard as Lizzie stood there with her emerald eyes shimmering through the darkness. Lizzie reached out her hand, slowly seeming to beckon Jenny closer. Shyly Jenny stepped closer and it was then that Lizzie broke the magical spell that she was casting over Jenny's heart. "Towel?" was all that the blonde said.

Jenny's heart sank as she tossed a towel to Lizzie. She had to throw the fluffy beast since she was far too afraid to get any closer to Lizzie. Her heart was racing and her hands shook uncontrollably. Once again she found herself fighting to regain her composure. She reached for the buttons on her blouse. Battling to at least look normal, Jenny struggled to free those damn buttons. She just needed to stop her hands from shaking and she would be fine. She was on the verge of tears as the buttons refused to yield.

"Here, let me help you," Lizzie said softly as she stepped over to her and slowly began to undo each button. With each one, Jenny was certain that her heart would explode. She felt it pounding uncontrollably in her chest; never before had the teenager felt her heart beating so fast or so hard. Her mind was racing, fearful that Lizzie would somehow know what she was thinking. If Lizzie discovered her secret then she would most certainly be disgusted by Jenny's thoughts and their friendship would be over.

Then it happened. Lizzie unbuttoned the last button that was exposed and the blonde didn't step away. Instead she reached down and undid the copper button of Jenny's jeans. Then she gently lowered the zipper. Nothing this intimate had transpired between them before. Jenny's mind was swimming in confusion as her body ignited.

Lizzie freed the tails of Jenny's blouse from her well-fitting jeans. Then she undid the lower buttons of the blouse. Lizzie didn't look at Jenny as she reached up and lowered Jenny's blouse off her shoulders. Jenny's skin was tingling as her damp blouse slid down her arms. Lizzie seemed to be breathing heavily as she dropped the wet garment to the floor.

Jenny failed to notice that Lizzie's heart was also beating out of control. She was breathing far too heavily herself and hiding her face from her friend. When Lizzie did finally look up and their eyes met, Jenny saw the same flushed confused expression that she possessed. Lizzie's face was a mirror of her own. Lizzie felt the same way! She wanted what Jenny wanted.

Lizzie slid her arms around Jenny's waist, sliding her strong hands up and around Jenny's long back. Never taking her sparkling green eyes off of Jenny, Lizzie gently unhooked the clasp of Jenny's bra. Jenny once again swallowed hard, curious as to why her mouth was suddenly so dry. Lizzie slid Jenny's bra down, across her long arms, until it fell to the floor next to her blouse.

Feeling suddenly exposed, Jenny broke the tender gaze the two shared. Lizzie reached up and gently swept the damp brunette hair from Jenny's brow. The feel of Lizzie's fingers warmed her skin and she found herself turning to look back at the blonde. They leaned into one another, neither of them making the first move. The two girls simply moved in unison as their arms wrapped around one another.

Their lips brushed with a soft tremble. Their first kiss happened so quickly, and before either of them could understand what had happened, they kissed again. The second kiss exploded into a fiery passion. Their thighs slipped between the other's legs and they began to sway in rhythm as their wetness coated the other's thigh. Lizzie tugged insistently on Jenny's lower lip. Jenny's lips parted as Lizzie's tongue slid inside her mouth.

Up until that moment in time, Jenny had only dreamt of holding Lizzie and kissing her. Her self-control had prevented her from wishing for more. Now she wanted so much more.

As their lips parted they were left standing there, breathing heavily. Their bodies were so close that Jenny could feel the rapid beating of Lizzie's heart. Lizzie lowered her arms and took a small step back. Jenny panicked, fearful that Lizzie now hated her for what she had just done. Or perhaps she was simply a lousy kisser, or Lizzie thought that she was some kind of freak? Jenny was certain that Lizzie was about to bolt out of the room and that she would never see her again. Her youthful mind conjured up those and a thousand other fears.

Lizzie quieted them all when she took Jenny's hand and led her across the room to the bed. She lowered Jenny onto the bed. Neither of them spoke as Lizzie gently removed Jenny's wet shoes and socks. Jenny gasped as Lizzie leaned over her and slid Jenny's wet jeans off her body.

Lizzie stood there admiring Jenny's body. "Take yours off too," Jenny said in a voice that frightened her. There was something so different in her voice; it was so sure and so very hungry. "I want to see you naked, Lizzie," she commanded. Lizzie smiled before obeying her instructions.

Lizzie lowered her body onto Jenny's. The brunette moaned deeply as her lover's body touched her own for the first time. Their hearts raced uncontrollably as their hungry lips met once again. Lizzie's lips parted, inviting Jenny in. Gasping, as they broke apart, Lizzie leaned down and tenderly began kissing Jenny's neck. She *moved even closer to Jenny, pressing between Jenny's quivering thighs. Jenny groaned deeply as her own thigh found its way between Lizzie's legs.*

They pressed against one another's wetness as their bodies began to move in rhythm. They moved slowly at first before the passion exploded in a wild frenzy. Jenny could feel Lizzie's breath against her ear as the blonde whispered in a deep inviting tone. "I want you, Jenny."

"Yes, oh yes," Jenny answered with a moan.

Lizzie continued to kiss Jenny's swan-like neck, tracing her tongue down to her shoulders. Jenny could only whimper as Lizzie's mouth moved to her breast and captured Jenny's breast. As Lizzie gently teased her nipple with her tongue and her teeth, Jenny wondered how Lizzie knew what she needed. Jenny's hips arched against Lizzie's firm thigh.

Driven by pure instinct, their bodies responded to one another. Lizzie slid her hand down Jenny's long firm body. Jenny's body pulsated as Lizzie's fingers shyly ran through her damp curls. Jenny's desire grew even stronger as her lover dipped her fingers along her slick folds. She clutched the blonde's shoulders as her fingers pressed against her aching center. "Lizzie," she gasped in a needy tone.

"Yes, Jenny. Yes," her lover panted against her breast.

"I want you inside of me," Jenny moaned, not understanding where the words or the desire had come from. "I want you now," she pleaded hungrily.

Lizzie responded without hesitation. First with one finger and then a second, she gently slid inside of Jenny's wetness. Jenny felt the walls of her center closing around Lizzie's touch. Her hips arched up off the bed as Lizzie plunged in and out of her. She was moaning and calling Lizzie's name over and over again, begging her not to stop. She whimpered as Lizzie's mouth abandoned her breast. The blonde began to work her way down Jenny's body, first to her ribs, then her abdomen, and finally to her quivering thighs. Lizzie's kisses grew more insistent as she worshipped the inside of Jenny's thighs.

Jenny opened her legs, inviting Lizzie's mouth to join her hand. A delightful shudder passed through her, as Lizzie's tongue tasted her for the first time, fumbling at first until it found its way to the spot that neither of them knew existed. "Yes. There," she begged. Her hand pressed Lizzie's head closer to her passion as she begged for more. Lizzie held her steady as her body thrust against her lover's mouth. Jenny cried out as her body shook. The brunette's body arched even higher as her legs trembled wildly. Her nerves were pushed to the breaking point as she felt her soul explode.

Jenny collapsed on the bed as the waves trickled through her. Lizzie rested her head on her stomach, kissing her softly. She whimpered as Lizzie's touch left her center. Jenny felt alive as she pulled Lizzie up to her. Kissing her lover deeply, she rolled her onto her back. Moving her mouth to Lizzie's neck, she began to taste the blonde's skin. She kissed her way down to Lizzie's breasts. Her tongue flickered across her lover's already erect nipple. Jenny was amazed as the rose-colored bud became more erect from her touch.

Jenny captured Lizzie's nipple in her mouth and suckled it greedily. Her body pulsated as her lover's body arched against her own. Jenny could feel her own excitement growing as she hungrily feasted on one breast and then the other. She couldn't hear her lover's words as she lost herself in her breasts.

Unable to contain herself any longer, she began to work her way down Lizzie's body. She hungered to taste all of her lover. She licked and tasted her way lower and lower, her mouth and tongue savoring every inch of Lizzie's naked body. She could see and smell her lover's desire as she ran her fingers through the golden tufts of hair. She gently parted Lizzie before taking her into her mouth, tasting her deeply as she drank in her passion. Lizzie moaned as Jenny's tongue found it's way deep inside her center.

Jenny could feel Lizzie's thighs quivering against her as her body rose. Lizzie whimpered as Jenny's tongue departed her warmth. Her fingers soon replaced it and her tongue fumbled until it found the quivering bundle begging for her touch. She suckled the button in her mouth as her fingers slid in and out of Lizzie's wetness. She could feel the walls closing around her fingers as Lizzie screamed out. She held her lover tightly and continued to pleasure her as Lizzie's body rose against her. Lizzie cried out as her hips began to thrust in a wild rhythm. Lizzie had screamed as *she released her passion, finally collapsing onto the bed.*

Jenny could still remember how they'd held each other, exchanging tender kisses until they drifted off to sleep. Even with the way their love had ended, Jenny still couldn't let go of the images of that night.

Now, seventeen years later, Jenny felt like death warmed over as she looked out the window at the steadily falling rain. "Crappy weather," Jenny grumbled as she fought against the warmth that had invaded her body since her mind decided to relive the night she gave away her innocence.

"I like the rain," Lizzie responded softly.

Jenny turned and flashed her former lover an amused smirk. Lizzie just continued to watch the rainfall. "So, Sister, what brings you to Boston?" Jenny inquired tersely.

She watched as Lizzie's body stiffened and her jaw clenched. Jenny knew that her tone had been harsh, and that the blonde had been nothing but kind to her since they'd been reunited a few short hours ago. Yet at that moment in time Jenny disliked every female on the planet with the possible exception of Jodie Foster. *'Hey, Jodie would always be a hottie,'* she reasoned.

Jenny felt the room grow smaller as she watched Lizzie just stand there in silence. She could tell by the brilliant color in the blonde's eyes that she was angry. "I'm going to take a shower," Lizzie said softly as she finally shifted her position.

"Still running?" Jenny spat out bitterly.

"I never ran, Jenny," Lizzie said softly as she turned to face the brunette. "I screwed up. I made a mess of everything back then, and I'm still doing it now. I'm here to see if I can get my life back. I'm here to see my family that I've only seen a handful of times since I was sent away. "

CHAPTER FOUR

Jenny didn't know what she should be feeling. A part of her wanted to reach out to Lizzie and a part of her hated the blonde for the hell she had put her through. "It's still early. Why don't you get some more sleep? You were tossing and turning all night," Lizzie offered in a comforting tone ignoring the tension that had filled the tiny apartment.

Jenny scratched her aching head as she perused the clock hanging on the kitchen wall. "Just after nine thirty," she grumbled, thinking that maybe a couple more hours of sleep just might be a good idea. Her blue eyes widened suddenly as she looked around the tiny apartment. There was the small living room with a coffee table, a chair, and the futon that she was reclining on. The tiny kitchen, which was separated from the room by an island, was so small that it wasn't really another room. The small bathroom and Kate's bedroom were the only other rooms. It was typical for Boston. It left one nagging question. In such a small space, just where had Lizzie slept last night? "Uhm," she stammered. "Did we bunk together last night?"

"Yes," Lizzie answered shyly as she chewed nervously on her bottom lip.

"I was naked," Jenny gasped. *'Okay, this is not a major problem. It's not like Lizzie hasn't seen me naked before,'* her mind reasoned. Still there was a sudden recall of holding a warm body very close to her during the night. Her mind sifted through the images and she realized that her hands had drifted as well. "Oh my God," she shrieked. "I felt up a nun. That's it; I'm going to Hell," she muttered bitterly.

"Jenny." Lizzie chuckled as she approached her cautiously. "First off, you don't believe in Hell," Lizzie continued, chuckling as she sat beside Jenny.

"After the past twenty-four hours, I've become a believer," Jenny moaned.

"You didn't feel me up," Lizzie protested. "You were just very snuggly."

Jenny glared at the amused blonde in disbelief. "Out with it, Sister," she demanded as she felt a wave of panic rush over her.

"Well, perhaps slightly," Lizzie responded in a strange tone.

"Slightly?" Jenny pushed. "Just how does someone get slightly felt up?"

"Oh Jenny." Lizzie laughed. "Trust me; it wasn't anything I would need to go to confession over."

"This day just gets better and better," Jenny grumbled as she pouted. "Hey, how do you do that? That voice, it's all nun-like. One minute you're the same goofball I grew up with, and the next you sound like a nun."

"I am a nun," Lizzie said with a smirk. Jenny watched as the blonde's smile grew brighter.

"What?" Jenny questioned as green eyes twinkled at her.

"I can't believe that you're here," Lizzie confessed. "I've thought about you over the years."

"Really?" Jenny snorted in disbelief.

"Yes, really," Lizzie responded sincerely. "Sleep. I'll wake you in a couple of hours, and we can see about getting some of your belongings."

Jenny nodded in agreement as she climbed back under the covers. Lizzie stood and tucked her in before heading off towards the bathroom. "Lizzie?" Jenny called out as she snuggled into the soft pillow.

"Yes?" Lizzie responded softly.

"I thought about you too," Jenny confessed as her weary eyes fluttered shut. She was asleep before the blonde could respond.

Jenny slept soundly, and a few hours later she was awakened by someone gently caressing her shoulder. "Jenny," the voice whispered softly against her skin. Jenny's eyes snapped open as she recognized the voice. She sat up, her body still aching from the abuse she'd subjected it to the night before.

"Hi," she said brightly to the blonde kneeling beside the futon.

"Feeling better?" Lizzie asked softly as she stroked Jenny's arm.

"A little," Jenny answered as she yawned and stretched. "Are you up for a little trip?"

"Are you sure that you're up for this?" Lizzie asked in concern. "Perhaps you should talk to *her* first."

Jenny raised her eyebrows quizzically, not missing the harsh way Lizzie had referred to Wendy. "I just want to get this over with," Jenny said dryly. "Besides, I need to get some clothes." Lizzie simply nodded as she stood. Jenny stood and grabbed her work jacket.

"Do you want to talk about it?" Lizzie inquired tenderly.

"Not much to say," Jenny grunted, knowing that Lizzie was the last person she wanted to discuss her unfaithful lover with. "I came home early from work and found her in our bed with another woman. No scene, no yelling, I just turned and walked away. However I did kick her girlfriend's Lexus and then beat it with a dozen roses. I bet when the alarm went off it finally got the two of them out of bed." She chuckled wryly.

"She's a fool," Lizzie said dryly.

"Strange words coming from you," Jenny spat out. Lizzie just stared at her oddly before putting on her own jacket.

Later, after circling the block of what was now her former residence, Jenny finally found a parking space for Kate's truck. She was relieved when she didn't see the Lexus parked out front. As they entered the building and walked upstairs to the apartment, Jenny was surprised that neither of them had spoken since her biting comment earlier.

Jenny received another surprise when she saw two cardboard boxes sitting in the hallway outside her apartment. She snatched the note from the top of one of the boxes. "Sorry you had to find out this way. I've packed your stuff. Wendy," she read aloud. 'Well, she's direct; I'll give her that." She sighed, feeling a strange sense of relief that she was finally free.

"Uhm, Jenny?" Lizzie said slowly. "I don't want to seem

snotty or anything, but I have more stuff than this and I've taken a vow of poverty."

"Right you are, my friend." Jenny smirked as she dangled her keys. "Let's hope Wendy hasn't changed the locks yet." She smiled as her key turned easily in the lock. "Oh Wendy, where are you? Are you home, you little troll?" she called out. "Looks like you won't get to meet Wendy," she said sarcastically.

"Pity," Lizzie droned.

"You may need to go to confession yet," Jenny quipped as she headed towards the bedroom. "How does that work?" she asked as she began to search for her jewelry.

"Confession?" Lizzie responded as she began to scan the bookshelf. "This is yours," she said as she tossed an old copy of Victorian poetry onto the bed. "I bought it for you," Lizzie added with a shrug.

"Yes, you did," Jenny said as she smiled at the memory. "Not confession," she continued with her earlier thought. "Your vows - what are they actually?"

"You take three vows when you enter the order," Lizzie explained as she placed more books on the bed. She held up a tiny stuffed kitten and shook it gently, making the tiny bell around its neck jingle.

"Jingles." Jenny smiled as she took the animal. "What were we, twelve when you won him for me at that carnival? I can't believe she tried to keep him." She held the tiny animal tightly as she resumed her search for her missing jewelry. "What are the three vows?"

"Poverty, chastity and obedience," Lizzie explained. "Isn't that your grandmother's rocking chair?"

"Yes," Jenny responded as she stared at the blonde with a dumbfounded expression. "How do you deal with that?" she managed to choke out.

"Poverty is a snap." Lizzie shrugged. "I'll bring the chair down to the truck."

Jenny was dying to ask how Lizzie was faring with her other vows, but the blonde lifted the chair with ease and made her way out of the apartment quickly. "Oh, this is going to be fun," Jenny quipped as she continued to search for her jewelry. "Jenny, focus on cleaning up this mess before you start dealing with the past," she scolded herself.

"Okay, boss, what's next?" Lizzie called out as she entered the bedroom. Jenny found herself staring at the blonde. "There was a tarp tucked behind the seat; I covered the rocker with it," Lizzie continued as she stared back at Jenny. "Seventeen years," Lizzie stammered. "I can't believe it."

"I know," Jenny responded softly.

"I had prepared myself for the possibility that we might run into one another," Lizzie began to explain as Jenny continued to sort through her belongings. "I didn't know that you'd become a cop and worked with Kate."

"You seem to be taking everything in stride," Jenny said thoughtfully.

"Not really." Lizzie laughed lightly. "I've been through a lot over the years. I'll tell you about my life, and I'd like to hear about yours. And I would really like to get some coffee."

Jenny couldn't help but laugh at the blonde's last comment. "Still a caffeine junkie?" Jenny taunted her.

"You have no idea," Lizzie droned.

"Tell you what, let's finish sorting through this mess, and on the way up to Haven we'll stop for coffee," Jenny explained.

"Good. You're buying." Lizzie wiggled her eyebrows playfully. Jenny flashed the amused blonde a mock look of indignation. "Hey, vow of poverty." Lizzie chuckled as she held up her hand in protest.

"Yeah, about those vows . . ." Jenny began with renewed interest as Lizzie rolled her eyes.

"Pack," Lizzie instructed her firmly.

"I'm just curious," Jenny continued as she began to collect more of her belongings. "How chaste is chaste?"

"That's what you want to know?" Lizzie grumbled. "Not what it was like teaching children in an impoverished village? What do you think about the trouble going on in the church? Nope, you want to know about my sex life?" Lizzie teased as she poked Jenny playfully. "Did you get taller?"

Jenny laughed as she swatted Lizzie away. "No, maybe you got shorter," Jenny, taunted her.

41

"Still a brat," Lizzie chastised her.

"Come on, let's get moving. I want to get out of here before Wendy shows up," Jenny said. Her mind was still contemplating the question that Lizzie hadn't answered.

A strange energy filled the room as they continued to work. Jenny found her jewelry hidden in Wendy's bureau. She didn't feel any bitterness; her emotions were busy handling the way her body was reacting to Lizzie's presence. "Does it bother you?" Jenny finally asked as they were packing some boxes.

"Are we back on the celibacy thing?" Lizzie chuckled lightly.

"No," Jenny said quietly although she was more than a little curious about Lizzie's celibacy, only because Lizzie's libido when they were dating was the size of the Aegean Sea. "Does it bother you that I'm gay? That's a pretty big no-no for your bosses. The church has a major problem with it," Jenny pointed out. "Of course, they have a major problem with most everything."

"Not fond of the clergy, are you?" Lizzie snorted in amusement.

"Oh no, I think you folks are great bunch," Jenny snarled.

"I know that the Holy Father has some strict views," Lizzie continued casually.

"The Holy Father?" Jenny choked, unable to believe that she heard Lizzie speaking this way.

"I don't have a problem with your sexuality," Lizzie stated firmly. "How could I? You were my lover. I didn't forget you, Jenny. Nor did I forget what we once shared."

"I guess we need to add that to the things we need to talk about," Jenny responded calmly. There was something in Lizzie's eyes that made the ice around her heart melt slightly. She glanced at her watch quickly. "But not now. I really want to get out of here as quickly as possible. I need to put this part of my life behind me."

"I've waited a long time to talk to you again," Lizzie said quietly. "A little while longer won't hurt."

They finally finished. While Jenny was locking up the apartment, Lizzie went to check on the truck. "Jenny?" Wendy's sickeningly sweet voice called to her as the tall blonde descended down the hallway.

Jenny groaned in disgust as her now former lover smiled at

her. "I'm glad you're here," Wendy purred as she approached. Jenny brushed away her hands as she tried to hug her. "I see you got your things." Jenny looked at the floor where the two boxes had been waiting for her. *'Oh goodie, she thinks I just got here,'* her mind growled. She was about to subject Wendy to some very choice language when she saw Lizzie enter the hallway.

"Yes, I got all my things," Jenny retorted with a sly smile.

"What?" Wendy choked.

Jenny didn't pay any attention to Wendy; she was too busy watching Lizzie's approach. The small blonde seemed to be seething. She stopped behind Wendy and folded her arms across her chest in a defensive manner. Jenny rolled her eyes in amusement as she wondered just what the little nun was going to do.

"You've been inside?" Wendy inquired in a hostile tone.

"Yes," Jenny responded flatly as she watched Lizzie's eyes get darker. She knew that look and it only meant trouble. "Here's the key so you won't need to change the locks." She handed the key to Wendy in the hope that it would end the conversation.

"What did you take?" Wendy fumed.

"Only what's mine," Jenny snapped. "Look, it's over. Fine I hope you're happy with your new girlfriend. Goodbye."

"Jenny, we should really talk about this," Wendy continued, oblivious to the small blonde behind her who was about to burst. "You know if you had been around more . . ."

"Hold it," Jenny yelled. "I wasn't around because you said we needed more money. Look, you got what you wanted from me. You can keep the apartment."

"What about your half of the rent?" Wendy whined.

"My half?" Jenny blurted out. "For starters, you never paid rent. The apartment is yours and so is next month's rent."

"Let's go," Lizzie growled from behind Wendy.

"Who are you?" Wendy asked in confusion.

Lizzie's face grew hot as she slowly lowered her arms. "No," Jenny cautioned Lizzie. "Go wait for me downstairs." Lizzie looked as if she was about to protest. "Go, before I have to arrest you," Jenny growled. Lizzie chuckled slightly at the comment as she held her hands up in surrender. "I'll be fine," Jenny offered in a reassuring tone. Lizzie nodded in understanding and walked away,

43

but not before she cast one last icy glare at Wendy.

"She hasn't changed a bit." Jenny laughed lightly.

"Who was that?" Wendy said accusingly.

"I really am in Hell," she groaned as she prepared herself for whatever Wendy wanted to talk about.

Jenny was exhausted by the time her conversation with Wendy had concluded. The gist of the conversation was that somehow Wendy blamed Jenny for her infidelities and wasn't thrilled about Jenny informing the cable company, the electric company, the gas company, and the landlord that she was no longer living there. When Wendy realized that Jenny was going to close all the accounts and remove her from her credit cards, she actually suggested that Jenny stay so they could work things out. Apparently Wendy's new love interest wasn't ready to co-habitat. That's when Jenny finally exploded and told Wendy exactly what she could do with her suggestion. Although Jenny doubted that her advice was physically possible, she would certainly enjoy watching her try.

When she reached the street, she noticed that the rain had stopped and Lizzie was pacing up and down the sidewalk. *'Okay, I've dealt with one and now it's time to deal with you,'* her mind fumed. "You were going to hit her," she blurted out when she caught up with Lizzie. "Don't lie. I've seen that look in your eyes before."

"I don't like her," Lizzie explained flatly.

"So you were just going to pop her one?" Jenny asked incredulously. "Don't they teach you gals to turn the other cheek?"

"Yes," Lizzie responded slowly. "But when I was sent up to a convent in Saskatchewan, there was this Mother Superior who certainly knew the value of a good whooping. I'm sorry. She was just so mean to you. I hate bullies. And I hate seeing you hurt."

"They sent you there?" Jenny said slowly as her mind began to process little bits of information that Lizzie had given her. "Your other assignments out of the country - you were *sent* there as well?"

"Yes," Lizzie responded nervously.

"You didn't volunteer?" Jenny pushed. "You didn't choose to stay away from your family? You were sent away. Why?"

"Jenny, it's a long story." Lizzie sighed in exasperation. "Mostly I was sent to difficult assignments as a form of punishment."

"Punishment?" Jenny pried further.

"Well, the joke is on them." Lizzie said, trying to make light of the situation. "I loved teaching those kids in areas where running water is unheard of."

"What were you being punished for?" Jenny said as she held onto Lizzie's shoulder tenderly. "What happened, Sister? Did you get *caught* again?"

They looked deeply into one another's eyes as a spark of electricity flowed between them. Lizzie swallowed hard before answering in a soft simple tone, "Yes."

CHAPTER FIVE

As they drove along Route One, both women remained silent as the neon images lining the roadway flashed past them. Jenny found Lizzie's quiet reflective mood a bit disconcerting. The girl she had known in high school had been a constant chatterbox. She added this observation to her growing list of things that were muddling her emotions. Since that morning she'd seen the woman that Lizzie had become, and yet there were still traces of the girl she had once known and loved. What was troubling the brunette the most was how they kept bouncing from easy conversations to emotional conflict. One moment they were talking like old friends and the next they were snapping at one another.

She couldn't believe the way that Lizzie had jumped in to defend her honor when Wendy had shown up. Lizzie, her brave little warrior, had reemerged. Jenny was smiling as she recalled the murderous look in Lizzie's eyes. *'Oh yeah, you were going to punch her lights out. Some things never change,'* Jenny thought with pride. Despite the fact that Jenny stood a good half a foot taller, since the first day they'd met Lizzie had always acted like Jenny's protector. Jenny laughed as once again the images of their first encounter flashed through her mind.

"What's so funny?" Lizzie inquired quizzically.

"Just remembering the day we met and how you punched Robby to stop him from pouring sand on my head," Jenny explained merrily. "You had the same look in your eyes this afternoon."

"I still hate bullies," Lizzie responded with a slight smile.

After that brief moment, silence once again filled the truck. Jenny was surprised that she didn't feel uncomfortable by the lack of conversation. Wendy had always felt a need for conversation. Of course Wendy's version of communication consisted of her talking about herself and what she wanted and Jenny simply agreeing. She sighed heavily as a sudden sense of relief filled her.

She felt really good for the first time in a long time. She hadn't had the opportunity to fully cope with the events that had been sprung upon her in the last twenty-four hours. And now that she could stop and think, she felt good. During her relationship she hadn't really taken the time to think about how Wendy had controlled her. In many ways Jenny had simply been wandering through her days with a strange sense of stagnation. She was simply following the road that Wendy was leading her down. Jenny followed her blindly simply because she didn't want to jeopardize the first long term relationship she'd ever been in.

Now she was finally free. Closing the door on her life with Wendy gave her back a strange sense of herself. Perhaps it was seeing her first love again that fueled her newfound desire to get her life back. Jenny had endured the pain of betrayal once before only to emerge stronger. In some bizarre way, when Lizzie broke her heart she'd led her to take that first step towards becoming a woman. Not that she was by any means thankful for the pain.

Jenny glanced over at Lizzie who was watching the passing restaurants and hotels in fascination. The woman sitting next to her now clearly wasn't the girl who had hurt her; still, she had been that person once. Jenny wondered if she could ever forgive the girl and become friends with the woman. Jenny had a lot to think about. *'When did I decide to simply be content with my life?'* she wondered as the sense of relief continued to trickle through her body.

Jenny caught a glimpse of Lizzie smiling. The vision of her first love sitting next to her with the gray skies passing behind her took her breath away. Jenny couldn't help but notice that Lizzie was a stark contrast to Wendy. Lizzie was smaller yet confident and full of life. Wendy, on the other hand, possessed a self-absorbent brooding quality that Jenny now found very unattractive. *'What am I doing? Why am I comparing two of my former lovers?'* Jenny questioned herself in bewilderment. She shook her head in an effort to clear her thoughts.

Jenny spotted the familiar pink sign marking a Dunkin' Donuts just up ahead. "Dunkies!" Lizzie exclaimed gleefully as Jenny pulled into the parking lot. "I haven't had a cup of Dunkin' Donuts coffee in years," Lizzie continued babbling as she unhooked her seatbelt. "There was one at Logan, but I didn't have enough time to grab a cup. Father Desposa was in a hurry when we landed. He hadn't seen his family in years either and he just wanted to get going," the blonde spoke in a hurried tone without pausing to take a breath. Jenny's head was spinning.

"Go on inside," Jenny interrupted her with a smile. Seeing a small glimpse of the girl she'd once been very much in love with warmed her heart.

"Sorry; I'm just a little excited." Lizzie laughed.

"It's okay. Go on inside," Jenny offered as she handed Lizzie some cash. "I'm just going to check the back to make sure my stuff is still dry."

"Do you need any help?" Lizzie offered. Her eyes were glazed over as she looked at the interior of the donut shop.

"Go," Jenny responded in a firm yet reassuring tone. Lizzie hopped out of the truck and dashed into the shop. Jenny couldn't hold back the smile as she watched the blonde bounce with excitement.

Feeling certain that her belongings were safe, Jenny joined Lizzie inside. "You know it's the little things I've missed," Lizzie explained as she tried to look over the other patrons to see the menu.

"Like what?" Jenny asked.

"Like taking a shower, good smelling shampoo, shaving your legs, or running water for that matter," Lizzie explained. "And of course a good cup of Dunkin' Donuts coffee," Lizzie said as she licked her lips in anticipation.

"They must have had coffee where you were," Jenny noted, realizing that Lizzie had been living in Central America.

"Oh yeah," Lizzie groaned in an almost erotic tone. "Really good coffee in fact. It's just that Dunkin' Donuts is like having breakfast at Dante's Diner. It means that I'm home. Large coffee, black, no sugar," Lizzie ordered her coffee quickly.

"Large Dunkaccino and a chocolate honey dip donut," Jenny

ordered. "Don't you want a donut?"

"I'm not really into sweets anymore," Lizzie explained as the counter girl handed them their order. "Besides, donuts are for cops."

"Ha ha," Jenny snorted as Lizzie handed her the change.

They took a booth in the corner and sipped the coffee quietly. There was something nagging at Jenny. It was what Lizzie had said earlier, and the way she left the door open regarding her sexuality. Jenny looked at the golden-haired woman, trying to figure out what was going on in that pretty little head. She watched as Lizzie savored every last drop of her coffee, clinging to the Styrofoam cup and licking her lips with pleasure. Jenny's crystal blue eyes widened as she watched the pink tongue swirl between Lizzie's full lips. *What am I thinking?'* Jenny questioned herself frantically.

"What?" Lizzie asked as she caught Jenny staring.

"Nothing," Jenny lied as she ran her fingers through her long raven hair. "You just seem to really be enjoying that coffee."

"Sorry," Lizzie responded with a blush. "It's just what I said before; a good cup of Dunkin' Donuts coffee reminds me that I'm finally home."

"For how long?" Jenny asked carefully.

"I'm not certain," Lizzie said with a heavy sigh. "Possibly just until the fall, or it could be forever." Jenny blinked in surprise. "I'm going to substitute teach at Xavier until the end of this term." Jenny nodded in response, familiar with the Catholic school located in the heart of the city. "Then I'm taking a sabbatical, and *if* I return to the order, I'm off to Zaire."

"If?" Jenny choked on her beverage.

"That's why I'm taking a sabbatical," Lizzie explained carefully. "I'm thinking of leaving the church. I've been thinking about it for years, but my superiors kept putting off my sabbatical. It was never the right time. I insisted this time, and I've been allowed to take a few months to figure out if I wish to continue with my vocation."

"Does Kate know about this?" Jenny inquired quickly, her mind whirling from what Lizzie had just told her.

"Yes." Lizzie smiled. "She's thrilled and she's hoping that I leave the church. My dad feels the same way. The only one who doesn't know is my mother."

"I'm sure the news will go over big with her," Jenny snorted in disgust.

"Right." Lizzie smirked. "The few times I've been home, she insisted that I wear my habit just so she could show me off."

"There's something wrong with that woman," Jenny grumbled as she collected her trash.

"No kidding," Lizzie groaned.

They stood and deposited their trash in the waste receptacle. Both women walked somberly out to the truck. Once inside Jenny placed the key in the ignition and paused. She just sat there while her mind spun. "Why?" Jenny whispered softly.

"Why what?" Lizzie responded in a tired voice. "Why did I become a nun?"

"That's a good place to start," Jenny encouraged her as she stared blankly through the windshield, her hand still firmly locked on the keys lying stagnant in the ignition. "Was it your parents?"

Lizzie rubbed her temple in a tired motion before she answered. "Mother pushed, yes. My father simply withdrew even further. In the end I was the one who took the vows and entered the order."

"But you haven't managed to keep your vows," Jenny responded bitterly.

"No," Lizzie confessed in a sad quiet tone.

"Was it . . .?" Jenny stammered. "Was it a woman?"

"Are you asking if I'm gay?" Lizzie laughed. Jenny turned to find Lizzie smiling at her. "Jenny, the last time I had any questions regarding my sexuality was a rainy night a very long time ago."

"Isn't that a major no-no?" Jenny pried.

"Yes, it is," Lizzie, explained in an amused tone. "But it's a little bit like the military; you know - don't ask, don't tell. Of course with the recent turmoil none of that seems to matter anymore."

Jenny's mind began to spin as her headache returned. She had no idea what she should say or do at that moment. She was trying to convince herself to let it go; Lizzie was just someone from her past and none of this mattered anymore. "Jenny, I need you to understand something," Lizzie continued seriously. "I've been

Sister Rachel almost as long as I was Lizzie Carrington. This sabbatical isn't a vacation. It's a leave of absence that I've been granted so I can make a very important decision."

"What's to decide?" Jenny snapped, unable to comprehend why Lizzie just didn't walk away.

"I need to decide whether or not I can continue in my vocation. At this time my superiors will allow me to return if that's what I decide to do."

Jenny was stunned into silence. *'Why are you thinking about this? Get out and don't look back!'* Jenny's mind screamed as her heart began to beat frantically in her chest. "Jenny," Lizzie began slowly, seemingly prepared to answer Jenny's unspoken questions, "for the first time in my life I need to think things through. In the past, every one of my life-altering decisions was based solely on emotion. I've spent my entire life jumping into things without stopping to think about what I was about to do."

As Jenny listened, she couldn't help but wonder if she'd been one of those unknowing jumps. "My life choices . . . "Lizzie continued, ". . . were reactions to love, hate, jealousy, rage, and lust. I need to know this time that I'm making the right choice, and that I'm making it for me."

Jenny tried to take it all in. She really did understand what Lizzie was saying. Her own life choices had been just that - choices. Since the night they were discovered in the Carrington's kitchen, Lizzie's life had been thrust upon her. "Now having said all that, I feel down right silly," Lizzie concluded.

"Why is that?" Jenny inquired.

"I just blurted out all my troubles to you," Lizzie explained. "It's not like you don't have a full plate already."

"It's okay," Jenny reassured her as she finally turned the keys in the ignition. "Well, you did take my mind off my own troubles."

"Yeah, and all you wanted to know was if I'm gay or not," Lizzie teased as Jenny slowly pulled out of the parking lot. "Of course my first reaction was to just look at you and say *Duh*."

"Well, some things never change." Jenny laughed heartily as she waited to reenter the rushing traffic on Route One.

"Yeah, like the drivers up here," Lizzie, noted with interest.

They finally arrived in Haven; the little seacoast town nestled on the North Shore. Jenny was weary by the time she pulled the truck into the driveway. Both women stretched as they exited the truck. "The hoop is still up," Lizzie noted as they began to untie the tarp.

"Oh yeah, Dad still thinks I'll end up playing for the WNBA," Jenny teased as she pulled back the tarp.

"The what?" Lizzie asked in confusion.

"You have been away a long time." Jenny sighed deeply, thinking about how much they'd both missed out on over the years. "Women's National Basketball Association. It started right after the U.S. women kicked butt at the Olympics."

"It's about time," Lizzie noted as they began to unload Jenny's belongings. "Does Boston have a team?" she asked eagerly.

"No," Jenny grumbled in disappointment. "But New York does."

They worked in silence as they stored Jenny's meager belongings in her parent's garage. Jenny was fighting a loosing battle with her libido. The occasional brushing against the smaller woman was causing her pulse to race. Neither of them had touched intentionally; it was just inevitable due to the close quarters they were working in. Yet the quick glances she made whenever she was certain that her companion was not looking were solely her own responsibility.

Jenny watched the sway of Lizzie's hips as she left the garage for the last time. Jenny was mentally chastising herself when she spotted the familiar orange ball out of the corner of her eye. She smiled wickedly as she scooped up the basketball. She pressed her fingers into the rough rubber and smiled when she discovered that her father had maintained the air pressure.

Jenny stepped out of the garage and hid the ball behind her back. Lizzie was facing away from her, seemingly lost in her own thoughts. "Hey!" Jenny called out. Lizzie spun around quickly. "Think quick," Jenny shouted as she pulled the ball out from behind her back and tossed it at her startled companion.

"Brat." Lizzie giggled as she caught the ball easily and began to dribble it on the driveway. "So what do you say, Stretch? I think you still owe me a rematch," Lizzie taunted her.

"I always owed you a rematch," Jenny scoffed as she pulled

down the garage door. "You could never beat me."

"That's because you're abnormally tall," Lizzie protested as she continued to dribble the ball.

"Right," Jenny snorted in amusement. "Come on, Sister; let's see what you've got," Jenny challenged the smaller woman.

Lizzie creased her brow in determination as she removed her jacket and began to dribble the ball. Jenny took on a defensive stance in an effort to block the feisty blonde's advancement. The taller woman managed to block Lizzie as they raced around the small driveway. Lizzie grunted as she spun around and tried to fake to Jenny's left. The brunette was onto her and quickly jumped up to block Lizzie's shot.

Their bodies collided as they both sprang up. Jenny felt the air escape from her lungs, knowing it wasn't the force of the impact that caused her distress. Lizzie's body covered her own completely. As their bodies began their descent back to the ground, she felt Lizzie slipping away. Instinctively she reached out and wrapped her arms around the smaller woman's body.

They stumbled as they clung to one another tightly, each balancing the other so that they would land on their feet. The basketball was forgotten as it rolled down the driveway. Jenny could feel Lizzie's heart beating against her chest as their breasts pressed together. She looked down and found herself locked in a smoky haze of green. She knew she should pull away; instead she tightened her hold on the smaller woman.

She watched as Lizzie's lips parted slightly. Jenny was unable to control herself as she bent her head down. She was so close to capturing Lizzie's full lips that she could feel the blonde's breath on her skin.

"Hey, did you lose something?" an irritatingly familiar voice called out.

Both women pulled apart quickly as if they'd been burned. Jenny's crystal blue eyes darkened and she cast a menacing glare at Robby who was trotting up the driveway, holding the basketball up proudly. "You have got to be kidding me," Lizzie hissed as Jenny rubbed her now throbbing temple.

"Robby," Jenny greeted him coldly.

"Here you go," he responded brightly as he handed her the

ball.

Robby turned pale when he finally noticed Lizzie standing there; Jenny watched in fascination. "Robert," the blonde managed to greet her former nemesis politely.

"Lizzie," the man said as he clenched his jaw.

"Actually, it's Sister Rachel now," Lizzie corrected him calmly.

"I suppose you think that's funny?" he barked at her.

"I thought it was appropriate," Lizzie responded with a shrug as she walked over to the truck.

Jenny was more than a little confused by their exchange. She was thankful that Lizzie had walked away in an apparent effort to diffuse the situation. "Robby, we need to get going. Thanks for the ball," Jenny said quickly as she tossed the basketball into the back of the truck. Robby stood there dumbfounded as Jenny climbed into the truck and they drove off.

"I'm sorry," Lizzie apologized. "I should have been more cordial."

"What?" Jenny chuckled. "It's not like the two of you ever got along. Come to think of it compared to the way you used to talk to him, I thought you were very polite. I still remember the way you used to stand on your toes so you could scream at him. The two of you never liked each other."

"I guess you're right," Lizzie said thoughtfully. Jenny turned to the small blonde with a questioning look. "Some things never change," Lizzie explained flatly.

"What was the whole thing about your name?" Jenny pressed as she pulled up to a stop sign.

"You really should read your bible," Lizzie offered in an amused tone.

"My last name is Jacobs," Jenny grunted. "We're not exactly bible folk."

"True," Lizzie said absently as a mischievous smirk formed on her angelic lips.

Jenny drove along in frustration, knowing that she wouldn't be getting any answers to her questions. A small part of her was thankful that Robby had interrupted them. Jenny knew that if she'd kissed Lizzie it would have been a huge mistake. Then there was another part of her that was screaming loudly for her to find Robby and beat him senseless for destroying a perfect moment.

CHAPTER SIX

When they arrived back at Kate's apartment, Jenny had managed to convince herself that the intimate contact she'd had with Lizzie was nothing more than a shared lapse in judgment. As Lizzie unlocked and opened the door, Jenny had decided to simply forget that it had happened. She wasn't prepared for the sight of Kate staring at both of them with an angry expression. For a brief moment Jenny feared that Kate had discovered the truth about their past and present, although Jenny was confused as to what exactly was happening in the present. Still enduring the wrath of Kate Carrington was not on her list of things to do.

"Lizzie," Kate hissed and Jenny breathed a sigh of relief when she realized she wasn't the one who was in trouble.

"What?" Lizzie spat out; suddenly sounding very much like the teenager Jenny had once loved with all of her heart.

Kate's eyes drifted to meet Jenny's. The look of fear in her superior's eyes made Jenny's heart beat faster. "Charles Englewood," Kate said in slow careful tone.

Jenny felt a rush of panic run through her at the name. *'Dear God! She's been in South America! Please tell me she didn't do anything stupid,'* Jenny thought frantically.

"You've heard of him?" Lizzie responded calmly.

Jenny stood there wondering how Lizzie could be so relaxed. *'Maybe she's lost her mind? That's it; she's crazy. It would certainly explain everything,'* Jenny mentally reasoned.

"Heard of him?" Kate shouted, barely able to contain herself. "Lizzie, this guy gives the other drug lords a bad name!"

"Yes. Well, he can be a most disagreeable person," Lizzie responded thoughtfully.

"He's a sadistic killer!" Kate bellowed, her body trembling.

Lizzie just stood there the picture of calm. Jenny blinked as her jaw hung open, trying to understand just what was happening. "Lizzie, I'm damn glad to see you but just what kind of trouble did you get yourself into?" Kate pleaded as Jenny watched the scene unfold, feeling completely helpless. "How did this happen?" Kate wept as Lizzie wrapped her arms around her taller sibling.

"It's okay," Lizzie comforted her older sister. "Kate, it will be okay."

The words sent a shiver down Jenny's spine. *'Why did I leave you that night?'* her mind screamed as she blamed herself once again for failing to be there for her young lover. Lizzie led her sister over to the futon and sat her down. Jenny's feeling of hopelessness grew as she watched the tiny blonde take her sister's hand in her own. Kate seemed to relax slightly from Lizzie's touch. "Just over three years ago, the church sent me to a very rural community just outside of Columbia," Lizzie began her story.

"But you're a teacher?" Kate protested. "Why did they keep sending you to places like that?"

"Because they need teachers," Lizzie responded in a calm voice.

Lizzie was a teacher?' Jenny still found the concept hard to grasp. Lizzie was the one who'd never wanted to go to class. When they were growing up, Lizzie never once mentioned wanting to become a teacher. Of course, back then Jenny had never considered becoming a cop either.

Jenny began to pace nervously as Lizzie continued her story. "The place they sent me to was as I said, very rural, and it was a bit of a hot spot. " Jenny was amazed at how calm Lizzie's voice remained. "I was needed there. These were good people caught between politics and criminals. Everyone wanted to exploit them. Very often the criminals and the politicians were one and the same. That's where Englewood comes in. He wanted the villagers to grow crops for him - the wrong kind of crops. They resisted. Father O'Brien, Father Desposa, and I helped them refuse. When things began to get tense, the Peace Corp workers were pulled out. Our superiors had warned us to stay out of what they referred to as the local political climate. I'm certain in light of recent events that you're aware, that the church can be really good at burying their collective heads in the sand." Kate nodded in understanding as she silently encouraged her younger sister to continue. "We couldn't. We lived there with these people. How could we just stand back and allow them to become a part of something they didn't want? How could we simply stand by while innocent people were murdered and forced into slavery? Englewood failed to take over the village. And with our small help, his hired guns ended up behind bars."

"Which pissed him off," Kate added with a hint of pride.

"You could say that," Lizzie sighed in agreement. "So how do you know about this?"

"My boss called me to talk," Kate explained. "O'Brien has taken the church's offer to be placed out of the country in an undisclosed location. You and Father Desposa refused. The DEA wants to put both of you in protective custody. Inspector Gillette thought that I might be able to talk some sense into you."

"No," Lizzie flatly refused. "I know Englewood, and I'm not going to be locked away because he has a grudge against me. I came home to get my life back, and I'm not going to delay that again. I want to live my life, starting with having dinner with you and Dad tonight."

"Lizzie, the Catholic church can hide you anywhere in the world," Kate vehemently protested.

"No," Lizzie argued. "I'm tired of running and hiding. I'm over thirty years old, and I have no idea who I am. Plus Englewood seems to have a lot of other problems that don't include one pesky little nun. He's under investigation, and from what I understand, it's just a matter of time before he's locked up."

"True," Kate conceded with a hint of hesitation.

"A man like that doesn't just ignore it when his pride's been hurt," Jenny interrupted, unable to remain silent any longer.

"I've been home for a couple of days," Lizzie pointed out. "I've been out in the open. I'm staying with two cops. He's too busy trying to keep his sorry butt out of prison. The only thing that worries me is that even if they do lock him up for the rest of his life some other low life is just going to take his place."

The room fell into a heavy silence. Jenny knew that Lizzie's reasoning was true. If Englewood had wanted her dead, he would have at least tried before now. Fear still gripped her heart. "Please stop pacing," Lizzie addressed Jenny, finally breaking the uneasy tension that hung over them. Jenny scowled as she halted. Her fingers reached up to her long dark tresses, which she absently began to play with. It was a nervous habit she'd had throughout her entire life. "And don't twirl your hair. It drives me nuts," Lizzie scolded her.

"Whatever." Jenny scowled as she rolled her eyes.

"Bite me," Lizzie shot back.

Jenny was suddenly lost in the familiar playful banter they'd shared in their youth. She bit back the urge to inquire just where Lizzie would like her to bite her. Yet she was unable to keep the question out of her smoldering gaze. Lizzie blushed as she pursed her lips in response to Jenny's unspoken teasing. "Lizzie, may I suggest something?" Kate's question broke through the growing intensity of their feelings.

Lizzie cleared her throat and tore her gaze from Jenny's. "Uhm, sure," Lizzie squeaked out and Jenny stifled a giggle.

"I've already discussed it with the DEA; they're not thrilled, but they agree that it might work," Kate carefully began to explain. "What if Jenny and I kept an eye on you? It would only be until Englewood is locked up or you go off to Zaire. That is, if you go to Zaire."

"What do you mean?" Lizzie asked. She seemed to be considering the suggestion.

"I mean that the department gives us a little extra assignment, and we hang around you," Kate explained. "We could take the boat out and just enjoy ourselves and keep an eye on you."

"So the two of you would be babysitting me?" Lizzie pressed with a hint of discomfort. "I don't want to disrupt either of your lives."

"It wouldn't be like that," Kate stressed. "Plus it would look good for both us. The Feds are planning on calling you as a witness since you have direct knowledge of Englewood's illegal activities. Think of it as a chance to hang out with your big sister and an old buddy from high school who'll just happen to be armed."

"I still have my teaching assignment," Lizzie pointed out.

"Which is only a couple of days a week," Kate argued. "In the meantime we can go sailing, do some camping, fun stuff like that. You can help Jenny look for an apartment."

"Sounds reasonable," Lizzie agreed. "And it would give me an excuse to avoid Mom. All right. But only if the two of you swear I won't be putting a crimp in your lives."

"What life?" Jenny snorted, relieved that Lizzie would be under their watchful gaze.

'Wait! Did I just agree to spend my days and nights watching over my ex-lover?' Jenny's mind suddenly panicked as Kate excused herself to get ready for dinner. *'What am I thinking? I almost kissed her after spending a few hours with her!'*

"You should be ashamed of yourself," Lizzie teased her in a husky tone from her spot on the futon. Jenny's eyes widened in surprise as a shiver traveled down her spine. "Teasing a nun." Lizzie wagged her finger at her playfully.

"What did I do?" Jenny feigned innocence as she recalled the look they'd shared.

"Don't try to play innocent with me, Miss Jacobs," Lizzie cautioned her as the blonde's tone maintained it's teasing quality. "I know that look you gave me." Lizzie's emerald eyes darkened. Suddenly Lizzie's face turned ashen and her eyes filled with the same sense of panic Jenny was feeling. "Forgive me," Lizzie said in a frightened tone just above a whisper. "Maybe this isn't such a good idea."

"Too late," Jenny responded harshly, somehow blaming Lizzie for the new predicament they found themselves trapped in. Lizzie seemed flustered as she turned away to get ready for dinner with her father. Left alone with her thoughts, Jenny tried to steady herself. *'Just keep reminding yourself how she broke your heart,'* Jenny's inner voice instructed her harshly.

***

A few hours later Jenny found herself unable to sleep; Kate and Lizzie were still out. The thought that she would once again be bunking with Lizzie made her uncomfortable. "I need to find my own place," Jenny muttered as she absently flipped through the television channels. "I don't know why this is getting to me," she grumbled as she tossed the remote down with a frustrated growl. "It's not like I can't control myself," she berated herself, wondering if she should be concerned with the fact that she was talking to herself.

Once again she invoked the image of a younger Lizzie lying in the arms of another woman. Her teeth clenched in hatred. "Still, as bad as what Lizzie did, at least she wasn't the freak Erika turned out to be." Jenny rolled her eyes at the memory of the tall Nordic woman she'd met her freshman year of college. "Now women like Erika should come with warning labels." Jenny scowled as she recalled the first time she'd seen the tall blonde strolling across campus.

The blonde stood over six feet tall and she strode confidently across the lawn. The autumn sun had illuminated her fair skin and her long blonde hair. Jenny's eyes were glued to the upper class woman's firm backside, which was accented by her tight blue jeans. "Wow," Jenny exclaimed in amazement, thinking that the woman looked like she'd just stepped off a magazine cover. Jenny was elated later in the week when she discovered that she was actually in the same literature class as the older woman.

For weeks Jenny had lustfully watched the leggy blonde from afar. She almost went into a full panic attack when Erika actually spoke to her one day after class and invited her to study with her. For the life of her, Jenny couldn't understand why the vision of beauty would want to talk to her. Everyone noticed Erika. Heads spun whenever she walked by. If Jenny had paid closer attention, she might have noticed that several women shied away when they saw Erika approach.

Jenny had been so enamored with Erika's beauty that she never noticed the chilly reception the blonde received from other women. If she had only taken the time, she might have been prepared for what happened. They studied together for a couple of weeks, and Jenny had to fight to keep herself focused on the study topic. Inevitably her mind would wander to lustful images of Erika.

It didn't help that Erika was always touching her. The one thing Jenny was grateful for was that they always studied in the busy college library.

Then one day Erika invited Jenny to come over to her dorm room to just hang out for the evening. Jenny was both terrified and thrilled at the idea of spending time alone with Erika. Jenny recalled how she had to wipe her sweating palms on her jeans before knocking on the door to Erika's room. She checked her attire quickly as the door slowly opened. It was too late to change, plus she had already tried on five different outfits before she had to dash out of her own dorm room.

Jenny's mouth went dry as she drank in the sight of Erika standing in the doorway clad in a pair of faded jeans and a loose-fitting black cotton oxford; it hung slightly open, giving Jenny an ample view of Erika's cleavage. "I've been waiting for you," Erika offered with a sensual purr that reverberated through Jenny's body.

"Hi," she squeaked out in embarrassment.

Her pulse was beating rapidly as Erika guided her into her dorm room by taking her by the hand. Jenny's body tingled as her eyes adjusted to the dim lighting of the room. Erika had forgone electricity in favor of candlelight. Ironically Jenny's body was humming with enough energy to light a city block as she sat on the floor dangerously close to Erika.

Jenny reluctantly accepted the glass of wine Erika offered her; she wasn't much of a drinker and she was underage. Still, she hoped the alcohol would help calm her nerves. She struggled to hold up her end of the casual conversation as Erika leaned her long body slightly into her. Jenny's eyes continually drifted to the swell of the older woman's cleavage.

Against her better judgment, Jenny accepted another glass of wine. She wouldn't have refused Erika anything when she whispered the request hotly in her ear. Jenny's body was trembling, and her hard nipples strained against the material of her silk blouse. She suppressed a deep moan when Erika's hand came to rest on her quivering thigh. "Do you like the wine?" Erika whispered in her ear as Jenny's clit began to throb in a steady rhythm.

"Yes," Jenny managed to choke out as she felt her jeans become damp with desire. Jenny was terrified that she was going to

spontaneously combust when Erika dipped her index finger in her own glass of wine and traced Jenny's trembling lips with the sweet nectar. "Taste it," Erika growled into her ear, her lips brushing Jenny's skin.

Jenny was trembling as she slowly licked her lips, savoring each drop. "It's good, isn't it?" Erika offered huskily as her tongue began to trace Jenny's ear. Jenny's eyes fluttered shut as Erika dipped her tongue playfully into her ear. She was panting heavily as she felt Erika's mouth explore her neck; Erika relieved her of the glass of wine that was threatening to spill on the carpet. "You're very beautiful, Jenny," Erika whispered against her skin as she lowered Jenny down onto the worn carpet.

Jenny gave herself over to Erika's touch as strong hands began to explore her body. She opened her eyes, wanting to capture the vision of Erika making love to her. Jenny's body was crying out as Erika's hands became more insistent, cupping Jenny's breasts. Jenny was lost in the feel of Erika unbuttoning her blouse, kissing her newly exposed skin. It had been so long since she'd felt or invited another woman's touch. Not since . . . her mind ground to a halt as a familiar pain stabbed at her heart.

"Just relax," Erika encouraged her softly. "I'm going to teach you." Jenny was far too busy trying to expel Lizzie's image from her thoughts to grasp what Erika was saying. She felt her blouse being opened and her bra undone. Erika's tongue traced her nipple slowly as Jenny's demons slipped from her mind. The feel of Erika's mouth capturing her nipple and her long blonde hair tickling Jenny's skin freed her from the past. "I'm going to make love to you, Jenny," Erika promised as she released Jenny's nipple from the warmth of her mouth. Erika lowered her body down and Jenny arched in response. "I'm going to show you what it means to be loved by a woman," Erika promised as she feasted upon Jenny's neck. "Then after you've learned the pleasures of being loved by a woman, I am going to teach you how to make love to a woman."

Jenny's eyes flew open as she finally grasped what this woman was saying to her. Thoughts of correcting Erika's misunderstanding flew from her mind as Erika once again suckled her nipple greedily. Jenny's body arched as her hips swayed against Erika's firm body. Jenny was thrusting urgently as Erika teased her aching nipple with her teeth and her tongue. "That's it, baby. Let go. Let me show you," Erika encouraged her as she began to kiss her way further down the swell of Jenny's breasts.

Despite her body's urgent need to continue, her heart couldn't. A misconception was no way to start things off with Erika who was being so gentle and loving. "Erika?" Jenny pleaded as she tried to squirm away from the taller woman.

"It's all right," Erika reassured her as she lifted her head. Erika's hazel eyes gazed deeply into Jenny's crystal blue eyes. She leaned down to capture Jenny's lips. Jenny stopped her by placing her fingers against Erika's soft lips.

"Erika," she repeated softly. "I've made love to a woman before," she reassured her soon-to-be lover with a sweet smile.

She was completely unprepared for what happened next. Erika yanked her body away and jumped to her feet. "What?" Erika demanded bitterly as she glared at Jenny.

"I said I've made love to a woman before," Jenny repeated in bewilderment as she sat up.

"How could you deceive me like this?" Erika demanded as she stormed across the room and flipped on the lights.

"Deceive you?" Jenny stammered as she blinked at the sudden brightness.

"What about the guy who keeps coming to visit you all the time?" Erika fumed as Jenny scrambled to her feet.

"Robby?" she questioned as her mind tried to understand just what was happening. "I dated him for a short time last year after my girlfriend and I broke up," Jenny tried to explain.

"You had a girlfriend?" Erika spat out as Jenny just stared at her. "I think you should leave," Erika demanded. Jenny was speechless as Erika threw open the door.

In a mass of confusion and humiliation, Jenny stumbled out into the hallway. Erika slammed the door behind her. "What the hell just happened?" she blurted out as she quickly began to button up her blouse, noticing a woman averting her gaze. Suddenly the woman stopped and turned to the bewildered and embarrassed Jenny.

"You must have just been introduced to the ice princess," the woman commented in a sorrowful tone.

65

Jenny hastily tucked her blouse back into her pants. "I don't think I'm going to like this," Jenny grumbled as she approached the small brunette. "I'm Jenny by the way."

"Emily, and welcome to the club," Emily explained as she guided Jenny towards her room.

"The club?" Jenny choked out in horror as she stepped into Emily's room.

"Yes, the club," Emily answered with a heartfelt sigh. "The 'I'm a notch on Erika's bedpost' club."

"But I'm not," Jenny protested, realizing that Erika had just played her for a fool.

"Huh?" Emily responded in confusion.

"Almost," Jenny confessed as she sat down next to Emily on her bed. "But she kicked me out."

"That's not like her." Emily blinked in confusion. "Normally she wouldn't toss aside a chance to deflower some young thing."

Jenny's jaw clenched in anger as reality slammed into her thoughts. "Now I get it," Jenny fumed as Emily looked at her curiously. "Erika only sleeps with women who haven't slept with a woman before?"

"Yes," Emily sadly confessed. Jenny's heart dropped as she realized that Emily had been one of Erika's conquests. She captured Emily's trembling hand and offered her a shy smile. "So why did she throw you out?" Emily asked.

"Because when things started to . . . well, you know," Jenny began to explain.

"Unfortunately I do," Emily confided.

"I told her that she didn't need to show me the way," Jenny explained in amusement. "I had a girlfriend in high school." Jenny smiled at how good it felt to just be able to say it after all the years of hiding the truth.

"She must have freaked," Emily exclaimed in glee. "Tell me everything. It's not often I get hear about someone taking the ice princess down a notch."

Jenny smiled at the memory of the night she and Emily became friends. They'd talked all night long and still remained friends to this day. "I need to call her," Jenny said thoughtfully.

"She'll probably do a happy dance about Wendy. I should have listened to her about that one. Maybe she'll have some advice about Lizzie," she pondered. A scowl formed on her lips as she realized that she'd never told Emily everything about Lizzie. She'd never told anyone the whole story. It had just hurt too much. "Still does," Jenny confessed in the darkness.

Jenny was suddenly stirred out of her musings as the front door opened and the light flipped on. Lizzie and Kate entered the apartment, each sporting a smile. "Hey, kiddo," Kate greeted her with a smile as Lizzie's expression dropped slightly.

"You two have fun?" Jenny offered as Lizzie looked at her in concern.

Kate told Jenny about the dinner while Lizzie kept a watchful eye on her. After Kate excused herself to go to bed, Jenny looked at Lizzie. "Yes?" Jenny asked.

"Are you all right?" Lizzie asked in concern.

"Fine," Jenny clipped.

"Sorry. You just seemed a little . . ." Lizzie began to explain.

"Just a lot on my mind," Jenny cut her off gently. "You know, the breakup and all."

"She was a fool," Lizzie offered. Jenny stared at her in bewilderment as her mind screamed, *'What was your excuse?'*

CHAPTER SEVEN

Jenny tossed and turned all through the night. She fought to get comfortable so she could get some much-needed sleep. The stress of the last twenty-four hours preyed heavily upon her. The cause of all her turmoil and stress was lying beside her on the tiny futon. To Lizzie's credit she did suggest that she bunk down with her sister Kate. Jenny was very much in favor of the idea. However Kate was not so gracious; she explained that despite the fact that she loved her baby sister dearly, she wasn't about to share a bed with a blanket-thieving, snoring, body-heat-sucking little pest.

What could Jenny do? She certainly couldn't argue the point. She had shared a bed enough times with the little blonde to know that Lizzie was all of those things and more. Lizzie had an annoying habit of not only stealing all the blankets during the night, but also wrapping and tucking them around her body so tightly that it was impossible to retrieve them. Jenny had spent many an evening before and after they'd become lovers fighting for the tiniest scrap of bedding to stave off the cold night air.

So far that night Lizzie had yet to commit this transgression; of course that was because she was wide-awake. "We could talk," Lizzie suggested quietly.

"Don't want to," Jenny grumbled as she fluffed her pillow and turned her back to Lizzie.

"Watch television?" Lizzie persisted. "I haven't seen much in the past decade. Anything good on?"

"Not since the X-Files went off the air," Jenny grunted as she

69

rolled over to find Lizzie lying on her back, staring at the ceiling. "I need to sleep so I can go to work in the morning," Jenny groused.

"Me too," Lizzie sighed in response.

"On Sunday?" Jenny inquired in surprise. She was working weekends because the money was better and Wendy had insisted.

"I always work on Sundays," Lizzie noted wryly.

"Oh yeah, I guess you would." Jenny blinked in surprise. "That must suck. I'm guessing you don't get overtime like I do."

"No." Lizzie chuckled as she rolled over to face Jenny. "That whole pesky vow of poverty thing kind of messes with that."

Jenny smiled as she watched Lizzie's emerald eyes twinkle in the darkness. She felt a strange sense of comfort from the familiarity of the situation. "This kind of reminds me of when we were younger," Lizzie continued with a shy smile. "We'd stay up all night talking and then drag our tired carcasses into class the next morning."

"That's not all we used stay up all night doing," Jenny whispered softly as she held Lizzie's gaze. She hadn't meant to say it, yet the words just slipped out. She also hadn't intended to say it in such a sultry tone.

She felt bad as she watched Lizzie's gaze drift away from her own, a small frown crossing her full lips. "Sorry," Jenny muttered shyly. She watched in horror as Lizzie alternately opened her mouth to speak and then quickly retreated into a heavy frown. "Hey, no big deal, right?" Jenny blurted out, trying to cover up her mistake.

"Jenny, I," Lizzie stammered.

"Like I said, no big deal," Jenny repeated, cutting off whatever Lizzie was about to say. She caught a glimmer of Lizzie's crestfallen look before she rolled over. "Good night," she muttered over her shoulder, unable to look at Lizzie. Jenny felt miserable as she tried to understand how she had been caught in Lizzie's charm so quickly. She wondered if perhaps the breakup with Wendy was messing with her ego or perhaps it was just seeing Lizzie again.

Somehow Jenny did manage to fall asleep for a few short hours. She awoke alone and stumbled off the futon. The tall brunette stretched her body in an effort to ease the tension and cramps caused by sleeping in such a small space. A small smile creased her lips as she detected the faint aroma of coffee. She blinked her weary eyes as she shuffled towards the kitchen. She wasn't completely aware of her movements; she simply followed the enticing aroma calling out to her.

Jenny released an orgasmic groan as she took her first sip. Then she rested against the kitchen encounter and began to savor each drop. Jenny yelped suddenly as Lizzie entered the living room dressed for work. The tall brunette cringed as hot coffee spilled across her torso. "Oh my God," she sputtered as she scrambled to clean up the mess.

"I'm still a couple of promotions shy of that job," Lizzie quipped as she approached Jenny who was fighting to keep her wet T-shirt from further burning her skin.

"Funny," Jenny grumbled as she continued to hold the wet shirt away from her skin.

"Stop that." Lizzie swatted her hands. "Just take it off before you burn yourself any further."

"What?" Jenny squeaked as the damp shirt scalded her once again.

"Take it off," Lizzie repeated vehemently.

"I can't," Jenny protested. Her skin was burned once again as she stepped away from Lizzie.

"Why not?" Lizzie asked in confusion.

"Because you . . ." she stammered as she motioned to Lizzie's black habit. "Turn around," Jenny demanded, seeing it as the only solution to her dilemma.

"You're kidding me?" Lizzie laughed heartily.

"Just turn around," Jenny demanded.

"Fine." Lizzie chuckled as she held up her hands in defeat.

"I don't understand why people get so flustered when they see me in my habit," Lizzie prattled on as Jenny yanked her shirt up over her head and tossed it into the sink. "I mean, it's basic black; how can you go wrong?" Jenny rolled her eyes at Lizzie's running commentary as she ran her fingers over her burned flesh.

"It just surprised me," Jenny mumbled as she tried to plan her escape from the kitchen without Lizzie seeing her breasts. "I wasn't prepared for you looking like a nun." She knew her explanation sounded feeble, but it was how she felt.

"I am a nun," Lizzie teased as she sneaked a peek over her

shoulder.

"Don't do that," Jenny squeaked in horror as her hands flew to her breasts. "Would you not look until I've put on something decent?" Jenny pleaded as she tried to push past Lizzie.

Much to Jenny's horror, Lizzie turned around and laughed. "Jenny, you're being silly." The little nun chuckled. "We used to wear one another's underwear."

"Well, that won't be happening again," Jenny flared as she darted past the laughing blonde. She held her hands to her breasts and Lizzie laughed harder while she searched for something to cover her body. The tears rolling down Lizzie's face miffed her. "Glad you find this so amusing, Sister."

"Jenny," Lizzie choked out as she fought against her laughter, "I've seen them before. In fact I saw them the other night."

"Not dressed like that you haven't," Jenny protested as she snatched a shirt up off the floor and covered herself.

"What is going on out here?" Kate demanded as she stumbled into the living room. She cast a wary glance at both of them. Jenny blushed furiously as she looked for a place to hide from the laughing little nun and her sergeant.

"Jenny won't show me her boobies," Lizzie teased, as Jenny's blush grew deeper.

"Lizzie!" Jenny hissed as she tried to cover more of her body.

"Oh," Kate responded with a yawn. "It's my day off. I'm going back to bed."

"I'm taking a shower," Jenny grunted indignantly.

"I'm going to church," Lizzie added brightly.

"Freaky, isn't it?" Kate whispered to the still flustered Jenny. "Seeing her dressed like that still wigs me out."

"You have no idea," Jenny muttered before making a quick retreat to the bathroom.

Later that day Jenny still felt exhausted while she waited for Nuru to return with their coffee. "How are you holding up, partner?" Nuru inquired as she handed Jenny the steaming paper cup.

"I've been better," Jenny confessed as she took a careful sip of her French Roast. "I'm relieved that Wendy's gone for good," she explained as Nuru started the cruiser.

"Well, that's a bonus," Nuru commented with a slight smile. "I was afraid you might actually forgive that witch and take her back."

"No, it's over for good," Jenny reassured her.

"Can I ask you about something?" Nuru inquired carefully as she pulled out into traffic.

"Sure," Jenny agreed, savoring her coffee, still regretting the loss of her first cup.

"The other night you were talking about someone named Lizzie," Nuru began hesitantly.

Jenny cringed as the memory came back to her. "Kate didn't hear what I said, did she?" she inquired fearfully.

"No," Nuru reassured her. "So you and the Sergeant's little sister, or was it one of those unrequited things?"

"I don't want Kate to hear about this," Jenny cautioned her partner and friend.

"I won't say a word," Nuru vowed.

"We were lovers," Jenny confessed with a heavy sigh. "She was my first. We were just kids and thought the sun rose and set because the other one said so."

"Wow." Nuru blinked in surprise. "So what happened?"

"Like I said, we were kids," Jenny grumbled, not wanting to discuss what really happened. "It doesn't matter now. She's a nun and I don't want my commanding officer to find out I took her baby sister's virginity."

"Understandable," Nuru responded with a chuckle. "She freaks out when someone takes the last Boston Cream donut."

"No kidding." Jenny laughed. "Remember poor Randy? I'm amazed the guy can still use that hand. Oh, you haven't heard the best part. I'm crashing at Kate's place until I get resettled and guess who's in town for a visit?"

Nuru released a hearty laugh. "Your life just gets better and better, doesn't it, girlfriend?" Nuru commented gleefully.

"Don't you wish you were me?" Jenny teased as she spotted a Toyota running a red light. "Ah look at that," she noted as Nuru hit the lights and siren. "I'll run the plates."

It was late that evening when Jenny stumbled up to Kate's apartment, her arms loaded down with the Sunday edition of the

73

Boston Globe and a bag of takeout from Kelly's. She knocked as she juggled the items in her arms. Jenny breathed a sigh of relief when Lizzie opened the door dressed in a pair of sweatpants and a T-shirt. She wasn't prepared for the wide-eyed expression Lizzie cast her. She was confused by the fact that Lizzie's eyes were darting up and down her body as she stood there blocking the doorway. "Can I come in?" Jenny inquired in confusion.

"Sorry," Lizzie blurted out with a deep blush as she stepped aside.

"You okay?" Jenny asked as she settled her stuff on the coffee table.

"Fine," Lizzie squeaked as she closed the door behind her.

Jenny looked at the little blonde strangely as she shrugged off her jacket. As she collected her sleeping attire, she tried to understand why Lizzie looked so flustered all of sudden. Jenny shrugged off her strange behavior as she made her way to the bathroom. Once Jenny had showered, she hung up her uniform and secured her gun. She was happy to see that Lizzie seemed much calmer than when she'd answered the door. "I picked up some fried clams from Kelly's. Want some?" she offered as she settled down onto the futon and opened up her dinner.

"No thanks." Lizzie waved her off as she settled down on the chair by the window.

"Where's Kate?" she asked as she began to search the paper for the real estate section.

"Out with friends," Lizzie offered as she picked up the remote and began to flip through the channels. "Wow, there are so many channels now."

"Still nothing on," Jenny grunted as she scanned the paper and dug into her clam plate. She didn't miss Lizzie watching her each time she took a bite. "Sure you don't want any?" Jenny teased her.

"Maybe just a bite," Lizzie conceded as she crossed over to the futon, shutting off the television as she crossed the room.

"Some things never change," Jenny, responded with a light laugh, as she held up a forkful of clams that she had lightly dipped in some tarter sauce. Lizzie opened her mouth and accepted the offer eagerly. A small amount of mayonnaise dribbled out the side of Lizzie's mouth. Jenny smirked as she grabbed up one of the flimsy paper napkins that came with her dinner and wiped away the errant drops. Lizzie moaned in pleasure as she savored the deep-fried food.

A jolt of familiarity ran through Jenny and her hands quickly retreated. She handed Lizzie the napkin and plastic fork. "Why don't you finish? I'm full," she offered in an off-handed manner.

"Are you sure?" Lizzie asked quizzically.

"Yeah," Jenny lied, unable to meet Lizzie's gaze. There was something all too familiar about the situation that sent Jenny's body into turmoil. Jenny leaned back and rested her hands over her eyes as the far away memory began to replay in her mind.

Her parents were gone for the weekend and Lizzie was on her way over so they could spend the weekend together. It had been easy to convince their respective parents to allow them to have the house to themselves for the weekend. They were seventeen and neither had gotten into serious trouble. Of course, if their parents only knew the real reason they were so eager to spend the weekend alone together, they would have freaked.

The doorbell rang and Jenny let her lover in, assisting her with her overnight bag and two large shopping bags. "What's all of this?" she asked as she carried the bags filled with plastic containers of food into the kitchen.

"My mother is afraid that we're going to starve to death," Lizzie explained with an exasperated sigh as she flipped her long blonde hair.

"It's only for two days," Jenny quipped as she loaded enough meals to feed a family of four for a week into the refrigerator.

Once she'd completed her task, Jenny stood back and looked at the overstocked refrigerator. "So what do you want to eat?" Jenny asked in amusement. She turned to her lover and found herself locked in a fiery gaze. Lizzie flashed a sly smile, took Jenny by the hand, and led her out of the kitchen into the dining room. Jenny's body was pulsating as she bemusedly followed her lover. Lizzie guided her until the back of Jenny's legs bumped into the dining room table.

The raven-haired teenager was certain that she was going explode when Lizzie placed her hands on her shoulders and molded her body to hers. "You know I've really been looking forward to this weekend," Lizzie murmured softly as she began to unbutton Jenny's blouse. "We can be as loud as we want," Lizzie explained in a voice heated with desire as she opened Jenny's blouse. Jenny blushed deeply as Lizzie removed her blouse and tossed it onto the floor. It always amazed her that her sweet innocent-looking girlfriend could be so direct when it came to their passion.

Lizzie began to slowly trace the swell of Jenny's breasts with the tip of her tongue. Jenny's heart raced as she entwined her fingers in Lizzie's soft golden locks. She bit back a moan as Lizzie's talented fingers danced along the straps of her bra while her tongue continued to tease the curve of her breasts with her tongue. Jenny parted her thighs and pulled her lover closer as the clasp of her bra was released.

Her breathing became labored as Lizzie removed her bra and threw it across the room. "You asked me what I wanted to eat," Lizzie murmured against her skin. She flicked her tongue across one of Jenny's nipples until it puckered in response. Lizzie lifted her head slightly and Jenny's body burned from the lustful look in her lover's eyes. "This is what I want," Lizzie demanded in a breathy tone. Jenny allowed her deep moan to escape as she watched Lizzie's tongue peek out once again. This time it teased her other nipple until it was fully erect as well.

Jenny could feel her thighs trembling as Lizzie lowered her down onto the cool surface of the family's mahogany dining room table. The family only dined at the elegant table on special occasions. Lizzie seemed determine to turn this afternoon into a special occasion as she nestled her body between Jenny's thighs. Jenny supported her body by placing her hands flat on the table with her arms behind her; her body was raised just enough that she could watch Lizzie's movements.

Lizzie ran her fingertips slowly along Jenny's exposed flesh, watching intently as the brunette's skin erupted in tiny goose bumps beneath her touch. Jenny's crystal blue eyes darkened with desire; they were focused on Lizzie's breasts that strained against the soft cotton material of her black T-shirt. Jenny felt another moan escape her lips as Lizzie ground her body against her center. The seam of her jeans pressing against her aching clit caused Jenny's faded blue jeans to become even damper as her desire grew.

Jenny's body thrust into Lizzie, needing to feel more of her lover. "This is what I want," Lizzie repeated as her small hands drifted down Jenny's trembling body. Lizzie captured one of her nipples in her mouth and began to suckle it greedily while her hands busied themselves undoing the zipper of her blue jeans. Jenny was whimpering as Lizzie teased her nipple with her teeth and her tongue and her hands urgently yanked Jenny's jeans down her body.

Lizzie nudged Jenny's body down onto the cool surface of the table while she suckled her harder and pushed the rough material of her pants down past her hips. Jenny was sprawled out on the dining room table and her lover's teeth taunted her aching nipple as one of her hands roamed across her passion-soaked panties. Lizzie pressed the palm of her hand against Jenny's mound as she kissed her way over to her other nipple. Jenny's body was thrusting urgently against her lover.

"God, you're so wet," Lizzie growled against her skin as she pressed harder against Jenny's clit. "I want you so much," Lizzie panted as she began to kiss her way down Jenny's body.

Jenny's skin tingled as Lizzie's mouth blazed a determined trail down her body until she was running her tongue along the elastic waistband of her underwear. Lizzie tugged playfully on the band with her teeth while she continued to rub the palm of her hand against her wetness. Lizzie's hand slipped away and she began to caress Jenny's quivering thighs with both hands while she nuzzled her face in the brunette's wetness. "Please," Jenny pleaded as Lizzie's tongue snaked out and began to tease the inside of her thighs.

Jenny's head fell back slightly as her lover knelt before her and removed the last vestiges of her clothing. Jenny fought to stop her body from shaking as Lizzie began to taste her way up her long legs, eventually nestling herself between her thighs. Jenny opened herself as her heart pounded loudly in her heaving chest. She whimpered as Lizzie's tongue dipped into her wetness.

Jenny released a strangled cry as Lizzie's tongue flattened and ran the length of her sex. Before they'd become lovers, Jenny was complete unaware of what it meant to feel with such intensity. Lizzie's tongue drank in her desire with an agonizing slowness as it ran along her slick folds. Once again Jenny was fighting not to lose control of her body, needing the moment to last as long as possible. Her quivering body warned her that it was impossible.

Lizzie draped Jenny's legs over her shoulders as her tongue plunged deeper into the brunette's wetness. Jenny panted and moaned as she felt Lizzie's soft tongue pressing against the opening of her aching center. "Please," Jenny repeated, her voice dripping with need as Lizzie curled her tongue and slowly entered her lover. Lizzie began a slow sensual rhythm, plunging deep inside her lover and withdrawing. Jenny was lost in the sensation of her lover filling her while her hands roamed along Jenny's body.

Jenny ached with desire as she thrust into Lizzie's touch. Her hips arched up as Lizzie drew her closer. Lizzie's tongue slipped from Jenny's warmth. The brunette whimpered in disappointment as her body hovered above the table. She cried out once again as Lizzie's fingers replaced her tongue while her mouth began to suckle her clit. Jenny's body thrust urgently as Lizzie's rhythm grew in intensity. Jenny's urgent cries seemed to fuel Lizzie and she plunged deeper inside the brunette while she suckled her clit harder. Jenny gasped for air as Lizzie pleasured her with a fiery passion. Her ears were ringing as the room spun and her body exploded against her lover's touch.

Lizzie held Jenny tightly while she continued to pleasure her. Her mouth and fingers grew more demanding and Jenny crested once again before collapsing onto the hard surface of the table. Lizzie began to lick away the last traces of Jenny's passion. "It's so good to hear you," Lizzie murmured softly against trembling thighs as her fingers slipped from Jenny's wetness.

Jenny struggled to breathe as she felt her lover's breath caressing her skin. Her body still trembled as her need to sate her lover's passion grew steadily. "I want you," Jenny choked out with a throaty growl. Jenny lifted her still quivering body up and pulled her lover into a lingering kiss as her hands began to explore Lizzie's body, removing as much clothing as she could along the way.

Frustrated by not being able to feel her lover's skin, Jenny slipped down off the table and began to tug Lizzie's clothing off. Lizzie gave herself over to Jenny's demands until she was clad only in a pair of cotton panties. Jenny's tongue traced Lizzie's lips while *she cupped the blonde's wet mound. She parted Lizzie's lips and plunged her tongue deep inside the warmth of her mouth. While she explored Lizzie's mouth, she ground the palm of her hand roughly against Lizzie's mound. The feel of Lizzie's desire soaking through her underwear was making Jenny's body pulsate with renewed passion. Jenny pressed harder as her lover moaned into her mouth. She yanked on the soft cotton material. Lizzie's moans grew deeper as her panties pressed against her clit.*

Jenny tore her mouth from Lizzie's lips and began to lower the blonde's panties. She could see that Lizzie was trembling as she tried to assist Jenny in removing the last barrier that remained between them. Unable to harness her aching need any longer, Jenny tore Lizzie's panties from her body; the blonde released a passionate cry as her body swayed. Jenny assisted her trembling lover up onto the table. Lizzie was balancing herself on her hands and knees, her feet dangling off the edge of the table as she faced away from Jenny.

Jenny's clit throbbed urgently at the sight of her lover kneeling on the table, her long blonde hair cascading down her body. Jenny ran her hands along Lizzie's firm backside, feeling each curve as she tried to resist the urge to take her lover with the fiery intensity that was raging inside of her. Jenny's fingers dipped lower until they were coated with Lizzie's desire. The blonde groaned as her thighs parted, inviting Jenny in.

Jenny stood above her lover's trembling body, and as her fingers dipped into Lizzie's wetness, her tongue began to trail its way up and down the blonde's spine. She felt Lizzie open herself up further as she savored the taste of her skin. Jenny's fingers glided along Lizzie's slick folds until they pressed against the blonde's warm wet center. Jenny entered her lover as her tongue dipped lower and began to trace Lizzie's backside. Lizzie's hips thrust against Jenny's touch as the brunette plunged deeper inside her lover. She could feel Lizzie's thighs trembling and the walls of her center tightened around Jenny's touch.

Jenny plunged in and out of her lover; Lizzie's body matched her wild rhythm while the brunette began to drink in her wetness. Jenny took her lover harder and deeper; she lost herself in the taste of Lizzie's wetness while the blonde cried out in pleasure and begged her for more. Jenny tasted all that Lizzie had to offer, and her fingers filled her while her body rocked wildly. Nervously Jenny added another digit deep inside of Lizzie as her lover loudly begged her for more. Lizzie cried out her name as she collapsed on the table.

Jenny's body was pulsating as the memory played over in her mind. She would never forget how incredibly desirable Lizzie looked perched up on that table as she pleaded for more. To this day Jenny still blushed when she shared a meal with her parents at that same dining room table. "That was incredible," Lizzie moaned in pleasure.

"Yes, it was," Jenny absently responded.

The brunette lifted her head and smiled when she discovered that Lizzie had managed to polish off the last of her fried clams. "You okay?" Lizzie asked her in concern. "You look a little flushed."

"I'm fine," Jenny lied. Her body still hummed from the memory of their youthful passion. She shook her head in an effort to erase it. She wasn't certain what had invoked the memory. If simply watching Lizzie dining on some takeout food was going to have this kind of effect on her, she was going to need to find a new residence very quickly.

Jenny sighed deeply as she lifted herself into a sitting position and once again began to look over the ads for available apartments in the area. Lizzie cleaned up the remnants of their dinner and took them to the kitchen. A knock on the front door startled both of them. "I wonder who that can be." Lizzie asked as she made her way over to the doorway. Jenny smiled in amusement as she watched her ex-lover stand up on her toes to see through the peephole.

Her smile quickly faded as she watched the small blonde's body tense. Lizzie's face had turned ashen when she spun around. Her emerald eyes were filled with fear as she clutched her heart and leaned against the door. "What is it?" Jenny asked fearfully.

"My Mother," Lizzie choked out in fear.

CHAPTER EIGHT

"It's my mother," Lizzie gasped again as she leaned against the door. Jenny's chest tightened.

"I'll get my gun," Jenny offered coldly.

"That's not funny," Lizzie snapped.

"Who said I was joking?" Jenny responded dryly as her face and body tensed. She could see the fear and confusion marring Lizzie's angelic features. Jenny stood and crossed the room, her only focus and goal was to offer comfort to her friend. As Jenny wrapped the trembling smaller woman up in her arms, the brunette felt a strange wave of déjà vu gnawing at her. "If you don't want to see her, then we can just wait here quietly until she goes away," Jenny whispered tenderly in Lizzie's ear as the blonde clung to her.

"Mary Elizabeth Francis Carrington, I know you're in there," the overbearing matron bellowed. "Now open the door this instant."

Jenny's heart constricted as Lizzie slipped from her grasp. "What are you doing?" Jenny asked her in a horrified voice.

"She's my mother," Lizzie explained in a defeated tone.

"And?" Jenny flared.

"And I'm going to talk to her," Lizzie continued, a slight tremor slipping through the confident façade.

"Fine," Jenny responded, not happy with Lizzie's decision. "I'll be right here."

"No," Lizzie stammered. "Seeing you, or rather seeing us together, could set her off."

"I'm not leaving your side," Jenny responded sternly.

They stood there locked in an intense stare, each fighting their own inner demons. Jenny couldn't walk away again. "Not this time," Jenny choked out in a voice that resembled a pleading whimper. "I won't abandon you a second time. I can't."

"You didn't abandon me," Lizzie reassured her as she reached up and cupped Jenny's face tenderly. Jenny leaned into her touch and caressed Lizzie's hand. "I was the one who told you to leave."

"Mary Elizabeth Frances Carrington," the shrilling voice from Jenny's past repeated.

"Why does she do that?" Jenny asked as she gave the door an incredulous look. "Oh well, it did give us an extra few moments to discuss the merits of letting her in or not." Lizzie snorted in amusement at Jenny's strange sense of logic. "I'm not hiding in the other room. There is no way I'm leaving you alone with that woman."

"I've been alone with my Mother before," Lizzie reasoned as the pounding continued. "I'm not looking forward to seeing her. In fact I've been trying to delay it as long as possible. But I can handle this."

"Fine," Jenny responded with a shrug. "Open the door," she instructed her former lover as she folded her arms tightly across her chest, adding to her defiant stance.

"Could you at least wait over there?" Lizzie pleaded.

Jenny nodded in agreement as she started to cross the room. She thought for a moment about pulling the futon up so Mrs. Carrington couldn't see that it was set up for sleeping. Lizzie was smoothing out her sweats and taking calming breaths. As Jenny reclined her long body across the futon in a casual manner, she knew what she was doing would only anger Mrs. Carrington even further, but she couldn't stop herself. She leaned up on her elbow and smiled sheepishly at Lizzie who was giving her a very harsh look. Lizzie was infuriated as she turned to open the door.

Feeling a pang of guilt, Jenny pulled herself up into a more respectable position. Lizzie had barely opened the door when the short stodgy woman pushed her way into the apartment. Mrs. Carrington had gained more weight; considering that she was shorter than Lizzie, it must be affecting her health. Her hair was almost pure white and her once vibrant eyes had dimmed. Her face was bright red and the veins in her neck were bulging as she started to back Lizzie into a corner. "How dare you leave me standing in the hallway!" she growled at the truly frightened blonde.

Jenny leapt from the futon and crossed the room as Mrs. Carrington continued to berate her child in a demoralizing fashion. "Back off," Jenny hissed as she approached the irate woman who had been unaware of her presence. Mrs. Carrington turned and stared up at the fuming policewoman.

"What are you doing here?" Mrs. Carrington spat out, as her face grew redder with each passing moment. Jenny briefly wondered if she was about to have a stroke. "Mary Elizabeth, what is this person doing here?" she demanded in an accusing tone as she turned back to Lizzie.

Jenny clenched her fist as she tried to calm herself. It wasn't easy with so many memories screaming through her mind. She had to try and defuse the situation before history repeated itself. "Mrs. Carrington?" Jenny began in a controlled tone.

"I said answer me, Mary Elizabeth," the woman flared, ignoring Jenny's presence.

Jenny watched in horror as Lizzie, the woman who had recently stood up to a drug lord, cowered in the corner. Jenny reached around the older woman and pulled Lizzie away from the corner and wrapped her arms around her trembling body. "Stay out of this," Mrs. Carrington hissed as she wagged her finger at Jenny. The policewoman wanted to laugh at the woman's theatrics.

"Mrs. Carrington, I'm a guest in your daughter's home," she explained as she fought the urge to simply haul off and slap the woman. "Lizzie is very upset. If you want to talk to her, I suggest you lower your voice or leave." Jenny gently guided Lizzie away from her mother as she spoke.

"I told you to stay away from her," the older woman said bitterly to Lizzie in a slightly lower tone. "You remember what the judge said."

Lizzie's body tensed before she pulled herself from Jenny's grasp. "Mother, you need help," Lizzie offered in a soft pleading voice as she slowly approached her.

"I need help?" Mrs. Carrington laughed in response. "You are sick. How dare you tell me that I need help?"

The slap happened so suddenly Jenny could do nothing to

prevent it. Jenny wasn't certain what was tearing at her insides more - the fact that Mrs. Carrington hit her daughter or the way Lizzie didn't even flinch from the hard slap. Jenny quickly maneuvered herself between the two women. "Go before I arrest you," Jenny informed the woman she hated most in the world. The sight of her was making her stomach turn, but she had to maintain her focus. Years of training were paying off as she kept a towering stance over the woman.

"You are not leaving the church, young lady," Mrs. Carrington informed her daughter who was still standing numbly behind Jenny's protective stance. "You will not bring shame to this family again."

"I said that it was time for you to leave," Jenny repeated authoritatively. "I'm not kidding. Unless you want to spend the night in jail, you will leave now."

"You think you can come between me and my family?" the short robust woman challenged her.

"Your family doesn't want anything to do with you," Jenny responded, finding the woman's challenge completely absurd.

"If you think for one moment I'm going to leave my child alone with a depraved pervert, you are sadly mistaken," Mrs. Carrington challenged her once again with a cold stare and a fierce growl.

"Now you're concerned about your children's well being?" Jenny choked out in disbelief.

"I will not allow you to corrupt her again," Mrs. Carrington asserted.

"You can't be serious," Lizzie muttered in disbelief as she moved to Jenny's side. "I think you should leave," she told her mother who looked at her in disgust. "Jenny is a guest in Kate's home, and I doubt that she would appreciate you treating her friends in such a manner."

Jenny watched as the woman's face exploded in beads of perspiration as her hand started to rise. "You raise that meat hook again and I will lock you up," Jenny informed her as she cast an icy gaze down at the smaller woman. She pinned the woman with her glare as Lizzie once again stood there without flinching. Jenny almost wished that the older woman would try something so she could arrest her. She knew the look on Lizzie's face; she'd seen it many times before. It was the look of a battered child, cowering when her mother screamed at her yet standing idly by while her mother beat her.

They stood there in an eerie silence as Lizzie's eyes turned blank and distant. Mrs. Carrington and Jenny held each other's gaze, waiting for the other to blink. "Fine," Mrs. Carrington conceded with a callous smirk. "Mary Elizabeth, I want you to gather your things."

Jenny was horrified when Lizzie began to obey her mother's request. "What are doing?" She asked in disbelief. Lizzie stumbled slightly as she halted her movements. Lizzie stood completely still as Jenny and Mrs. Carrington glared at one another.

"It seems I missed all the fun," a cold voice announced, ending the standoff.

Jenny lifted her gaze to find Kate standing in the doorway. "Jenny, would you please put some clothes on and take my sister for a walk?" Kate instructed her sternly. Jenny knew it wasn't a request. She didn't care; getting Lizzie out of there was something she looked forward to doing. "Liz, are you all right?" Kate asked as Jenny pulled her jeans up over her shorts and grabbed a jacket. Lizzie simply nodded mutely with a vacant look. "Put something warm on and go with Jenny." Lizzie moved like a zombie into the bedroom. "Not a word from you, old woman," Kate cautioned her mother who was staring at her in disbelief. "I told you before that if you ever laid another hand on her, I'd lock you up."

Jenny put on her shoes; Lizzie reappeared, having found a jacket and shoes. The brunette silently prayed that Kate would make good on her threat. She placed a comforting arm around Lizzie's shoulders. It broke her heart when the blonde flinched at her touch. She took a deep breath and walked the dazed woman out of the apartment. She didn't miss the fierce scowl Mrs. Carrington cast upon her.

They walked in the cool night air without speaking. Jenny simply allowed Lizzie to be alone with her thoughts, praying that she would see the spark return to her eyes as they walked along the Charles River. Finally she could see a glimmer of life returning to the normally vibrant eyes of her former lover. She guided Lizzie to a bench and they sat in silence.

When she saw Lizzie starting to shiver from the cold, she pulled her closer and wrapped her arms around her. Lizzie blew out a heavy breath. "Better?" Jenny inquired carefully.

"A little," Lizzie responded wearily.

"Was she violent before that night?" Jenny asked softly.

"No," Lizzie responded flatly.

"Has she hurt you since then?" Jenny inquired as her throat constricted, already knowing the answer.

"Yes," Lizzie answered her weakly. "Please don't tell Kate."

"I can't promise you that," Jenny responded as she pulled the shivering blonde closer.

Lizzie snuggled closer, seeming to accept Jenny's choice. "What did she mean when she mentioned the judge?" Jenny asked as she comforted the smaller woman by making soothing circles across her back. Lizzie's body tensed as she pulled slightly away from Jenny's touch. Her eyes were puffy, and she had tears running down her face.

"Oh, Jenny Jacobs, it seems the past has caught up with us." Lizzie sniffed as she wiped away the tears. "We need to talk."

'Now that is the understatement of the century,' Jenny thought as she looked deep into Lizzie's saddened eyes. "Whatever you want to talk about is okay," Jenny offered, letting her old friend know that she could share her deepest secrets with her or tell her nothing at all. Jenny was going to be there. "But remember, I already know that it was you who let the snake loose in Principal Skinner's office," Jenny added playfully.

"That's because you were with me," Lizzie noted with a hint of a smile. "Who knew that big man could scream like a girl?"

They both fell into light chuckles as Jenny wrapped her arm around Lizzie's shoulder, and the blonde leaned into her. As the light laughter faded, Lizzie snuggled deeper into the warmth of Jenny's body. There wasn't anything sexual about the way they were holding one another. Jenny had a sense that her friend had returned to her; that one person from her youth whom she had shared all of her secrets, dreams, and fears with, not to mention the blood oath to stay best friends forever that they'd made when they were seven. "This reminds me of when we were kids," Jenny murmured absently as she pulled Lizzie closer.

"I know," Lizzie agreed with a relieved sigh. "You didn't abandon me that night," Lizzie assured her. "There was nothing either of us could have done."

"I could have . . ." Jenny began to protest.

"Nothing," Lizzie cut her off. "We were seventeen years old; we had no options. Other than running away, and trust me, that is no option."

"What are you saying?" Jenny asked fearfully. "What happened, Lizzie?"

"My mother flew me out to St. Paul and took me directly to the school," Lizzie explained softly. Despite her outwardly calm demeanor, Jenny could hear the raw pain hiding behind the words. "Dad didn't come. I don't think he fully understood what was happening. He never went to Bingo with my Mother. I found out years later that he had a weekly poker game on those nights." Lizzie smiled at the memory before the darkness returned once again. She cleared her throat before she continued. "When we left I wasn't allowed to bring anything with me, just the clothes on my back. My Mother didn't speak to me the entire time; she didn't even look at me. She just dumped me off and left. That night I did the only thing I could think of doing. I ran."

"You ran away?" Jenny blurted out.

"Yes. I didn't think about what I was doing; I just took off," Lizzie explained in a distant tone. "I had no money and no real idea of where I was. I just wanted to go home and be with you. Seeing you again was my only goal. I was stupid."

"Really?" Jenny grumbled, thinking that Lizzie was talking about her.

"Yes," Lizzie explained softly. "But not about needing to see you. I was just another kid on the streets of St. Paul with no money and no one to turn to. Autumn nights in Minnesota are cold." Jenny felt Lizzie shiver from her memories.

"How did you survive?" Jenny asked as the fear that was welling up inside of her threatened to choke her.

"I slept in abandoned warehouses and stole food from the local supermarket," Lizzie explained. "I kept trying to figure out how I was going to get back home. Without money, it was impossible. I tried hiding on a train but got caught. I ran before the cops showed up. I'd been on the streets for almost two months before I was finally arrested for shoplifting. Since I wasn't forthcoming with any information, it took them over a week to track down my family. I spent the entire time locked up in a juvenile detention home. I don't have to tell you what that's like. When my mother finally showed up, she used my lawyer to arrange a deal with the judge - twenty-four months of probation."

"For a first time shoplifting offense?" Jenny shouted bitterly. "How much did your dear sweet mother have to do with the harshness of your sentence?"

"Everything," Lizzie confessed shyly. "I think she embellished a few things to get the judge on her side. While I was on probation she was in complete control. And she held it against me. She sent me back to the convent school. I wasn't allowed to go home, and I was shipped off to a convent to begin my training as a novice while I attended a Catholic college. I figured I would just get my degree and bide my time."

"What happened to change that?" Jenny asked, unable to believe everything Lizzie had been forced to endure. The thought of the sweet young girl she knew trying to survive on the streets was making her sick.

"Life," Lizzie explained flatly.

"And?" Jenny pressed, wanting to know what had happened and why Lizzie had betrayed her trust in her. If she had loved her enough to live on the streets facing unspeakable danger, what had made her turn her back on the love that they'd shared?

"And nothing." Lizzie shrugged. "I jumped from one rash decision to the next, and now I have no idea who I am. The only good thing that happened was when a local school needed more teachers. The order I had joined was a cloistered sect. Which meant that I was almost completely cut off from the outside world."

"Let me guess who chose that," Jenny grumbled.

"My Mother," Lizzie conceded. "But when this other order needed teachers for their school, I used my education and joined it. That order was a lot more in touch with the real world. Unfortunately I got into trouble again. That was the first time I got shipped up to Saskatchewan. I hated it. All the nuns looked like lumberjacks and it was cold. I hate the cold."

"I can imagine you would after sleeping on the streets," Jenny said in concern as she pulled Lizzie closer to her in an effort to keep her safe and shield her from the night air. "Wait! The first time they sent you to Saskatchewan? How often were you in trouble?"

Lizzie chuckled lightly. "On and off. I taught at a series of parochial schools in St. Paul and then Chicago. Not all of my troubles were caused by my sexuality. I had allied myself with a movement in the church known for its untraditional beliefs. We believe that women need more of a say in what is happening in the church, and that the Holy Father needs to realize what century we're living in. I also made a shift in my assignments from the more prestigious schools to the inner city where I felt I was more needed. For the first time in my life, I was good at something that I really enjoyed doing. I was sent to Los Angeles then back to Chicago. They began to send me all over the country, each time to a school that was poorer than the last. The funny thing was they thought they were punishing me. In reality they were doing me a favor."

"And just what were you being punished for?" Jenny pried.

"Let's just say I had a knack for finding kindred spirits," Lizzie explained sheepishly as Jenny chuckled. "Every time I got busted they'd ship me up to Saskatchewan so I could see the error of my ways. The Mother Superior there is really strict and worked us to the point of exhaustion. She also enjoyed lecturing me daily on the evils of homosexuality. She made a point of reminding me that I wasn't the first to turn to the church because of sexual confusion."

"How did you put up with that?" Jenny asked in disgust.

"I held my tongue," Lizzie explained seriously. "Of course the whole time I was thinking, *'No kidding! I'm not the only one. Where do you think I keep meeting these women?'* It was all really silly when you think about it," Lizzie added with a light laugh.

"So all your girlfriends were other nuns?" Jenny asked with a hint of jealousy clouding her words.

"Well, I wouldn't call them girlfriends," Lizzie explained thoughtfully. "They were more like special friends, and there weren't that many of them. Each time I broke my vows, I just couldn't stop myself. What's wrong with me?"

"Nothing," Jenny admonished her. "You're human."

"I think that I was trying to get caught," Lizzie continued, lost in her own thoughts. "That somehow it would be easier if I was asked to leave. I ended up being sent to New York. That's when things really hit the fan, so to speak. I was teaching at a school in Harlem during the day, and at night I was taking classes at NYU. I wanted to get my Master's degree. When I wasn't teaching or going to school, I did some volunteer work at this clinic. I didn't go there as Sister Rachel. The clinic wasn't the type that the archdiocese would have approved of since they taught family planning and gave counseling to gay teens. I got involved after one of my students committed suicide. I had to keep my work there a secret; it seemed like the right thing to do. I met this other volunteer there. She was a lawyer and married, and I should have known better. She didn't know I was a nun until we already felt an attraction to one another. My superiors discovered my visits to the clinic and my relationship with her. I was off to South America by way of Saskatchewan. Biggest mistake of my life."

"Did you love her?" Jenny asked, certain that she really didn't want to know.

"No," Lizzie confessed with a heavy sigh. "That's why it was a mistake. If I had been, my actions would have made some sense. I didn't sleep with her either. Yet there was something between us. In the end I ruined both of our lives."

Hey," Jenny cut her off. "You're acting like this woman didn't have a mind of her own. What did she have to say about all this?"

"She said that I helped her realize who she was," Lizzie admitted.

"I thought so," Jenny said with a heavy sigh. "Stop blaming yourself."

"I will if you will," Lizzie offered hopefully.

Jenny's lips curled as she tried to reconcile everything she and Lizzie had said since being reunited. It was true that they both needed to stop blaming themselves. It wasn't easy. Jenny also felt that there was still a major piece missing. Then she found herself smiling and released a light laugh.

"What?" Lizzie inquired curiously.

"Special friends?" Jenny offered in a droll tone. "In the

outside world we have quite a different term for that."

"Really?   What is it?" Lizzie asked with a wide-eyed innocence.

"Never mind." Jenny cringed. There was no way she was going to explain to her high school sweetheart, the nun, about fuck buddies.

"So, Jenny, tell me about your life," Lizzie encouraged her.

"Maybe tomorrow." Jenny yawned as once again the events of the past few days overwhelmed her. "It's late. We should start heading back before Kate begins to worry." Jenny found herself wrapped up in a soft hug.

"Thank you," Lizzie whispered softly before releasing her.

Jenny shrugged off her friend's gratitude as she stood and helped Lizzie to her feet. Lizzie looked out over the flowing water of the Charles River. "It's beautiful here," she said with a sense of serenity.

"Yes, it is," Jenny, agreed as she looked out over the calm waters and the lights of the University gleaming across river. She smiled at the sight of Lizzie looking out at the water. Jenny realized that it was one of those moments when you look around and realize you are home.

CHAPTER NINE

Jenny braced herself for whatever awaited them when they returned to Kate's apartment. Thankfully Mrs. Carrington was gone. Kate was visibly upset. She could see the look of guilt in Lizzie's eyes. "Kate?" Lizzie approached her sister carefully.

"Why don't we all go for a sail tomorrow?" Kate inquired distantly.

Jenny and Lizzie gave her an odd look. Jenny had a feeling that Kate was up to something. "Kate?" Lizzie repeated with a slight tremor.

"Listen, kiddo, this isn't your fault." Kate turned to her younger sibling and wrapped her arms around her. "And no, I didn't arrest her, although I thought about it," she added wryly. Her face clouded over with a sad expression. "There is so much I need to talk to you about." Kate's tone almost sounded like a plea. "Tomorrow we can take the boat out, and the three of us can have a good time. I've already cleared Jacobs and myself. We're on protective duty," Kate added with a sly wink.

"What boat?" Lizzie asked in confusion.

"My boat," Kate informed her. "It was my gift to myself after the divorce."

"You were married?" Lizzie blurted out in surprise.

"Briefly," Kate responded with a laugh. "Roger, the guy I was involved with a few years ago, and I went to Las Vegas for a vacation. After winning big at the black jack table and drinking far too many cocktails, we decided to get married that night. By the time we flew home we both knew it was a mistake. A few months

93

later we got a divorce."

"A quickie wedding in Vegas and a divorce? I see you're still trying to give Mom an aneurysm," Lizzie teased, seeming to relax slightly.

"I do what I can," Kate retorted gleefully. "Now why don't we all get some sleep? I think we've had enough excitement for one day."

Lizzie and Jenny simply nodded in response. Jenny was still exhausted and a little hungry since she gave her dinner to Lizzie. "Jacobs?" Kate motioned for her to come over while Lizzie ducked into the bathroom.

"What's up, Sarge?" Jenny asked with a slight yawn.

"Thank you," Kate offered softly. Jenny looked at her in confusion. "For protecting my sister. I want to thank you. My mother is out of control."

"I've noticed," Jenny commented wryly. "As far as Lizzie is concerned, I would never let anything happen to her. After all we did sell Girl Scout cookies together," Jenny added with a smile.

"Well, be that as it may, thank you," Kate answered with a chuckle and a warm smile. "I just wish I knew what started all of this." Jenny's heart sunk as guilt crept up on her. She had the answer her friend was seeking, but she was unable to reveal the truth. "You want to tell me?"

"I can't," Jenny responded with a grimace. "You should talk to your sister."

"Fine," Kate answered her, seeming to understand why she was holding back. "Good night, Jacobs."

"Night, Sarge," Jenny replied, guilt gripping at her insides.

Lizzie emerged from the bathroom just in time to say goodnight to her sister. Jenny could hear them whispering. The tall brunette gathered up her things, brushed past the whispering siblings, and ducked into the bathroom. Her hasty retreat into the bathroom gave everyone the space they needed. "I need to find a place to live," she muttered as she turned on the shower. Jenny undressed and stepped into the soothing spray of water. She was tired; her mind and body ached from the emotional roller coaster she'd been on for the past couple of days.

All she wanted was for her mind to stop spinning, to stop

reliving the past so she could just get some sleep. As she washed her long dark hair, her mind refused to idle. She found herself recalling the night she and Lizzie had made love for the first time. They had fallen asleep in one another's arms.

Jenny was fast asleep, holding her lover in her arms, when the sound of the front door opening and closing jolted her from her blissful slumber. "It's my parents!" she gasped in horror as she jostled her lover.

"Damn it!" Lizzie choked out. "What time is it?"

Jenny reached for the clock that was resting on the table beside her bed. The red glowing numbers glared at her in the darkness. "It is a quarter past twelve," she stammered nervously.

"I have to get out of here," Lizzie squeaked as she bolted out of bed. "I was supposed to be home over an hour ago."

Jenny's heart was hammering in her chest as she heard her parents' footsteps approaching her room. "They're coming upstairs," Jenny whispered in a horrified tone. "They'll look in on me," she explained as she leapt out of bed and helped her lover find her clothing. "Quick! Hide!" she instructed the frightened blonde as she gently pushed her into the bathroom. Jenny raced around her room, trying to be quiet as she grabbed a T-shirt. She spied Lizzie's underwear lying on the floor. She snatched up the garments and tossed them into the bathroom. "Thanks," Lizzie responded as she bent over to collect her belongings.

Jenny's stomach clenched. Lizzie's movement gave the flustered brunette a full view of her assets. "Oh my," she gasped and then she broke out in a deep blush as Lizzie turned to her and flashed her a saucy grin. The sound of the doorknob to her bedroom alerted her. She quietly closed the door to the bathroom, leapt across the room, and dove under the covers.

Jenny felt her heart racing as her parents peeked into her bedroom to find their only child supposedly fast asleep. Jenny was far too terrified to move as she heard them whispering. After they closed the door, she listened to her parents' retreating footsteps. Finally convinced that the coast was clear, she sprang from the bed and listened at the door for a few moments.

Jenny blew out a sigh of relief. Her moment of reprieve

quickly vanished when she heard her father tell her mother that he was heading downstairs to his office to finish up some paperwork. "Shit," she muttered as she turned to her bathroom and quietly opened the door. Jenny's crystal blue eyes widened in surprise as she looked into the dark bathroom and discovered that it was empty. Her tiny private bathroom had no windows so she knew that the blonde couldn't have escaped without her seeing her. She gently pulled back the plastic shower curtain that sported a picture of the Bionic Woman.

Jenny almost burst out in laughter when she found Lizzie cowering in the bathtub. "Is it safe?" the blonde whispered urgently.

"No," Jenny responded with a scowl as she assisted the small blonde out of the bathtub and back into her bedroom. "My Dad went downstairs to his study," she explained in a worried tone. "There's no way to get you downstairs without him seeing you."

"I am so dead," Lizzie whispered as her emerald gaze drifted to Jenny's bedroom window.

Jenny watched in horror as a mischievous smirk emerged on Lizzie's face. The small blonde opened the window and looked down. "Are you insane?" Jenny protested as her young lover lifted the screen and started to crawl out the window.

"I'll be fine," Lizzie reasoned as she crept further out the window. "I'll just climb down the trellis. Don't worry," Lizzie reassured the stunned brunette.

Jenny was smiling as she stepped out of the shower. Lizzie had fallen of course, managing to break her ankle in the process. It turned out to be a lucky break. Somehow the spunky little blonde managed to convince her parents that she'd broken her ankle while running home so she wouldn't break her curfew and get grounded again. Lizzie's parents believed her. The injury did leave her in a cast for over a month. Lizzie spent the last few days of the school year being chauffeured around by her mother. Between Lizzie's lack of mobility and Robby's sudden increased attention towards Jenny, the two girls hadn't had an opportunity to talk about what had happened between them.

Jenny sighed heavily as she leaned up against the bathroom

vanity. She wasn't ready to go back out into the living room to face Lizzie. All she could think about was how anxious she'd been back then to talk to Lizzie. Well, not just talk to her; she wanted to wrap the small blonde up in her arms and kiss her senseless. She'd been terrified that Lizzie might reject her.

She had to see Lizzie. She wanted to tell her that she wasn't sorry that they'd made love. She needed to express to the energetic blonde just how deeply she loved her. Jenny also wanted to show Lizzie that she wanted to be with her again. Terrified that Lizzie would not return her feelings; she gathered up her last ounce of courage and forced herself to face her fears. Jenny had to know one way or another if she had a place in Lizzie's heart.

Unfortunately it took almost two weeks before Jenny had the opportunity to be alone with Lizzie. They were in Lizzie's bedroom, and Mrs. Carrington had a church function to attend. Lizzie looked like an angel, lying on her bed with her foot propped up on a pillow and her long golden hair cascading down her shoulders. They didn't get the chance to talk about what had happened between them just a few short weeks ago. From the moment they heard Lizzie's mother close the front door, they were in one another's arms, kissing each other with a newfound passion.

Jenny unbuttoned Lizzie's blouse and unhooked her bra, freeing her beautiful breasts. She captured Lizzie's nipple in her mouth and teased it gently. Lizzie lifted Jenny's face to her own and kissed her deeply. She unbuttoned Jenny's blouse and reached down to unhook the clasp on the front of her bra. "I like this," Lizzie remarked with a sly smile. "Easy access," she added as she cupped Jenny's breasts in her hands. Jenny playfully pushed Lizzie's hands away and then proceeded to completely undress her lover, using care as she lowered Lizzie's shorts over her cast.

Then she slowly undressed herself and lowered her long body down into her lover's embrace. There was no need for words. Jenny knew what Lizzie wanted and the blonde definitely knew what she wanted. Lying side by side they felt completely at ease as they gently touched each other's bodies with soft caresses. They stared deep into one another's eyes as they moaned with pleasure. They replayed everything they'd learned their first night together. Jenny knew that they belonged to one another. She also understood that they had to be careful and hide the love they shared.

Jenny shook her head furiously in an effort to banish the thoughts. The memory of Lizzie's lips still burned so intensely. It was all too confusing. The breakup with Wendy and Lizzie's sudden reappearance plus the demonic Mrs. Carrington - Jenny was lost in the turmoil of the past. "That is all it is - the past," she said, trying to convince herself that her attraction to the small blonde emerged only because of what they'd lost in the past. "Making love to her again would be the worst thing I could do, even if she does leave the church," she assured herself. "She left me and found someone else," she continued to babble at her image in the bathroom mirror. Her heart failed to feel the conviction of her words. A part of her did feel a little better after talking with Lizzie by the chilly waters of the Charles River. Still, she had a masochistic need to know why Lizzie had given up on their love. Young wounds take the longest to heal and the vision of her first lover wrapped up in another woman's arms still haunted her.

Jenny groaned as her inner turmoil reemerged. Shaking her head clear once again, she dried off and dressed in a pair of sweatpants. Finally she exited the bathroom and crawled under the covers next to the source of her torment. Lizzie's steady breathing gave the brunette a small sense of relief as she snuggled into her pillow. Jenny smiled as she heard the tiny whimpers Lizzie released in her slumber. "Some things never change." She chuckled softly as her eyelids grew heavy.

Jenny drifted off to sleep only to become lost in the past. Her dreams evoked visions of rainstorms and Lizzie's body lying before her as she pulled Jenny closer. Jenny hovered above her lover and kissed Lizzie's naked body. She kissed her milky white shoulders and worked her way down her lean body before teasing her nipple with her tongue. Jenny's desire grew as her tongue slowly flickered across the tiny rose-colored bud.

Once Jenny had drifted off to sleep memories invaded her thoughts. Suddenly the vision turned dark as faceless women invaded her thoughts. The faceless women called out, *'Beth.'* She beckoned her in a sultry voice. Jenny's eyes flew open as her body sprang up. She'd broken out into a cold sweat and she was struggling to breathe. Jenny gasped for air as she held herself in an effort to calm down.

"Jenny? Are you all right?" Lizzie asked in a quiet yet frightened voice. Jenny's body shook violently as Lizzie wrapped her arms around her.

"I'm fine," Jenny choked out. "Bad dream," she gasped as her chest tightened painfully.

Lizzie pulled her closer and rocked her gently as she made soothing circles along Jenny's back. Jenny relaxed as Lizzie held her. Feeling her breathing return to normal, she turned to the blonde to thank her. Jenny's mouth went dry as they sat there in the darkness, simply staring at one another. With almost no space separating them Jenny could hear the rapid beating of Lizzie's heart. Unaware of what they were doing, they leaned towards one another. Jenny felt Lizzie's breath caressing her skin. As their lips were just about to touch, Lizzie jerked back and turned away.

"I'm sorry," the blonde whimpered helplessly. "I can't."

Jenny was far too stunned by her own lack of control to speak. "If I break my vows again, I won't be permitted to return to my order. This time there would be no going back," Lizzie explained in a confused voice.

Jenny was torn between offering comfort and exploding in anger. She wanted to ask why it was all right for her to break her vows in the past and not now. She took a calming breath and reached out to place a comforting hand on the blonde's quivering shoulder. Jenny jerked her hand back before she could touch Lizzie; she realized that touching one another was far too dangerous for both of them. "It's all right," she offered in a comforting tone. "I understand," Jenny lied. She could see Lizzie nodding in response. They crawled back under the covers and pulled the blankets up, forming an invisible barrier between them. They spent the rest of the night lying there stiffly, each pretending to sleep.

Just before the sun was about to caress the morning sky, Jenny climbed off the futon and was greeted by an overly cheerfully Kate and one cranky little nun. "Come on, ladies. The weather might turn later so we need to get going," Kate chimed gleefully.

"Bite me," Lizzie grumbled as she tried to retreat under the covers.

The sight of tufts of blonde hair peeking out made Jenny smile. The smile quickly vanished as once again a rush of memories overwhelmed her. "Coffee," Jenny grunted as she stumbled into the kitchen.

"We can get some on the way," Kate suggested as she engaged in a tug of war with Lizzie for the blankets.

"No," Jenny snapped in a harsher tone than she'd intended. "I'm not heading up to Salem until I have some coffee in my tired old body."

"I'm with Stretch," Lizzie agreed from beneath her blankets.

Jenny began to put on a pot of coffee as she muttered under her breath. "Stretch!" She scowled. "Why, I ought teach that little rodent a lesson."

"I heard that," Lizzie bellowed as Kate dragged her from the futon.

"Good," Jenny grunted in response. She watched the steady drip of the coffee maker as she leaned against the counter.

"Who are you calling a rodent?" Lizzie grumbled as she stumbled into the kitchen.

"You, Pee Wee," Jenny snorted, as her crystal blue eyes remained focused on the coffee maker. She could hear Lizzie growling next to her. "Behave or no coffee," Jenny chastised her.

"You suck," Lizzie quipped as she leaned against Jenny's body. Jenny could feel her body warming from the blonde's touch. "Didn't sleep either?" Lizzie whispered softly so Kate couldn't hear her.

"No," Jenny confessed in a feeble voice.

"Why is this happening?" Lizzie asked in a troubled tone.

"Just old feelings," Jenny reasoned. "I'll find a place soon and then we can put things in perspective."

Jenny's body tensed as Lizzie wrapped her arms around her from behind. "I'm sorry about last night," Lizzie choked out.

"Please don't touch me," Jenny pleaded as her body trembled with desire. She felt cold as Lizzie quickly retreated. Jenny swallowed hard as she steadied herself, gripping the kitchen counter tightly. "I know you only mean it as a friendly gesture," she explained softly, keeping her back to Lizzie. *'And that's what hurts,'*

Jenny's mind screamed.

"I'm sorry," Lizzie stammered from behind her.

"Me too," Jenny responded coldly.

CHAPTER TEN

Jenny stood patiently in the long line at Dunkin' Donuts. The morning commuters were eager to get their caffeine fix and Jenny was eager to get away from her traveling companions. When Kate suggested stopping for coffee, Jenny jumped at the chance to get away from the siblings. The long ride up to Salem with Kate and Lizzie was getting on her nerves. During the night Kate must have come to the misguided conclusion that a frontal attack would be what Lizzie needed to open up. Jenny adored her boss, but at times she was such a cop.

Lizzie's response was not to utter a single word. "This is going to be a fun trip," Jenny muttered as she continued to wait in the long line. If she just spent the rest of her day hiding in Dunkin' Donuts, would the Carrington sisters simply leave her there to enjoy the peace and quiet? She knew that if she took much longer one or both of them would barge in and hunt her down. She had already slipped to the back of the line three times.

The thought of spending the day trapped on a sailboat with one woman badgering her sister and the other not speaking just wasn't an appealing concept for the already over-stressed brunette. Suddenly Kate appeared at her side. "What happened? She throw you out of the truck?" Jenny quipped as Kate started to pout like a small child. Jenny didn't know whether she should laugh or cry at the sight of her boss. There was no mistaking the fear and frustration clearly written on the blonde's features.

Jenny sighed deeply as she prepared to step into some very

dangerous waters. "Kate, she's your sister. Just talk to her. Don't lecture her and don't badger her - just talk to her," Jenny said directly, hoping that Kate would listen to what she was trying to tell her.

"Jenny, you have got to help me out," Kate said in a pleading whimper.

"You have no idea what you're asking," Jenny grunted bitterly, angry at being trapped in this situation. "At one time in my life I knew Lizzie better than I knew myself. That just isn't true anymore. Up until a couple of days ago, I hadn't seen or spoken to your sister in over a decade. She isn't the rambunctious teenager I used to play 'truth or dare' with any longer. She's a grown woman with a new life and very adult problems."

Jenny watched in horror as Kate's pout formed into a bitter sneer. "Sorry," Kate snapped in a harsh tone. "I just thought that if anyone could get through to her it would be you. I just want to know what happened to my baby sister. I feel so helpless."

"So do I," Jenny willingly confessed in her own defense. "But you seem to think that Lizzie and I can just pick up where we left off." *Then again, if you knew just where we left off, you would probably beat the snot out of me,*' Jenny's mind screamed fearfully.

Jenny found herself at the front of the line and placed their coffee order with the overworked teenager who was manning the counter. Kate's scowl only seemed to grow as they waited. The deeper the scowl grew, the more Jenny knew that Kate had not listened to what she had said. "It's just that . . ." Kate began urgently.

"Just what?" Jenny groused in defeat. "Kate, listen to me. The last major issue Lizzie and I discussed was how much it sucked that we had to wait until we were sixteen to drive," Jenny lied, knowing that the last major issue they had in fact talked about was their past relationship and the still lingering attraction they both seemed to feel for one another. Much to Jenny's relief, Kate simply nodded in silent agreement with her observations. The tall brunette paid for the coffee order before following Kate out to the truck. She had a nagging fear that the conversation was far from over.

"It's cold," Lizzie grumbled as they loaded the gear up onto the deck of Kate's sailboat. Jenny would have agreed with the small blonde's comment if she hadn't been so startled by the sound of her voice. The irate little nun hadn't uttered a word in over two hours. Jenny smiled as she glanced over at Lizzie who was trying to bury her face inside her jacket. Jenny's smile quickly vanished; there was something about the way Lizzie was shivering that made her uneasy.

"You get used to it," Kate snapped in response as she went about her preparations to cast off.

"I don't want to get used to it," Lizzie said as her teeth began to chatter violently. "Can't we do this some other time?" she added with a whimper.

"No," Kate fumed as she continued with her work. "The sun just came up. Once we're out on the water and the sun is a little higher, it'll warm up."

"It's too cold," Lizzie protested.

"It's just a little brisk," Kate argued in response.

"Brisk?" Lizzie continued to protest. "Kate, it's cold."

"Why are you acting like such a baby?" Kate grumbled.

Jenny was ready to jump ship as the Carrington sisters continued to snipe at one another. She was about to do just that when she glanced over at Lizzie. There was something disturbing about the way the blonde was desperately trying to burrow herself deeper inside her jacket. The brief glimpse she caught of Lizzie's face made her heart stop as the reality of the situation hit her. Lizzie not only hated the cold; she feared it. Jenny could not understand why Kate seemed so oblivious to her sister's discomfort as she tossed life jackets at the both of them. "Let me help you," Jenny offered as Lizzie began to fumble with her life jacket. She took the jacket away from Lizzie and tossed it onto the deck next her own. Then she removed the heavy gloves she'd put on when they were unloading the truck.

"Put these on," she insisted as she handed her gloves to the trembling blonde. "No arguments," she asserted. Lizzie simply nodded in agreement as tears began to fill her emerald eyes. As Lizzie put on her gloves, Jenny reined in her anger as she turned towards the older Carrington. "Kate, does the heater in the cabin work on this bucket of bolts?" Jenny demanded.

"Yes," Kate conceded with a groan. "But once the sun is a

little higher in the sky, we'll be just fine," the blonde argued as she set about casting off.

Jenny stumbled slightly as the small sailboat left the dock. She wrapped her arms around Lizzie and tried to warm her as she fought the urge to beat Kate senseless. "Get down below," Jenny instructed Lizzie softly. Her heart dropped as a pair of frightened green eyes stared up at her. "Go on down below," she repeated. "There should be some blankets. Wrap yourself up in them and climb into the bunk. I'll be down there just as soon as I can to turn the heat on," she offered in a comforting tone as she guided the shivering blonde towards the hatch that led to the boat's cabin.

Jenny's blood was boiling with uncontrollable anger as she watched Lizzie's tiny body retreat to the lower deck. Jenny spun around to her sergeant whose physical strength seriously outmatched her own despite the fact she was shorter than Jenny. As Jenny stormed over to Kate, she was well aware of the fact that Kate could easily beat the brunette to a pulp without breaking a sweat. This did not stop Jenny from yanking the preoccupied woman by the arm and spinning her around. Kate's reaction wasn't unexpected; her body reacted to Jenny's assault and she swung a fist to defend herself. Jenny had anticipated her reaction and deflected the blow easily.

"Jacobs?" Kate spat out in confusion.

"Sarge, do me a favor and pull your head out of your ass for two seconds," Jenny demanded with a fierce growl as she kept a tight hold on Kate's arm.

"Excuse me?" Kate fumed as she cast a menacing gaze up at Jenny.

"She's cold," Jenny hissed as Kate looked at her in confusion. It was clear that Kate still didn't understand what the problem was as Jenny tightened her grip on the blonde's arm.

"And?" Kate asked in bewilderment.

It was at that moment that Jenny realized just how little the Carrington sisters had shared with one another over the last decade. Kate was acting like she didn't know what was going on because she truly didn't know what was going on. Jenny loosened her grip and released a frustrated sigh. "Do you know that she ran away from that school your mother dumped her in?" Jenny inquired carefully as her voice trembled.

"What?" Kate stammered as her face suddenly paled.

'Why do I have to be the one to do this?' Jenny's heart screamed. She braced herself so she could explain what was wrong with Lizzie without Kate going completely ballistic. "She ran away right after your mother abandoned her there," Jenny explained in a slow controlled tone. She watched for any sign that Kate understood what she was talking about. She was worried that she was about to betray Lizzie's trust in her. Jenny brushed the thought aside as she watched Kate's mind process what she'd just told her.

"She ran away?" Kate stammered. Jenny nodded shyly in response. "Where did she go?"

"Nowhere," Jenny explained. "She had no money and no street smarts to get help. Look, she can explain it to you later," Jenny added, trying to get Kate to focus on the immediate problem. She watched as the anger steadily began to cloud Kate's face. "She wasn't hurt," Jenny added quickly in an effort to placate the furious woman standing before her. "Work it out later," she added firmly. "Right now I have to get her warm." The only thing Jenny wanted or needed at that moment was to take care of Lizzie. "How do I turn on the heat in the cabin?" she asked calmly.

"I'll do it," Kate sputtered, trying to control her breathing. "I need to anchor us first. Go to her."

Jenny nodded in response as her throat constricted. The overwhelming anger she felt at that moment for Mrs. Carrington and what she'd done to her children's lives threatened to consume her. Stuffing her hands deep into the pockets of her jeans, she turned and went below to check on Lizzie. The sight that greeted the normally controlled policewoman broke her heart. Lizzie was bundled up under a pile of blankets on the bunk located towards the aft of the boat. She was shivering violently and whimpering like a small child. "Kate will be down soon to get the heater up and running," Jenny explained as she climbed up onto the bunk, crawled under the blankets and wrapped her arms around Lizzie's trembling body.

Lizzie turned into the comforting embrace and snuggled up against Jenny's chest. "I'm sorry," Lizzie whispered into her body. Jenny felt better as she felt Lizzie's breath seep through her clothing.

"For what?" Jenny asked softly as she rubbed Lizzie's back in a reassuring manner.

"For acting like this." Lizzie sniffed. "Kate's right; I am acting like a baby."

"No, you're not," Jenny answered her in a firm yet gentle tone as she continued to caress the smaller woman's back.

"I didn't know." Kate's voice echoed through the small cabin.

Jenny and Lizzie turned to look over at Kate. Jenny found it unsettling that her normally hard-as-nails supervisor was looking so forlorn as she shifted nervously on the balls of her feet. "Kate," Lizzie began in a shy quivering voice.

"We can talk about it later, kiddo," Kate quietly reassured her. "Why don't the two of you get some shuteye? Frankly, both of you look like crap," she added with a shy smile.

"Thank you," Jenny snorted sarcastically in response as she felt Lizzie snuggle closer to her. Unconsciously she tightened her hold on the smaller woman. There wasn't anything sexual about their embrace; Jenny was simply comforting a friend who was having some kind of bad flashback. This moment was very different in comparison to the exchanges they'd shared over the past few days. This time, sharing a bed with the small blonde was easy.

"The heat should kick up in a bit," Kate explained. "I've got the motor running and I'll be sailing us a little ways out towards Gloucester. Get some rest." Jenny watched as the blonde made a hasty retreat back up to the deck. Kate seemed to need to put some distance between her and Lizzie so she could wrestle with her own demons.

"Get some shuteye." Lizzie giggled against Jenny's chest. "She would have made a great drill sergeant."

"Tell me about it," Jenny agreed with a heavy yawn. "Lizzie?" she inquired softly as she continued to rub the blonde's back. There was something that had been nagging at her for the past couple of nights and she wanted to know what Lizzie thought about it.

"Hmm?" Lizzie murmured in response.

"Do you find it a little strange that your overprotective sister doesn't seem to have a problem with me climbing into bed with you?" Jenny asked thoughtfully.

"She trusts you," Lizzie reasoned with a hint of hesitation.

"Yeah," Jenny agreed, still feeling a little confused by Kate's actions. "But still, even though we don't talk about it, she knows that I'm gay. I know that she's cool about it and all, but ever since Wendy and I broke up she's been practically ordering me into bed with you. Is it just me or is that a little odd?"

"It's odd," Lizzie confirmed with a heavy sigh. She shifted her body so they could see one another while they spoke. "With everything else that's been going on, I hadn't really stopped to think about it," Lizzie continued thoughtfully. "The other day she didn't even blink an eye when I was teasing you about your breasts."

"Oh, you mean when you were whining about the fact that I wouldn't show you my boobies?" Jenny teased as she poked Lizzie's ribs playfully.

"Yeah, then," Lizzie confirmed with a giggle and a slight blush.

"You are such a brat," Jenny responded as she once again playfully assaulted Lizzie's ribs with her fingers.

"I am not," Lizzie protested vehemently as she tried to swat Jenny's teasing digits aside.

Jenny was surprised when the smaller woman quickly turned the tables on her and began to tickle the brunette furiously. Lizzie straddled her body and began a full attack on Jenny's over-sensitive sides. Lizzie's firm thighs tightened around Jenny's body, making it impossible for her to move. "No," Jenny squealed in protest, thinking it wasn't fair. Lizzie had known every ticklish spot on her body since they were six years old.

"You are such a wimp," Lizzie taunted her as she zeroed in on some of Jenny's more sensitive spots.

"Am not," Jenny fumed as she squirmed in a desperate need to free herself.

"Are too."

"Am not."

"Admit it," Lizzie demanded with a mischievous grin as she tickled Jenny harder. As Jenny tried to fight her off, their legs became entwined, capturing both women as they squirmed against one another's bodies while giggling hysterically. Tears were streaming down Jenny's face as she tried to capture Lizzie's wrists and cease her assault.

"I said sleep!" Kate's voice suddenly boomed from above.

Both women froze in sudden panic. Both of them looked up fearfully as they remained frozen in place. Slowly their gazes drifted down, and as their eyes met they broke out in gales of laughter.

"That was weird." Lizzie laughed as she slid her body off Jenny's. "I felt like I was twelve years old again and she was babysitting us."

"Oh man, she was so strict," Jenny agreed as she tried to steady her breathing. "Then again, every babysitter in the neighborhood agreed that they didn't want to watch the two of us at the same time."

"I never understood why." Lizzie snickered. "Didn't Debbie Collins say that together we were pure evil?"

"Do you remember what we did to poor Debbie?" Jenny asked as she rolled over to face Lizzie.

"No," Lizzie responded.

"We took Polaroid's of her and her boyfriend making out on your parents' sofa," Jenny supplied with an evil grin. "That was after we made water balloons out of the condoms we found in her purse."

"We didn't," Lizzie protested with a slight cringe. "Well, it serves her right for sneaking a boy into the house when she was supposed to be watching us. Whatever happened to her?"

"She's the president of a bank," Jenny replied as she brushed an errant lock of hair off Lizzie's brow.

"Now that's a scary thought," Lizzie grunted as she leaned slightly into Jenny's touch.

"I think she said the same thing about you becoming a nun." Jenny chuckled as her fingers lingered on Lizzie's face.

They gazed into one another's eyes and familiar warmth filled Jenny. Suddenly they both quickly withdrew as Jenny sensed the lines once again blurring. "Feeling better?" Jenny questioned in a clinical tone.

"Yes," Lizzie responded lightly. "I don't know what happened. It was like I was back there. I think the pressures of the last few days and seeing my mother again brought everything a little too close to the surface."

"Probably," Jenny agreed with a yawn. "I'm exhausted."

"Me too," Lizzie concurred as they both snuggled under the blankets.

Before Jenny realized what she was doing, she wrapped Lizzie up in her arms and drifted off into a blissful slumber. As the policewoman slept, images from her past crept into her subconscious. She was lost in a vision; a younger version of herself sat in her first car and her first love was wrapped up in her arms.

Jenny had parked the tan little car in the state park just a few miles away from their homes. She and Lizzie were kissing passionately until they bumped into the stick shift once again. "You couldn't get an automatic," Lizzie grumbled as her hands caressed Jenny's body.

"I like this car," Jenny offered weakly as she allowed Lizzie's hands to drift up under her sweatshirt.

"It's too small," Lizzie argued as she cupped Jenny's breasts.

"Lizzie," Jenny moaned deeply as her body arched in response. "Baby, if we stay here any longer we're going to be late for school. Again," she reluctantly pointed out. She didn't want to stop but one of them had to be the voice of reason. When Lizzie was in an amorous mood, she never thought clearly about anything except ravishing Jenny's body.

"So?" Lizzie murmured as she began to kiss Jenny's neck, eliciting a throaty moan from the brunette. "Both of my parents have left for the day. We could sneak back to my house," Lizzie suggested in a soft inviting whisper against Jenny's neck before she began to suckle the pulse point under her lips.

Jenny cried out as all thoughts of getting to school on time quickly vanished. Instead she slipped her hand between Lizzie's thighs and cupped her mound. After an intense groping session, Jenny drove back to Lizzie's neighborhood, parking her car a couple blocks away from her lover's home. They made a mad dash to Lizzie's house and snuck in through the backdoor. Once they confirmed that the house was empty, they quickly raced up to Lizzie's bedroom and made love until they forced themselves to finally go to school. They each produced a carefully forged note explaining why they were tardy.

The dream was so real that Jenny could feel Lizzie's body

responding to her touch. Her mind was filled with images of nestling between Lizzie's thighs as she feasted upon her lover's desire. Lizzie was moaning deeply as Jenny pleasured her. 'Oh . . . Jenny,' Lizzie moaned just as she had that day. The images in Jenny's dream shifted to Lizzie lying on top of her. Lizzie slipped her hands up under Jenny's clothing and began to gently roll one of Jenny's nipples between her fingers.

Jenny's body arched in response as she felt her desire dampening her jeans and the gentle waves of the ocean rocking her body against Lizzie's. *The ocean!'* her mind suddenly screamed as her crystal blue eyes snapped open. Her body was tingling with desire; Lizzie's hand had indeed crept up under her clothing and she was teasing Jenny's nipple. "Ugh!" Jenny cried out as she sat up. Lizzie's emerald eyes opened and she stared at Jenny in confusion. Jenny watched as Lizzie's look of confusion quickly shifted to one of horror as she discovered where her hand was resting.

"I'm sorry!" Lizzie quickly blurted out as her hand retreated from under Jenny's clothing. The small blonde was blushing furiously. Jenny stumbled off the bunk and crashed down onto the cabin floor. The brunette was completely flustered as she scrambled to her feet. "Bad nun!" She wagged an accusing finger at the embarrassed blonde as she scolded her. "Very bad nun!"

"I didn't mean to," Lizzie protested as her face turned an even deeper shade of red.

"That settles it. When we get back to your sister's apartment, you're sleeping on the floor," Jenny continued to fume.

"Why do I get the floor?" Lizzie whined as her blush began to fade.

"You copped the feel," Jenny hissed.

"Trust me; it won't happen again," Lizzie offered apologetically.

Jenny was so flustered that she was about to blurt out something she'd regret. *'How can I trust you? You broke my heart!'* her heart screamed. Fortunately her mind caught up with her anger and prevented her from uttering the hurtful words that would certainly open up another painful discussion. Jenny wasn't ready to deal with that part of their past yet. The emotions they'd been forced to face over the past few days were already taking a toll on her fragile state of mind.

"Do I want to know what's going on down here?" Kate called out frantically as she entered the cabin.

"No," Jenny managed to answer before storming past Kate and climbing up on deck.

The warmth of the sun was refreshing as Jenny took a deep breath, inhaling the sea air. She looked out over the glistening water and allowed the tension to slip away. Her body warmed as she felt Lizzie approach her. "I'm really sorry," Lizzie offered in a hushed tone.

"Forget it," Jenny responded softly, brushing away the last shreds of tension as she stared out at the ocean surrounding them. "You're still sleeping on the floor," she added with a wry chuckle.

"You two look like you're feeling better," Kate commented as she handed them their life jackets.

"It's beautiful," Lizzie said admiringly as she and Jenny put on the lightweight vests.

"I love it out here," Kate responded absently, getting lost in the pleasure of the beauty surrounding them. "Why don't the two of you relax and I'll get lunch started?" she suggested.

"Lunch?" Jenny said in surprise as she quickly glanced at her watch. "I guess it is lunch time," she agreed as Lizzie chuckled. "What?" Jenny asked the amused little blonde.

"Still into the seven dwarfs, I see," Lizzie pointed out. She tapped lightly on Jenny's watch, which displayed all seven of the little darlings.

"Yeah, whatever," Jenny grumbled as she tucked her hands in the pockets of her jacket. "I guess I have a soft spot for short things," she teased as she glared down at Lizzie who was scowling up at her. "It really did get a lot warmer," Jenny noted. She was uncomfortable wrapped in her heavy jacket. She hoped it was the air around her and not the way she woke up that was wreaking havoc with her body temperature.

Jenny and Lizzie both removed the life vests and the jackets that they were wearing and relaxed in the sunshine. "The weather's been so strange the last few years," Jenny commented as they stretched out on the padded seats located at the aft of the boat. "I remember my freshman year of college we had a huge snow storm in the middle of April."

"Where did you end up going?" Lizzie asked as she stared out over the ocean.

"BU," Jenny responded, lost in thought.

"Just like we always planned," Lizzie responded with a heavy sigh.

"Yeah," Jenny confirmed as a slight twinge of guilt hit her.

"So what did you do when it snowed in April?" Lizzie asked brightly. "I bet you did something crazy."

"No," Jenny lied.

"Come on, tell me?" Lizzie encouraged her. "We weren't allowed to do anything slightly rambunctious. Tell me what you did?"

"A bunch of us got together in a friend's dorm room and played strip poker," Jenny confessed shyly.

"Really?" Lizzie blurted out as her emerald eyes lit up.

"Yes," Jenny reluctantly confirmed. "It was nothing, just a little harmless fun."

Jenny was uncomfortable; she noticed Lizzie's eyes had gotten darker. Thankfully Kate reappeared with lunch and the conversation was forgotten. While they ate and chatted, Kate reminded them to put the lifejackets back on. Jenny complied with Kate's request; Lizzie did not. It amazed Jenny how Lizzie bounced from a mature responsible woman back into the brat kid sister whenever Kate ordered her to do something.

After lunch Kate cleaned up the mess and took the boat out a little further. Jenny and Lizzie relaxed against the rail while Kate pointed out the landmarks. "You should put your vest on," Jenny encouraged the smaller woman.

"I have to tell her everything," Lizzie said thoughtfully as she stared out over the water, ignoring Jenny's suggestion. She turned to Jenny and captured her in a troubled gaze. "Are you all right with me telling her about us?"

"I'm fine with it," Jenny agreed. "It does scare me just a little."

"Why?" Lizzie asked.

"I'm afraid that Kate's going to beat the snot out of me for . . . you know," Jenny said with a slight stammer.

"Deflowering her baby sister?" Lizzie teased her in a hushed tone.

"That would be it," Jenny confirmed with a heavy sigh. "You should put your vest on."

Lizzie once again ignored the suggestion as Kate anchored and approached them. "Put your vest on, Lizzie, and get away from the railing," Kate chastised her as she relaxed on one of the padded seats. Jenny joined her as she poured coffee from a Thermos. Lizzie ignored her sister's instructions, mesmerized by the sights and sounds that surrounded them.

"Lizzie, at least step away from the railing?" Jenny asked in exasperation as she sipped her coffee.

"Listen to her, kiddo," Kate chastised her as she stretched out her legs and sipped her own cup of coffee.

"So what were we talking about?" Kate inquired innocently.

"Oh, just some girl talk," Jenny hedged, not wanting to lie to her friend.

"Goodie, can I join in?" Kate beamed, eying her younger sister carefully. "Kiddo, get your butt away from that railing."

Lizzie turned to them, leaning her back against the railing and folding her arms across her chest in defiance. "So do you have any girl talk for us, Kate?" Lizzie asked in a cocky tone as she batted her eyes at her older sister.

"No, I have questions," Kate began slowly. "What happened?"

"When?" Lizzie answered shyly as she began to chew on her bottom lip.

"That night," Kate continued; she was treading very carefully. "When Dad called me in a panic because Mom had beaten you so badly that he thought he would have to take you to the hospital." Kate paused briefly; Jenny felt like she was going to be sick. Kate turned to her. Jenny knew that she'd turned pale. "You should have seen it, Jenny. I was a rookie back then and I rushed to the house still in uniform. Mom was screaming like a crazy woman. I'd never seen her like that. Dad, poor Dad was trying desperately to calm her down. I had no idea what was going on. I found Lizzie curled up in a corner of her bedroom closet."

'Lizzie, I never should have left you,' Jenny's heart screamed

115

as tears filled her eyes. She turned away from Kate, unable to look at her friend, feeling as if she'd betrayed them both. "Lucky me, my own mother was almost my first bust," Kate continued and Jenny could hear the panic creeping through the calm tone she was maintaining. "I swear, Lizzie, if you and Dad hadn't stopped me, I would have slapped the cuffs on her right then and there."

"Kate," Lizzie pleaded in an effort to stop her.

"No, Lizzie. No more lies. You're not putting me off this time," Kate argued in a firm controlled tone. "Now I want to know why. I know that Mom has always been a little out there. But what she did was total insanity. Then without talking to Dad about it, she ships you off to a convent school in Minnesota. Neither Mom nor Dad is willing to talk about this; all I get from you is, 'I got caught'. Tell me because I really need to know just what happened to my sister's life. And I want to know now."

Jenny knew that there was no way for Lizzie to get around it this time. She had to tell her sister everything. Jenny nodded to Lizzie whose face was filled with pain. She silently let her know that it was all right to tell Kate everything. They would survive the fallout. Lizzie sighed deeply before speaking. "Mom . . ." Lizzie began, choosing her words carefully. "Mom came home early from bingo that night and she caught me in a compromising position." She paused. "In the kitchen," Lizzie added shyly as she stared at her sneakers.

The thought ran quickly yet clearly through Jenny's mind. *'She's trying to protect me? Damn it, doesn't she see that it's okay? Everything will be alright.'* The words echoed in Jenny's mind and sent a chill down her spine. Her misery was suddenly broken as Kate broke out laughing. Both Jenny and Lizzie stared at her with stunned expressions.

"The kitchen?" Kate laughed, looking first at Lizzie and then at Jenny. "What were the two of you thinking?" Jenny and Lizzie were visibly shocked at Kate's outburst. It took each of them a few moments to completely understand what was happening.

"You know?" Jenny choked out first.

"How?" Lizzie stammered quickly.

"Sorry," Kate said as she shook her head before laughing once again. "First, let me explain something. I never said anything to

116

either of you about your relationship out of respect for your privacy. I assumed that if you wanted me to know you would have said something."

"How long have you . . . I mean when did you find out?" the flabbergasted Lizzie demanded.

"You're going to laugh," Kate said with a wry smile.

"I doubt it," Jenny threw in, deciding that Kate was far too amused by the situation. The two of them had spent over a decade hiding it from her, fearful of her reaction. Jenny had worried that Kate would freak out and hate her or worse. Laughter was the last thing the tall brunette had expected.

"Okay, so maybe you won't laugh." Kate giggled, which was something Jenny had never seen the stern policewoman do. "Here goes," Kate began once she calmed herself down. "It was when the two of you were still in high school. It was a weekday and I happened to have it off. So I figured that I could sneak home while the folks were out. You know, do some laundry and raid the refrigerator. Anyway, I drove in from the city and checked around to make sure Mom wasn't there. I was about halfway to the laundry room when I suddenly realized that I wasn't alone in the house. At first I was scared that someone might have broken in and they were upstairs in my baby sister's bedroom. I was just about to call the local cops when I realized that the person upstairs wasn't an intruder. It was Lizzie ditching school. I was pissed thinking that the little twerp cut school so she could mess around with her boyfriend. Or so I thought. I was about halfway up the staircase when I stopped. Hey, it wasn't anything I hadn't done when I was her age. I decided to sneak out so I wouldn't cause you any embarrassment. I was planning on sitting you down later for a long talk about safe sex and all of that other big sister stuff," she offered to Lizzie in a gentle voice. "Just as I started to make my retreat, I heard it."

"Heard what?" Jenny stammered fearfully.

Kate's response came in a low sensual tone. "Oh . . .. Oh . . . yes . . . yes . . .. Jenny," Kate panted. Jenny almost dropped her coffee mug while she and Lizzie each turned a brilliant shade of crimson. Kate erupted in gales of laughter as Jenny started to hyperventilate. "I swear . . . " Kate continued as tears streamed down her face, "it was the funniest thing. I mean, I was more than a little surprised at first. But once I began to grasp the situation, I thought it was hysterical. I had to stuff my fist in my mouth to keep from bursting out laughing. Come on, you two, it's funny. Mom always thought that Jenny was so sweet and such a good influence."

"So you just snuck out and never mentioned it?" Lizzie fumed as she crinkled her brow.

"Relax, kiddo," Kate retorted. "Turns out I never got the chance. Plus I didn't know if it was a phase or experimentation or the real thing for both of you. You have got to hand it to Mom though. It takes a certain type of genius to decide to send your daughter to an all girl school after catching her with another girl."

"Yeah, I know," Lizzie agreed, finally smiling at the situation. "Especially when you take into account that most of the other girls were there for pretty much the same reason."

"Way to go, Mom." Kate chuckled, still thoroughly amused.

Jenny on the other hand was fuming inside. Mrs. Carrington took Lizzie away from her and sent her to the one place she could easily meet another girl. Jenny's hatred for the misguided woman was growing with each passing moment. "Tell me about when you ran away," Kate asked, her voice suddenly tense. Jenny absently listened as Lizzie explained what had happened. As the sisters agreed that their father had probably been unaware of Lizzie's arrest and the deal her mother had made, Jenny was nursing old wounds. "Now that everything is out in the open, maybe we can all move on?" Kate suggested. Jenny realized that the comment was made for her as well. She nodded mutely, still feeling numb from the old memories that haunted her. "And step away from the railing, Lizzie," Kate chastised her sister.

"Fine," Lizzie agreed as she threw up her hands in exasperation.

Jenny watched in horror as Lizzie slipped the moment she stepped away from the railing and started to fall backward. She sprang up without thinking and captured the small blonde in her arms just before she tumbled overboard. A surge of warmth spread through Jenny's body as she held Lizzie tightly against her and assisted her over to where Kate was seated. "Thank you," Lizzie murmured against Jenny's chest. The tall brunette suddenly became aware of just how intimate her hold on the smaller woman was and quickly released her.

"No problem," Jenny responded with a nonchalant shrug.

"You're bleeding," Lizzie gasped.

Jenny looked down to find a deep gash on her elbow dripping blood. "Must have scraped it or something," she responded casually.

"There's a first aid kit down below," Kate offered. "Why don't you give our hero a hand, Lizzie?"

"I'm fine," Jenny protested.

"Nonsense," Lizzie chastised her as she took her by the hand and led her towards the lower deck.

Once they were down below, Jenny washed the cut while Lizzie retrieved the first aid kit. Lizzie guided Jenny to sit down and knelt beside her. The blonde's touch was sending delightful tremors through Jenny's body. "You're shaking," Lizzie, said softly, her warm breath teasing the skin on Jenny's forearm.

"I'm fine," Jenny responded coldly as Lizzie continued to tend her wound.

With each touch of Lizzie's gentle hands, Jenny felt the familiar ache of desire filling her. Once Lizzie had finished, she jerked her arm away, unable to stand the contact any longer. She saw the hurt look in Lizzie's eyes; it wasn't the small blonde's fault she was feeling this way. "Sorry," Jenny mumbled. Lizzie still knelt beside her with one hand resting on her thigh. Jenny fought to control her breathing as she stood suddenly, almost knocking Lizzie to the floor.

Jenny crossed the tiny cabin in an effort to put some distance between them. "I'm moving out of Kate's tonight," she said abruptly. "I can't do this. I can't be around you right now," she explained, wondering if Lizzie understood what she was saying and why.

"I understand," Lizzie agreed as a dark shadow crossed her face and she turned away from Jenny's look.

"It's for the best," Jenny tried to explain, her own emotions beginning to spin out of control. She turned away from the sight of Lizzie still kneeling on the floor of the cabin and retreated topside.

CHAPTER ELEVEN

Jenny was tired and cranky as she stood at the entrance to the police station. She hadn't felt well since the day she'd gone sailing with Kate and Lizzie. True to her word, she'd moved out that night and into a cheap motel. Kate was furious while Lizzie remained strangely quiet. It was for the best and both Lizzie and Jenny knew it. Since she'd left almost two weeks ago, she hadn't slept well. She'd finally found a new apartment that she could move into in another two weeks. "Jacobs," Kate called out to her.

"Hey Sarge," Jenny returned the greeting wearily.

"You all right?" Kate asked in concern.

"I think I'm coming down with something," Jenny explained. Her persistent headache was returning in full force as they walked into the station and towards the ladies locker room.

"Forgive me for saying it, but you look like crap," Kate added as they dressed and prepared for the evening shift.

"Gee thanks," Jenny grumbled as she rubbed her throbbing temple. "I don't know what it is except that I had to see Wendy today."

"Well, that would do it," Kate snorted in disgust.

"Tell me about it," Jenny agreed. "Against my better judgment, I've waited for her to switch the utilities over to her name. She didn't and I had to have them shut off. Now I'm stuck with her bills, and for some reason she thinks I'm a bitch and still wants rent money out of me."

"Don't give it to her," Kate cautioned her.

"I'm not," Jenny responded.

"I mean it. Don't give that witch a dime," Kate reasserted.

"I won't," Jenny spat back, feeling that Kate was scolding her like a child.

"I know you, Jacobs," Kate continued, ignoring Jenny's outburst. "You'll end up paying her off just to get rid of her."

Jenny released a heavy sigh, knowing that Kate's concern wasn't unwarranted. "Not one red cent, I promise," Jenny vowed. "Let her new girlfriend pick up the tab from now on."

"Good," Kate said firmly. "Since we both have tomorrow night off, why don't you come over for dinner?"

"I don't think so," Jenny declined as she put on her vest. She hated the bulky shield but she dealt with it because it could save her life.

"Why not? I know Lizzie would love to see you," Kate persisted.

"I'm just going to kick back and relax," Jenny lied.

"What about next Tuesday?" Kate inquired hopefully.

"What's up?" Jenny asked as a sudden gnawing feeling overcame her.

"Nothing," Kate responded with a casual shrug.

"Kate, what are you trying to do? Fix me up with your sister?" Jenny finally asked since this wasn't the first time Kate had tried to make plans for the three of them.

"Of course not," Kate answered her innocently. "But if I did, what would be so bad about the two of you getting reacquainted?"

"Well, let's think about why that would be a bad idea," Jenny said sarcastically. "Oh right, she's a nun!"

"She doesn't have to stay that way," Kate encouraged.

"Don't drag me into this," Jenny argued. "I'm not up for it. Lizzie and I both have a lot of stuff to deal with right now. Just let her make the decision on her own. That's all she's asking for - to be able to make a choice that affects her life without someone else pushing her into it. She's never had the chance to do that. Let her."

"I know," Kate grumbled. "Okay, I'll back off."

"Still helping me move on the 1st?" Jenny added brightly.

"Yes," Kate agreed. "So why did you take off that night?"

"I needed space," Jenny tried to explain, not wanting to give Kate false hope. "A lot has happened in the past few weeks, and I needed time by myself."

"Still going on the camping trip?" Kate asked, referring to the trip a bunch of them had planned.

"Wouldn't miss it," Jenny said with a smile as she locked her locker.

Later that day Jenny was once again waiting for Nuru to bring them coffee. "You don't look good," her partner commented.

"Everyone keeps saying that," Jenny grumbled. "I'm beginning to get a complex."

"Sorry," Nuru apologized. "You just look really tired these days."

"I am," Jenny confessed. "I'll feel better once I move into the new place. The neighborhood is a little iffy but it'll feel great to finally have a place where I can put my feet up and put my books on a shelf."

"I know what you mean," Nuru agreed. "I'm thinking of finding a place by myself. I'm too old to have roommates. It must have been cramped staying with Kate."

"It was," Jenny grumbled as she sipped her coffee. "Being trapped in such close quarters with my ex-girlfriend was the last thing I needed."

"You know what you need?" Nuru began in a knowing voice.

"To win the lottery and run of to someplace warm and tropical with Peta Wilson," Jenny quipped as her mind pictured a fun-filled afternoon on a beach with a mostly nude tall blonde actress.

"No that is what I need," Nuru scoffed. "You need a date."

Jenny was just about to argue with her partner about it being to soon for her to go out on a date when she realized that it wasn't such a bad idea. "You might be right," she agreed, thinking that going out with another woman might just be the ticket to help her get over the disastrous ending of her relationship with Wendy. It might also help distract her from thinking about Lizzie constantly.

"Really?" Nuru responded in surprise.

"Yeah," Jenny confirmed. "I need to start living again."

"Good, because . . . " Nuru began gleefully.

"Wait! You have someone in mind?" Jenny growled. "No, I will not go on a blind date. My life isn't that pathetic."

"Yes, it is," Nuru taunted her. "And it's not pathetic to allow one of your friends to set you up. She's a really nice girl."

"If she's so nice, why don't you go out with her?" Jenny inquired suspiciously.

Nuru performed a perfect imitation of a dying guppy as she tried to respond to Jenny's question. The ebony woman beamed brightly when their unit number was squeaked out over the radio. "That's for us," Nuru blurted out as she hit the lights and pulled out into traffic. Jenny gritted her teeth, knowing that she was going to be suckered into going out with Nuru's friend.

The tall brunette hissed slightly as she responded to the call. Her heart began to pound against her chest as she listened to the information. There had been some kind of assault at Xavier Academy. Normally this information wouldn't send the brunette into a tailspin; people slapped one another around on a daily basis. Having it happen at the school where Lizzie was teaching filled Jenny with an unexpected fear. As they sped over to the school, Jenny racked her brain in an effort to remember what days Lizzie taught there.

"What's wrong, partner?" Nuru inquired as they exited the patrol car after carefully securing it. Xavier was located in the heart of the city, and despite the school's stellar reputation, the neighborhood had changed over the decades. Leaving any vehicle unlocked, even a police cruiser, was unwise.

"Carrington's sister teaches here," Jenny explained as they ascended the stone steps and approached a very large and very angry-looking nun who appeared to be waiting for their arrival.

"Oh," Nuru responded with a shrug before she understood what Jenny had said. "Oh?" Nuru repeated this time with a hint of worry clouding her tone. "Don't worry. What are the chances that she'll be involved with this?" Nuru tried to reassure her.

"With my luck?" Jenny sputtered as they reached the top of the stairs.

The nun who greeted them made her displeasure at their arrival well known as she escorted them inside the cold sterile building that had housed the school for over a century. A smaller aging nun approached them in a flurry. She smiled as she greeted them. "Thank you for coming, officers. I'm Sister Agnes, the Mother Superior here," she informed them in a polite and friendly manner.

124

"We don't need them," the larger nun grumbled.

"Thank you, Sister Prudence," the Mother Superior said, dismissing the other nun politely.

"She doesn't seem happy to see us," Nuru commented wryly. Although Nuru towered over her, Sister Agnes gave her a stern look. Jenny watched in amazement as her partner actually shrunk back, her shoulders slumping as she stared at the floor. *'Now there is something I've never seen before,'* Jenny noted thoughtfully.

"Normally we're quite capable of dealing with the students without outside interference," Sister Agnes explained dryly.

"So I've been reading in the papers," Jenny muttered bitterly. She was surprised when the Mother Superior actually gave her a soft knowing smile in response.

"One of our male students attacked one of our female students," Sister Agnes explained in a worried voice as she led them down the long corridor. "She wasn't hurt as far as we know. What upsets me is that he's still acting out."

"Acting out?" Jenny responded in disbelief at her casual description.

"Ryan's behavior is so unlike him," the plucky nun continued, unfazed by Jenny's comments. "The girl is in my office. Ryan has locked himself in one of the classrooms with one of the sisters."

"Wait!" Jenny barked. "He's holding someone hostage?"

"Trust me. Sister Rachel can handle herself." Sister Agnes chuckled.

"Sister Rachel?" Jenny grumbled in a defeated tone as she rubbed her throbbing temple. "That's just great."

Sister Agnes turned towards the flustered policewoman. "I see you're familiar with my favorite problem child," the older woman noted dryly.

"She hasn't been here that long,' Jenny muttered as she wondered how Lizzie had become a problem child so quickly.

"I've had previous encounters with Sister Rachel," Sister Agnes confirmed in a tired voice. "They're in there," she explained as she pointed to a classroom door.

Jenny's palms were sweating as she peered into the tiny square glass window. She groaned as a full-fledged migraine threatened to consume her. "Nuru, why don't you go talk to the girl and I'll handle this."

"You're going in without backup?" Nuru questioned her.

"Look," Jenny instructed her partner.

She watched Nuru's dark eyes widen in shock as she spied the small nun holding the young man in a headlock; he must have been at least six three and built like a Mack truck. "That has got to be Carrington's sister," Nuru commented as she stepped away from the window.

"None other," Jenny confirmed. "Go talk to the girl and find out what happened. I'm going to rescue Ryan."

Nuru agreed and followed Sister Agnes down the hallway as Jenny braced herself to enter the classroom. She immediately discovered the door was blocked by some of the students' desks. She weighed her options as she peered through the glass. Despite the fact that Lizzie appeared to have the upper hand, Ryan was a very large young man and more than likely he would end up overpowering the small nun. "Here goes nothing," she reassured herself as she shoved her way into the classroom.

"Let go of me, you bitch," the young man hissed as he struggled against Lizzie's chokehold. Jenny climbed over the displaced desks and made her way over to the comical scene.

"Not until you calm down," Lizzie cautioned the angry teenager.

"Let him go," Jenny grumbled as she approached the struggling duo.

Lizzie looked up in surprise, tightening her hold on Ryan. "Hi," she greeted Jenny casually. "How've you been?"

"Sister Rachel, would you kindly let go of him," Jenny groaned.

"You don't want me to do that," Lizzie cautioned her.

"Sister, please release Ryan so I can do my job," Jenny implored her.

"He's very agitated at the moment," Lizzie explained firmly.

"Perhaps he's agitated because you're crushing his wind pipe?" Jenny tried to reason with the small blonde. "Let him go and step aside."

"All right," Lizzie agreed. She nodded to Jenny, informing her that she was about to release Ryan from her grasp.

126

Jenny tensed her body in anticipation; Lizzie released the angry boy and quickly stepped aside. Ryan's face was crimson as he reached out to grab Lizzie. Jenny moved quickly and grabbed the young man's flailing arms, pinning them behind his bulky frame. She pressed against the back of his knees with her own, forcing him down onto the floor. In a fluid motion, she handcuffed Ryan and held his squirming body on the floor. "What the hell were you thinking?" Jenny fumed at Lizzie who was looking on with interest.

Lizzie crossed the room and knelt beside the still-struggling teenager. She reached out and started to lift his school blazer and oxford shirt. "What do you think you're doing?" Jenny asked the obvious insane nun as she fought to hold Ryan down on the floor.

"What I was trying to find out earlier," Lizzie explained, unfazed by the events as she pulled the young man's clothing up to reveal his acne-covered back.

"Stay still," Jenny commanded the struggling boy as she stared down at the mass of acne on his skin.

"Ryan, you wouldn't be an athlete, now would you?" Jenny questioned him. She tightened her hold on him as she realized that the boy probably was not in control of his anger.

"Everyone told me that he's normally quiet and shy," Lizzie explained. "They also said he bulked up over the last term break."

"No one put it together before now?" Jenny fumed, having seen this scenario one too many times. "Sudden building of body mass and violent behavior are the first signs."

"I know," Lizzie agreed.

"Get off me, bitch," Ryan cursed as he continued to struggle.

"Ryan, you're in a lot of trouble," Jenny informed him. "I suggest you calm down and listen to me. First, I'm going to tell you what your rights are, and then I'm going to search your pockets. Is there anything in your pockets that could hurt me?" The boy grunted in response. "I'll take that as a no. Now after I finish with you we're going to search your locker and your backpack."

Jenny informed the violent youngster of his rights as she pulled him up to his feet. She dragged him into the hallway and out to her patrol car. She found the bottle of pills when she searched the pockets of his blazer. Then she forced him into the back of the squad car and locked him in. Ryan was like a wild animal as he kicked at the door while Jenny bagged the drugs in an evidence bag. Then she took Lizzie's statement.

"Is it what I thought?" Lizzie inquired after she signed her statement.

"Steroids," Jenny confirmed as she watched her partner, Sister Agnes, and a priest approach them.

"How's the girl?" Jenny asked her partner.

"She's pretty shaken up, but it seems that Sister Rachel intervened before she was seriously hurt," Nuru explained. "She's going over to the ER to be checked out. She said that he just exploded over nothing."

"Is it necessary to incarcerate him?" the priest questioned.

"This is Father Donavan," Nuru explained. "He's the Dean."

Jenny held up the evidence bag as Nuru looked at it. "That explains it," Nuru said in understanding.

"His back is covered in acne," Jenny added.

"Do I want to know what that is?" Father Donavan asked fearfully.

"Steroids," Jenny explained. "Do you test your athletes?"

"Yes, we do random drug tests, but we haven't run one for the new term yet," the priest explained wearily. "We'll run one today. I assume we'll be hearing from some detectives."

"Sister Rachel." Sister Agnes motioned to her.

Jenny watched in amazement as Lizzie allowed herself to be dismissed from the conversation and walked dutifully back inside the school. "Officer Jacobs, thank you for your assistance," Sister Agnes offered and Jenny realized that she was being dismissed as well.

Later Jenny and Nuru were taking a breather back at the station house. "Hey Carrington, I met your sister today," Nuru called out to the Sergeant.

"So I hear," Kate commented wryly. "What did she do now?" Kate directed the comment towards Jenny.

"Nothing," Jenny offered in an effort to placate the brooding policewoman. "She subdued that jock from Xavier."

"The no-neck tree that slapped the girl around?" Kate asked in a slightly worried tone.

"That would be the one." Jenny yawned as she looked at her

watch, happily noting that her shift was almost over. "Did the kid roll over?"

"Just as soon as his parents showed up with a lawyer," Kate explained. "He gave up everyone. He'll get treatment and no record if he behaves and the suits get the dealer. The guy is some stockbroker from Chestnut Hill trying to cover his losses in the market."

"He'll get a slap on the wrist too," Nuru grunted in disgust. "Time to clock out."

Jenny decided to work out at the station's gym then shower and change there before heading back to her dingy motel room. As she stepped outside the station house, she spied a familiar little blonde leaning against a tree just out front. Thankfully Lizzie had opted for her street clothes as well. Somehow Jenny didn't think it would boost her image to be seen with a nun.

"Lizzie," Jenny greeted the small blonde.

"Hey Jenny," Lizzie responded with a shy smile.

"Looking for Kate?" Jenny asked as she shifted her gear bag on her shoulder. "I think she has another hour or so left to her shift."

"Actually I was waiting for you," Lizzie explained. Jenny's heart unexplainably began to beat just a little faster. "I wanted to know how it went with Ryan Summers and I'm trying to avoid Kate since I know she's already heard I was involved." Her voice grew sheepish as she explained the last part.

"She's heard," Jenny confirmed. "What are you worried about? What's she going to do? Ground you?"

"She might." Lizzie chuckled. "It's just that she's so overprotective at times. I'm just not up for another lecture today."

"Sister Agnes gave you a stern talking to, did she?" Jenny quipped as she shuffled nervously from one foot to the other.

"You could say that," Lizzie groaned. "So, can I buy you drink or something?"

"Are you allowed to do that?" Jenny inquired, truly curious about the rules.

"Allowed to do what?" Lizzie responded in confusion.

"Drink?" Jenny explained.

"Yes," Lizzie answered with a laugh. "I'm just not allowed to have sex or money."

"Well, this should be a fun date," Jenny teased Lizzie as she nodded for the small blonde to follow her. "Oddly enough, it's the best offer I've had in long time. I just need to dump my gear off at the motel."

"This is nice," Lizzie said as she took a seat on the bed in Jenny's motel room. Jenny looked around the simple room. It had a bed, a television, a bathroom, and it was clean; other than that the motel room was not much to talk about.

"I keep forgetting how you've been living," Jenny commented as she hung up her uniform and secured her gun. Lizzie had already turned on the television and began to channel surf.

"You really are fascinated by television," Jenny commented as she continued to putter around and get ready to go out.

"Not really," Lizzie explained. "I still can't find anything I like. When we were kids, there were a lot fewer channels and some really good shows."

"Maybe the shows weren't really that good," Jenny commented as she stepped into the bathroom and began to brush out her hair. "Maybe we just watched them because you actually had to get up to change the channel."

"You have a point," Lizzie agreed. "Princess Di is dead?" Lizzie exclaimed in shock. "When did that happen?"

"Late summer in 1997," Jenny explained. "You didn't get a lot of news down in those villages you were living in, did you?"

"I wasn't exactly on the local paper route and we didn't have electricity," Lizzie called out as she continued to change the channels.

Jenny smiled as she emerged from the bathroom and found Lizzie with her brow creased in deep concentration as she watched an infomercial. "Why would anyone need that?" Lizzie asked before she continued to channel surf.

Jenny climbed up on the bed and folded her legs beneath her as she drank in Lizzie's profile. She couldn't help recalling how many times she'd sat on a bed next to Lizzie before they became lovers. Her palms would sweat, her heart would race, and she'd be terrified that Lizzie would learn the truth. A sudden wave of panic hit her as Jenny realized that at this very moment she was feeling exactly the same way she had all those years ago. Only now they were adults sitting in her motel room.

"We should go," Jenny suddenly blurted out as she jumped off the bed. Lizzie jerked her head up in surprise as she shut off the television.

"Am I making you uncomfortable?" Lizzie asked in concern.

"Constantly," Jenny admitted as she grabbed her black leather car coat. She handed the coat to Lizzie who was wearing a light charcoal-colored sweater and faded blue jeans.

Lizzie nodded as she accepted the jacket and climbed off the bed. They left the motel in silence and Jenny led the way towards the club. As they stepped inside the bar, Jenny prayed that it would be Claire's night off. As she spotted her friend behind the bar, the tall brunette decided that it wasn't the week for her to be playing the lottery.

It was still early in the evening as they took seats at one of the back corner tables. There was a small group of people hanging around. Since it was a weekday the crowd was still very thin. There was a rugby team in the opposite corner. Jenny assumed by their sour expressions that they hadn't won their match. Jenny spotted a few men and women in suits that had obviously ducked out of work early.

As she caught Claire peering over at her, she was thankful for one thing. Her friend wouldn't ask too many prying questions with Lizzie sitting right there. Jenny was just about to go get a round of drinks when she saw Claire approaching. "Oh crap, that's not a good sign," Jenny mumbled as she slid back down in her seat.

"Hey there, ladies," Claire greeted them brightly. She looked directly at Lizzie and worked her southern drawl for all that it was worth. "I don't normally do table service, but anything for our gals in uniform," she jested as she placed a comforting hand on Jenny's shoulder. "I'm Claire," she continued as she extended her hand to Lizzie who gladly accepted the kind offer. *Please say your name is Lizzie,'* Jenny silently pleaded, fearing that if word got out that her first date since the breakup was with a nun, she wouldn't get another date on the east coast even if she had Xena Warrior Princess strapped to her ass.

"Sister Rachel," Lizzie responded politely. "It is nice to meet you, Claire."

"Sister?" Claire said in confusion as Jenny watched the wheels in the woman's head spin. "Oh," she exclaimed in sudden understanding and Jenny braced herself for the fallout. "Well, if you don't mind me saying, Sister, what a waste."

"Thank you, I think." Lizzie laughed in response. Jenny considered climbing under the table and dying of embarrassment.

"How's the day job?" Jenny pried, hoping to change the subject.

"Good. The kids are a handful as usual," Claire explained. "Just wish it paid more so I wouldn't have to work nights."

"You're a teacher?" Lizzie inquired eagerly. "What subject?"

"Math," Claire explained proudly.

"I teach history and English," Lizzie explained. "Well, history is my specialty, but it all depends on where I'm assigned."

Jenny listened as they swapped classroom war stories. She was impressed as she realized just how impassioned both of these women were about their students. The brunette was also more than a little irked that Claire was flirting with Lizzie. Granted, Claire was a natural flirt who just couldn't help herself; it was all part of her southern charm. It still annoyed her that she was flirting with Lizzie.

"So how's the job market out here?" Lizzie asked. Jenny's ears perked up and she felt a small glimmer of hope that Lizzie was actually thinking of life outside the convent.

"Not so great," Claire confessed. "Do you have your Masters?"

"Yes," Lizzie confirmed.

"So you're a nun?" Claire blurted out suddenly. Jenny once again contemplated crawling under the table.

"Yes, I'm a nun," Lizzie confirmed with a sigh and a slight shake of her head. Jenny didn't miss the other patrons turning around at Lizzie's comment.

"My life is over," Jenny grumbled as she buried her face in her hands.

"I have to tell you, Sister, if more nuns looked like you, I'd convert," Claire teased.

"I'll see what I can do," Lizzie teased in response.

"Ah hem," Jenny cleared her throat loudly, rapidly growing tired of her friends flirting with one another.

"Right," Claire said with a slight cringe. "I guess I've wasted enough time over here. I suppose that I should take your drink orders so I can get back to waiting on the tip less wonders over there. What'll it be?"

"Club soda," Jenny grunted.

"Good call seeing as what happened the last time you were here," Claire teased her with a slight nudge. "Wouldn't want you playing in the traffic on Columbus Street again singing *'Don't Cry For Me, Argentina'*."

"I never liked you," Jenny hissed as Lizzie laughed. Jenny scowled as she tried to remember if she really did play in traffic that night?

"Sister?" Claire addressed the still giggling blonde.

"Do you have Patron?" Lizzie inquired.

"That I do," Claire confirmed.

"Great," Lizzie beamed. "I'll have a Grand Gold Margarita on the rocks, no salt."

"A woman who knows what she wants," Claire purred. "I'll be right back with your drinks, ladies."

"This is a nice place," Lizzie offered in a relaxed tone once they were alone again.

"Yes, it is," Jenny agreed. She tried to relax despite the curious glances they were still receiving.

"I've never been to a gay bar before," Lizzie added as she looked around. "Why is everyone looking at us?" She asked in a hushed tone.

"Oh I don't know," Jenny grumbled as she slouched further down in her chair. "Maybe it is because you're a nun and thanks to Claire everyone knows it."

"I'm beginning to feel like an opening to a joke," Lizzie said thoughtfully.

"What do you mean?" Jenny asked.

"You know, a cop and a nun walk into a bar," Lizzie explained with bright smile.

"So what's the punch line?" Jenny asked with a light laugh.

"Don't know yet," Lizzie responded seriously. "I missed your smile," she added so softly that Jenny wondered if Lizzie had meant to say the words out loud. Jenny tensed slightly as all too familiar stirrings began once again. "Sorry," Lizzie quickly apologized. "All of these mixed signals must be driving you insane."

"They are," Jenny responded honestly. "I've been doing the same thing. I just feel like the past is taking over when I'm with you."

"I know," Lizzie agreed as she began to fiddle with her napkin.

Jenny watched as the napkin was quickly reduced to shreds. "Sometimes I look into your eyes and it all comes back to me," Lizzie explained. "Before I can catch my bearings, one of us is stepping over the line."

"We can get through this," Jenny tried to reassure Lizzie, understanding what she was trying to say since she'd been dealing with the same whirlwind of emotions.

"The problem is that after all this time and everything we've been through, you still take my breath away," Lizzie choked out as her eyes began to fill with tears. "I'm sorry. I shouldn't have said anything." Lizzie stood suddenly. "Excuse me; I'm just need to use the washroom."

After Lizzie made her departure, Jenny found that she was clutching the edge of the table. She stared down at her hands to discover that she'd been gripping the table with such intensity that her knuckles had turned white. Jenny released her hold as she debated on whether or not she should follow Lizzie to the ladies room.

"So you want to tell me what's going on?" Claire questioned her bluntly as she placed the drinks down.

"Long story," Jenny muttered absently as she watched the doorway for Lizzie.

"Usually is," Claire agreed as she nudged a cocktail closer to Jenny.

The brunette finally tore her gaze away from the doorway. "That's not club soda," she said as she stared at the margarita.

"Very good, Officer," Claire retorted. "You're having what she's having. I'd thought I'd level the playing field. Now out with it."

"She was . . . ," Jenny began. Her voice trailed off as she tried to form the words. She didn't understand why all of this was so hard. "She was my high school sweetheart," she finally said as she realized it was the first time in her life she'd been allowed to call Lizzie that.

"I had a feeling," Claire concurred. "You said something about her the night you and Wendy split up. She's Kate's sister?"

"Yes," Jenny responded.

"You never forget your first girl," Claire said with a heavy sigh. "Poor baby, it still hurts, doesn't it?" Jenny could only nod in response. "My first was in high school too. Mary Sue Parker. We were on the basketball team together."

"What happened?" Jenny inquired sadly.

"Field hockey season," Claire explained with a snarl. "Bitch dumped me for the goalie. Last I heard she had shaved her head and was living with a group of separatists somewhere in the Ozarks. Love sucks."

"Amen," Jenny responded heartily as she raised her glass in agreement.

"But then again, if she hadn't broken my poor old heart, I wouldn't have come up here to go to college," Claire reasoned. "And I wouldn't have met Tina, the most wonderful woman on the face of the planet."

"I've always said Tina deserves a medal for putting up with your tired old carcass for all of these years," Jenny agreed.

"It's just that being around Lizzie has been so intense," Jenny tried to explain. "She hurt me more than I thought possible. I don't understand why it still hurts so much and why when I look at her . . ." Jenny allowed the words to die on her lips. "Forget it. None of it matters anymore."

"That's what you need to remember," Claire cautioned her. "Because if it does, you have a major problem on your hands that will make your troubles with Wendy seem like a trip to Disney World."

"She's thinking of leaving the church," Jenny argued.

"Thinking of leaving and leaving are two different things," Claire stressed. "Just ask any woman who's been involved with someone that's spoken for. And this gal is spoken for. She's also heading this way."

135

Jenny looked up and saw that Lizzie was indeed approaching the table. Claire made her departure before Lizzie reached the table. "Feeling better?" Jenny asked as Lizzie sat back down.

"Yes, thank you," Lizzie responded quietly. "Again, I'm sorry about everything."

"We need to stop apologizing to each other and move on," Jenny said with conviction. "Let's have a drink and I can tell you all about what happened with Ryan."

"Sounds good," Lizzie agreed.

As the night went on Jenny explained everything she knew about Ryan. They soon moved to other subjects. They talked about their lives and day-to-day stuff, carefully avoiding talk about their past relationship. Unfortunately as the night progressed, they also continued to drink. The tequila seemed to be impairing Jenny's judgment. They moved closer to one another over the evening, each finding an excuse to touch the other while they spoke. Claire's words of warning and Jenny's common sense were long forgotten as she found that she was sitting dangerously close to her ex-lover.

Once they decided that it was time to leave, they each wrapped an arm around the other's waist under the pretense of helping the other remain steady. Jenny could feel the heat emanating off of Lizzie's body as she guided her down the quiet streets. Jenny's hand began to caress Lizzie's stomach as they approached the motel. Her body pulsated with desire as Lizzie leaned closer. Somewhere in the back of her mind, a little voice was telling her that she should hail one of the many passing taxis and send Lizzie home.

The words of caution were drowned out by the rapid beating of her heart and the overwhelming desire burning in every fiber of her being. They stumbled to the door of Jenny's room. Lizzie turned into her embrace and leaned back against the door. Instinctively Jenny clasped the blonde's hips and leaned her body against the smaller woman's. Lizzie looked up at her through half open eyes that were burning with desire. Jenny's gaze drifted to Lizzie's lips; they were parted slightly as the blonde's breathing grew heavier.

Jenny swallowed hard and licked her lips. Her eyes remained focused on Lizzie's soft inviting lips. She was afraid to speak, knowing that if either of them said a word the spell would be broken. Jenny dug the key to her room out of the pocket of her jeans and unlocked the door. She never removed her hand from Lizzie's hip as they stumbled into the dark motel room.

She didn't realize that Lizzie's hands had been resting on her shoulders until she kicked the door shut and wrapped both of her hands around the small blonde's waist. The air in the room seemed filled with electricity as their bodies brushed against one another. Jenny lowered her head so she could feel Lizzie's ragged breath tickle her skin. *'I just need to kiss her,'* her mind screamed as their bodies melted together. Jenny cupped Lizzie's face in her hand and the two of them closed the gap between them. Their lips were about to touch when her cell phone chimed.

Stunned by the interruption, they stumbled away from each other as if they'd been burned. Jenny stumbled over to the bed and snatched up the phone. "Hello," she choked out in a breathy tone.

"Jacobs, it's Kate," the caller identified herself as Jenny's quivering body sat down on the bed.

"Hey Sarge." Jenny's voice creaked as she stared at the floor.

"Look, I know it's late, but Lizzie hasn't come home yet and I was wondering if you knew where she was," Kate asked in a panic.

"She's here," Jenny reassured her, still fighting to regain her voice. "Why don't you come get her?"

"Thank God," Kate said in relief.

"We've been drinking so why don't you just come on over and drive her home?" Jenny suggested once again. She continued to stare at the floor as she fought to control her breathing.

"It's late. Why don't I just pick her up in the morning?" Kate suggested.

"No," Jenny argued, knowing that there was no way she and Lizzie could stay in the room together without touching each other. "Come get her," Jenny hissed out in frustration.

"Uhm . . . okay," Kate finally conceded. "Do I want to know what's going on?"

"No," Jenny whimpered. "Thank you," she said before disconnecting the call. Jenny looked up to find Lizzie hiding in a distant corner with her arms folded tightly across her chest. "Your sister is on her way," she informed the frightened looking blonde.

CHAPTER TWELVE

Jenny's body was trembling uncontrollably from the events that had just occurred in her tiny motel room. What was shaking her to her very foundation was not so much what had happened but what had almost happened. She said a silent 'thank you' to Kate and her overprotective nature. Jenny was struggling to breathe as she muttered a feeble excuse to Lizzie who was still cowering in the corner. She quickly fled to the safety of the bathroom.

First she clenched the cool porcelain edge of the sink in a futile effort to calm her jagged nerves. When her knees started to buckle, she curled up next to the bathtub and pulled her legs tightly against her shaking body. She wrapped her arms around her knees and began to rock back and forth, trying to will herself to calmness and erase the need still burning inside of her. She needed to regain her composure before Kate arrived. "I have to let her go," she whimpered into her trembling knees. Her mind understood that she had to release Lizzie from her thoughts and heart, but still some part of her refused to let go. "Why is this so hard?" she whispered as she brushed the tears from her face.

After a long torturous debate between her mind and her heart, the tall brunette finally managed to pull herself up off the cold floor. Her body ached from the emotions still coursing through her and from being curled up in such a cramped space. She doused her face with warm water in an effort to conceal the fact that she'd been crying.

Jenny summoned up her last ounce of courage and dignity as

139

she checked her appearance one last time in the mirror. She flinched at her sallow complexion in the badly lit bathroom and swallowed hard as she mentally prepared to finally release Lizzie from her life. The first step was to get the blonde out of her motel room. With a false sense of strength, she gripped the doorknob and began to turn it.

Voices emanating from the outer room alerted her that Kate had arrived. Just as Jenny was about to open the door and join the other two women, she heard Kate's voice echoing her thoughts. "What are you going to do, Lizzie?" Kate asked, deeply concerned.

"I have no idea," Lizzie responded in a shaky tone. "I do know that I have a lot of thinking to do."

"What do you have to think about?" Kate fumed.

Against her better judgment, and throwing away her last shred of dignity, Jenny pressed her ear against the thin dusty wood of the bathroom door. She knew what she was doing was wrong and eavesdropping was beneath her, yet her curiosity won her over. Maybe Kate could get the answers that she couldn't.

"Lizzie, if it wasn't for Mom's fanaticism, you wouldn't be a nun right now," Kate stressed as Jenny pressed her body closer to the door. "So why stay a nun when it isn't the path you were meant to travel?"

Jenny strained to hear what Lizzie's response would be as she silently cheered Kate's bravado. "Face it, Lizzie. There's something wrong with our mother," Kate continued, hitting her stride. "The woman named both of her daughters Mary, for pity's sake. And you know why she did it - so we'd already have the right names when we became nuns. She planned on tossing us into convents from the moment we were born. That's not normal."

"No kidding," Jenny whispered in agreement.

"I know, I know!" Lizzie shouted in response. "I was there, remember? She didn't want girls; she wanted two sons - one to carry on the family name and one to become a priest. Her grand design failed when she had us and she never let us forget it. If we didn't become nuns, then we were supposed to act like nuns."

"People don't raise their kids that way in this day and age," Kate blurted out. "She never let us forget what a disappointment we were," she added bitterly. "How can you want to give in to her twisted desires? Lizzie, are you gay?"

"Yes," Lizzie responded with a slight stammer.

"How do you reconcile your homosexuality with what the church teaches?" Kate asked in confusion. "How do you handle confession? I heard what the Vatican said about homosexuals not having a place in the clergy. Why are you thinking of staying when they don't want you? Why are you letting our mother bully you into this?"

"Kate, I've spent far too many years being angry about the way things turned out," Lizzie flatly answered her sister's barrage of questions. "And I'm trying to make peace with our mother and get her the help that she needs."

Jenny was stunned. How and why Lizzie would want to make peace with that awful woman? "Why on earth do you think that woman is ever going to change?" Kate echoed her thoughts. "Look what she did to you. She beat you within an inch of your life and then she shipped you off to the frozen wasteland of Minnesota. She broke your heart so badly that you never returned home, not even for Christmas."

"That isn't entirely accurate," Lizzie said so softly that Jenny had to strain to hear her words. "Mom certainly set the wheels in motion, but it was Jenny who broke my heart. After I was sent away, she found someone else. That's the real reason I didn't come home after I was arrested. I wasn't allowed to see you, and after I lost Jenny I felt that there was nothing left for me to come back for."

Jenny stumbled back from the door feeling as if she'd been slapped. *That lying bitch! How can she do this? Why is she lying?*' Nothing made sense as Lizzie's accusation screamed through her mind. At that moment Jenny vowed that Mary Elizabeth Carrington had hurt her for the last time. Staying away from the blonde and resisting her charms would no longer be a problem. She wouldn't touch Lizzie Carrington if she was the last woman on earth.

Jenny had heard enough and now she felt violently ill. She sunk to her knees in front of the toilet and emptied the contents of her stomach as she began to cry once again. She staggered to her feet and washed her face. Catching a glimpse of her haggard appearance, she buried her face in a towel as she heard a light knock on the door. Still clutching the towel she staggered over to the door and opened it. She found Kate standing there giving her a harsh stare. Jenny brushed past the angry woman and was relieved to find Lizzie absent from the motel room.

Jenny plopped down onto the squeaky bed and twisted the flimsy towel in her hands. "You heard?" Kate inquired bitterly. Jenny nodded; she stared off into the distance as Kate approached her. The blonde policewoman towered over her with her arms folded across her chest in a defiant manner.

"It's a lie," Jenny said in weak voice as she continued to twist the towel violently.

Kate seemed to be taken aback by Jenny's comment and demeanor. "I never hurt her," Jenny said sincerely as she felt her heart breaking. "She was everything to me. I barely left my room after she went away. It wasn't until I caught her with another girl that I moved on. Why did she say that?" Jenny felt a strange sense of detachment as she spoke.

"This doesn't make sense," Kate responded thoughtfully.

"Doesn't matter," Jenny mumbled. She wished that Kate would just go away.

Kate seemed to understand Jenny's need to be left alone in her misery. Without a word she walked out the door. The moment Jenny heard the door shut, she crawled up onto the bed, curled up into a ball, and cried herself to sleep.

A week later Jenny found herself standing in her parents' kitchen while her mother peered over her cup of coffee at her. "What brings you by?" her mother inquired suspiciously.

"Can't a girl just visit her parents?" Jenny responded with feigned innocence. Her mother's crystal blue eyes just stared at her. "And bring twelve or thirteen loads of laundry?" she added with a sly smirk as her mother rolled her eyes.

"I suppose you want to be fed too?" her mother teased her with a dramatic sigh.

"Mommy?" Jenny pouted as her mother groaned.

"You're washing your own clothes," her mother informed her.

"Mom?" Jenny whined.

"Suck it up." The older woman laughed. "Start your laundry, and while I'm cooking you can tell me why you're really here."

Jenny shuffled down to the laundry room, eager to get started so she wouldn't be there all night. While she sorted out her clothing she mentally tried to prepare for the conversation she wanted to have with her mother. It was a familiar game with them. Jenny wanted and needed to talk to her mother but she was always shy about how to begin. Her mother would poke and prod until Jenny finally blurted out her troubles as her mother listened.

Jenny seated herself at the kitchen table, thankful that they wouldn't be eating in the dining room. The last thing she wanted was another reminder of her past exploits with Lizzie. "With all that laundry, why don't you just sleep over tonight?" her mother suggested as she busied herself with dinner preparations. "I could use the company since your father's in Buffalo."

"How's the case going?" Jenny asked as she sipped her coffee and avoided the conversation she'd really driven up there to have.

"The case is going well," Her mother responded.

"That's good news," Jenny mumbled as she began to twirl her hair.

"Who's car did you borrow?" her mother asked casually.

"Rental," Jenny responded with a shrug.

"You rented a car just to do your laundry?" her mother exclaimed as she continued to work on their dinner.

"I needed clean clothes," Jenny lied, knowing how ridiculous the whole thing sounded. "I have a date tomorrow and nothing to wear."

"A date?" her mother asked brightly as she spun around. "Someone special?"

"Blind date," Jenny informed her.

"Well, it's good that you're getting out," her mother encouraged her. "I was afraid that you might be stupid enough to take Wendy back."

"Geez, didn't anyone like her?" Jenny said as she choked on her coffee.

"Just you," her mother informed her directly. "And I'm not so certain that you did."

"What do you mean?" Jenny asked quickly.

"You didn't seem happy," her mother informed her. "So if it isn't Wendy or someone new, is there a problem at work?" her

143

mother encouraged her as she returned her attention to dinner.

"Work is good," Jenny responded in a casual manner. Silence filled the kitchen as Jenny fiddled with her placemat and her mother cooked. "Lizzie is back," she finally said in an off-handed manner.

"Your father mentioned that," her mother responded with a shrug. Suddenly she spun around and gave her daughter a frightened look. "Uhm, you two aren't together, are you?"

"Would it bother you?" Jenny snapped.

"Yes," her mother responded honestly. "Unless she's changed professions, then I have no problem. In fact, I always liked the girl."

"No, she's still a nun," Jenny grumbled. "Sister Rachel."

"That's interesting," her mother said thoughtfully.

"Why?" Jenny asked in confusion.

"I'll explain later," her mother answered her quickly. "First, tell me that you're not dating a nun so your grandmother can stop spinning in her grave."

"No, I'm not, and why would Grandma be upset?" Jenny answered.

"Sweetie, your Grandmother was Italian," her mother clarified. Jenny continued to look up at her in confusion. "She was Catholic."

"I didn't know that," Jenny said truthfully. "I thought she and Grandpa were Protestant."

"He was," her mother informed her. "English Protestant and your father's parents were Irish and Jewish."

"So that makes us what?" Jenny laughed.

"Yankee mutts like everyone else." Her mother chuckled. "So you're not involved with Lizzie. Is it seeing her again? You never really told us what happened."

"It's a long story," Jenny cautioned her mother.

"With all the laundry you brought, we have all night," her mother encouraged her as she placed a comforting hand on her shoulder.

After dinner, the dishes, and Jenny's endless piles of dirty laundry were taken care of, Jenny sat in the family room with her mother, feeling exhausted after telling her everything. Well, almost everything. She skipped over the parts about how she and Lizzie use to skip school so they could make love.

"Sweetie?" her mother asked softly. "Do you have your

nightstick on you?"

"No. Why?" Jenny inquired fearfully, not liking the menacing look in her mother's eyes.

"I want to go and beat Mrs. Carrington senseless," her mother fumed. "What the hell is wrong with that woman?"

"She's nuts," Jenny supplied.

"No kidding," her mother snorted in disgust. "Religious freedom and devotion to your faith can be a beautiful thing but zealotry is frightening."

"I know," Jenny agreed with her mother's observations.

"Okay, let's focus on you," her mother offered after taking a calming breath. "What may or may not be happening between you and Lizzie is a bit of problem."

"A bit of a problem?" Jenny echoed in an incredulous tone. "Mom, unwanted facial hair is a bit of problem. Almost making out with a nun is a freaking disaster."

Her mother chuckled wryly. "Perhaps," she agreed. "But it sounds like you're distancing yourself; that's a good thing until she decides just what she wants. If she decides to stay in the church and you let yourself start to care again . . ."

"I'm not," Jenny argued, knowing that in her heart she was lying.

After a long round of her mother's cautioning and Jenny's reassurance that she wasn't going to fall for Lizzie again, both women agreed that it was late and they were exhausted. Then her mother did the strangest thing. Just as Jenny was about to climb into her old bed, her mother knocked on the door and handed her a bible, informing her that it was her grandmother's. Jenny was bewildered as she accepted it. She thanked her mother and went to bed. Just as she was about to turn off the light, she remembered something Lizzie had said when Jenny questioned her about her new name. *'You really should read your bible.'* Jenny pondered the suggestion as she folded her long legs under her body.

She began to flip through the bible, not finding anything of interest as she quickly scanned the passages. Bored and frustrated, she tossed the bible aside and turned off the light. She relaxed into the comfort of her old bed and familiar surroundings. "I can't wait to move into my new place." She yawned as she started to drift off

145

to sleep.

Jenny slept well for the first time in weeks. She had the faintest recall of pleasant dreams yet couldn't quite grasp what she'd dreamt about that left her in such a good mood. She packed up the car and was preparing to leave when she spotted Robby making his way across the street. "Hi, Jenny," he greeted her with the same annoying boyish charm he'd possessed when they were dating.

"Robby," she responded politely. "Don't you ever work?"

"Just on my way in," he explained. "What brings you to town?"

"Visiting my mom and doing my laundry," she explained.

"Oh." He nodded as he leaned against her rental car. Jenny rolled her eyes as she wondered how long it would take her to get away from him. "I wish I'd known you were coming up; we could have had dinner."

"I just wanted to see my mother," Jenny explained, hoping that Robby would finally get it through his thick skull that she wasn't interested. *'You'd think that when I showed up at the class reunion with a woman he would finally gotten a clue,'* she mentally grumbled.

"Well, maybe the next time you're up this way we can get together," he eagerly suggested.

"Robby, we've been through this before," she said with a heavy sigh.

"I know," he offered in a pleasant tone that Jenny didn't buy. "But we're friends."

"We were in high school," Jenny clarified. "That was a long time ago and you didn't take our breakup very well."

"Oh, but hanging out with Lizzie is all right?" he hissed. Jenny cringed at the harshness of his tone.

"What is it with the two of you?" Jenny blurted out, not really wanting to hear what her old prom date had to say.

"She was always coming between us," Robby explained flatly.

"No, she wasn't," Jenny clarified, thinking that it was Robby who was always getting in their way.

"I don't know," he hedged. "I was shocked when my mom told me she'd become a nun."

"Your mom?" Jenny asked, not really thinking about what he

146

had said.

"Yeah, her and Mrs. Carrington used to work together at the church," Robby said as he shrugged. "Hard to believe that after she turned you she ended up becoming a nun."

"Turned me?" Jenny shouted. "You did not just say that?" He looked at her in shock. "Robby, nobody *turned* me. I was born gay. Now get off my car," she snarled as he stepped away with a sad look in his eyes. "Idiot," she groaned as she slammed the car door in his face.

On the drive back into the city, Jenny engaged herself in a very animated discussion on how big of a jackass Robby was. "Turned me," she scoffed in disgust. "Jerk." It wasn't until Jenny had unloaded the car that something occurred to her. "When did he find out about Lizzie and I?" she asked the empty room. "My own parents didn't know for years. Doesn't matter. He's an idiot and so is Lizzie," she reasoned as she tried to shake off the nagging feeling to get ready for her date.

During dinner with Nuru's friend Sandy, Jenny found it hard to concentrate on her date. Sandy was nice enough but the woman never stopped talking. It didn't help that Jenny was lost in her thoughts about what Robby had said and what Lizzie had told Kate. More than once the tall brunette found herself saying "Huh?" when she realized that Sandy had asked her something. Not surprisingly, once dinner was over Sandy decided to call it a night without offering to see Jenny again. Jenny couldn't blame the woman since she'd been about as entertaining as stick of gum during dinner.

A few days later, while she and Nuru were moving her things into her new apartment, the dark woman kept badgering Jenny with questions regarding what went wrong with the date. "Hey, I haven't had a date in a long time. Cut me some slack," Jenny finally blurted out.

"You need furniture," Kate finally noted.

The blonde had been helping Jenny and Nuru all day but had remained strangely quiet. "I have a mattress and box spring coming tomorrow," Jenny explained. "I'll just get the rest when I can afford it."

Throughout the day, while Nuru was nagging her, Jenny fought the temptation of asking Kate how Lizzie was. She was thankful that the blonde wasn't there to help and she was still hurt by what Lizzie had told Kate. Still, she wanted to know how she was. Nothing was making sense to the tall brunette.

"First you're buying us pizza," Kate informed her. "And beer."

"Damn right," Nuru agreed.

During dinner at Bertucci's the trio consumed a couple of pizzas and a few beers. They chatted away about nothing in particular. Jenny did notice that neither she nor Kate addressed one another directly. There seemed to be this wall between them that had never existed before. It didn't help that Jenny was dying to ask about Lizzie. She kept hoping that Kate would mention her so they could talk about her. When the blonde failed to mention her younger sister, it started to drive Jenny up the wall.

What was upsetting Jenny the most was that she kept trying to convince herself that she really didn't want to know or hear about the blonde. Still, she kept biting her tongue to avoid allowing the words to escape her mouth. "So what are you doing on your day off tomorrow?" Nuru inquired.

"Fixing up the new place, then I thought I might hit Avalon," Jenny responded casually. "You know, do a little dancing and scope chicks."

"Scope chicks?" Nuru laughed. "Yes, since you did so well on your last date I can see you doing that."

"My God, you're like a dog with a bone," Jenny grumbled. "We didn't hit it off. I hadn't dated in three years and I had a crappy day. Let it go."

"I'm just saying that Sandy is really nice," Nuru pushed.

"Again, I find myself asking if Sandy is so wonderful then why don't you ask her out?" Jenny taunted her partner.

"She's not my type," Nuru defended herself.

"Since when do you have a type, Stud Muffin?" Kate joined in.

"On that note, if you two will excuse me, I need to use the ladies room," Nuru grunted as she stood and made her way across the dining room.

"I think we hit a nerve," Kate quipped as Jenny chuckled.

Once it was just the two of them, Jenny suddenly felt nervous.

She fiddled with her napkin as her mind began to spin. *'Don't ask her. You don't want to know. Talking about Lizzie is just going to bring it all up again. You'll get over her if you put her in the past where she belongs,'* her mind reasoned as she knotted her cloth napkin in a tight ball. "How's Lizzie?" she asked, trying to sound uncaring. Mentally she kicked herself as the word *'loser'* screamed through her thoughts.

Kate didn't respond at first. She simply scrunched up her face seemingly lost in thought. "She hasn't said much to me since that night," Kate finally offered. "She seems even more withdrawn than before." Jenny didn't miss the underlying accusation in her friend's voice.

"Oh," Jenny grunted in a defeated tone.

"The two of you should talk," Kate suggested hopefully.

"The two of us should just stay away from one another," Jenny argued.

"You keep saying that but I don't think it's what you really want," Kate challenged her.

"Doesn't matter." Jenny shrugged as she lied.

"Really?" Kate pressed.

"Yes, really," Jenny asserted in an effort to convince herself.

"If you say so," Kate conceded as Nuru finally returned.

The following day Jenny's mattress and box spring were delivered. She had been shopping for a bed frame and headboard but failed to find anything she liked. She cleaned up, unpacked her meager belongings, and tried to organize the tiny studio apartment. She was tired by the time she'd completed her tasks but she liked the way the place was shaping up. The last time she'd felt at home in a place that she lived in was her old apartment before Wendy moved in. The funny thing was she never recalled asking Wendy to move in. She just kept coming over and not leaving. During each of her lengthy stays Wendy deposited more and more of her belongings. Before Jenny knew what was happening, they were living together.

Jenny reclined in her grandmother's rocking chair while holding Jingles, and for the first time in a long time she felt comfortable in her surroundings. "This could work," Jenny addressed the tiny stuffed animal with the bell around its neck. The image of a tiny Lizzie spending all of her quarters and tossing those baseballs at the milk bottles until she had finally knocked over enough to win Jingles for Jenny suddenly flooded her mind. Jenny laughed at how determined the small blonde had been. "Did I love her even back then when we were just children?" the brunette pondered aloud. Jenny couldn't honestly recall a time growing up when she didn't feel a need to be close to Lizzie. Jenny had no idea when she'd fallen in love with her best friend; perhaps it had always been there just beneath the surface. She remembered Lizzie's birthday party before they became lovers. She'd watched from a corner of the Carrington's backyard as Lizzie had danced the night away with her boyfriend Joel. She'd been so consumed with jealousy that she almost left the party. But she couldn't ruin the night for Lizzie. That night Jenny had slept over, and as usual, shared a bed with her friend. During the night as she slept she'd wrapped her arm around the blonde's waist. She'd been shocked when she awoke and discovered that she was spooning her best friend. Jenny had moved quickly away from cuddling Lizzie only to have the blonde capture her hand and hold it against her. Lizzie had told her to go back to sleep as she nestled closer.

Jenny chuckled at the memory of how frightened and excited she'd been to hold Lizzie while the blonde slept. She hadn't gone back to sleep that morning; instead she'd held Lizzie in her arms and watched her sleep. "So how did we go from all those innocent emotions to this?" Jenny asked Jingles, who was after all a very good listener. "Now we're all grown up and could end up hating each other. Enough," she scolded herself. "Tonight I'm going out dancing. And maybe if I'm really lucky, I'll find myself a feisty wench who will help me forget about my troubles."

The music and lights were overwhelming at the popular nightclub. Jenny spotted the blonde through the sea of gay men that flooded the dance floor. It hadn't taken her long to approach the woman and ask her to dance. They danced and got closer during the evening. Finally the woman invited Jenny back to her place for coffee; Jenny knew that the invitation was for more than a drink. She agreed as she allowed this stranger to lead her out of the busy nightclub.

Away from the thumping music of Lansdown Street, Jenny kissed the attractive woman as they rolled around on the blonde's bed. She pinned the woman's hands above her head as she began to kiss her way down the blonde's neck. Her companion was grinding her body into Jenny's as the brunette began to unbutton the woman's blouse. "Dams?" Jenny murmured against the woman's skin.

"Bureau," the blonde panted as Jenny struggled to recall her date's name.

Jenny sighed contentedly as she released her hold on the blonde's wrists. She kissed her companion deeply as the blonde sat up. Jenny noted how attractive the woman was as the blonde got up off the bed to retrieve the latex dental dams. They were still dressed but they both knew where the night was heading. She admired the gentle curve of the other woman's body as she searched her bureau.

Jenny frowned, knowing that there was something missing from the overheated encounter. "Wait," she said sadly. Her date turned to her with a surprised look. "I'm sorry," Jenny offered with a heavy sigh as she climbed off the stranger's bed and picked her jacket up off the floor.

"You're leaving?" the stranger stammered.

"I'm sorry," Jenny repeated as she put on her leather jacket. "I can't."

"But . . . ," the blonde stammered. She looked at Jenny in disbelief as her blouse hung open.

"I have to go," Jenny said honestly as she walked out of the confused woman's bedroom.

As Jenny walked the empty streets of the city towards her apartment, she knew that she'd made the right decision. As much as she craved intimate contact with another woman, there was just something missing when she touched the blonde stranger. The woman was a good kisser and very attractive; Jenny had been very excited when she'd kissed her. Still there was something just not right about the encounter. It was like looking at a picture and the person's face being blocked out. "Idiot," she chastised herself as she passed by an open coffee shop.

Jenny stumbled as she caught a glimpse of familiar golden blonde hair. "It couldn't be," she muttered as she stood frozen on the sidewalk. "Don't look. Even if it's her, you shouldn't see her," she scolded herself as she turned back and entered the coffee shop. "Is this seat taken?" Jenny asked as she leaned against the side of the booth where the small blonde was studying her book and sipping a cup of coffee.

"Hello, Jenny," Lizzie greeted her without looking up.

"How did you know it was me?" Jenny asked as she slid into the booth, seating herself across from the one person she knew she shouldn't be around.

"Just did," Lizzie said with a shrug as she closed the book she was reading and looked up at the brunette.

Jenny felt a shiver run down her spine as Lizzie looked deep into her eyes. She felt as if she was falling as she continued to look into her ex-lover's emerald orbs. Then suddenly Lizzie's eyes dimmed and she looked away. She began to shift nervously and seemed slightly agitated. "What brings you out this late at night?" Jenny asked, curious as to why Lizzie's demeanor had changed so abruptly.

"Couldn't sleep," Lizzie offered as she stared out the window.

"So you thought a strong cup of coffee would help?" Jenny teased her as she tried to figure out why Lizzie was purposely refusing to look at her.

"I just Uhm . . . ," Lizzie began to stammer as her eyes moved to the top of the table. "I've had a rough couple of days. I've managed to get into arguments with everyone - Kate, my dad, my mother, and of course my Mother Superior."

"Want to talk about it?" Jenny offered in genuine concern.

"No. It'll be all right," Lizzie stammered as her eyes darted around nervously.

"Am I making you uncomfortable?" Jenny finally blurted out defensively.

"Ugh," Lizzie grumbled as she buried her face in her hands. Finally she looked up at Jenny with a hint of anger in her eyes. "It's just that you have . . . ," Lizzie tried to explain as she made a motion to her neck.

"What?" Jenny asked as she felt her own neck, trying to figure out what she had on it that was upsetting Lizzie.

"It's . . . uhm . . . " Lizzie continued to stammer.

Jenny finally snatched up the stainless steel napkin holder to inspect her neck. "Oh man," Jenny groaned when she saw it. She slammed the napkin holder down on the table. "I can't believe she did that."

"So you didn't know," Lizzie said softly.

"No, I didn't know that I'm walking around with a huge ass hickey," Jenny groused loudly. She slipped down in her seat as the few other patrons and the youngster working the counter looked over at her. "Well, the guys at the station are going to love giving me a hard time about this," she muttered, knowing that Nuru was going to make her life hell.

"I didn't know that you were seeing someone," Lizzie said softly.

"I'm not," Jenny blurted out before she could stop and think about her words.

"Oh," Lizzie retorted coldly.

The anger pulsated through Jenny's body as she cast an icy glare at the woman who had reduced her to tears a few short days ago. "Sorry, it's none of my business," Lizzie apologized quickly.

"That's right, it isn't," Jenny snapped as Lizzie's words to Kate echoed in her mind.

Lizzie's accusation that Jenny had cheated on her was feeding her anger. There was something else feeding it as well - it was a nagging feeling of guilt. She felt guilty for having been with someone else even if nothing really happened. Her guilt was making her mad at herself for being such an idiot. They sat there glaring at each other as the tension grew.

"I'm sorry," Lizzie finally said in exasperation. "Well, it's official. I've managed to piss off everyone in my life in the last twenty-four hours."

Jenny's anger subsided as Lizzie's soft sincere words reached her. She rolled her neck and shoulders in an effort to release some of the tension. "What I don't understand is why you're mad at me?" Lizzie asked gently. Jenny's anger instantly returned as she clenched her jaw. She stared at the confused blonde sitting across from her.

"I'm mad at you because you cheated on me," Jenny finally spat out, feeling all the hurt of the past years rolling out of her. "I'm mad because you broke my heart and then lied to your sister about it."

"What are you talking about?" Lizzie asked in astonishment.

153

"I heard what you said to Kate the other night," Jenny hissed. "You told her that I was the one who had moved on and betrayed you."

"Because you did," Lizzie shouted back in a hurtful tone.

"What?" Jenny shouted. "So that girl I caught you in bed with was what? A study partner?"

"You've lost your mind," Lizzie fumed as she snatched up her book, bolted out of the booth, and stormed out of the coffee shop.

"Oh, not this time," Jenny grumbled as she followed the blonde. "This time I get answers," she vowed as she stormed after the angry woman who was walking down the street muttering to herself. "Freeze!" Jenny commanded.

Lizzie spun around with a brilliant fire in her eyes and threw her book at Jenny. The brunette jumped back as the book made contact with her shoulder. Lizzie stood there in the middle of the sidewalk with her hands on her hips and an angry gleam in her eyes. Jenny wasn't deterred as she stormed up to her. "I flew halfway across the country to find you," Jenny bellowed as she pointed an accusing finger at the blonde. "And when I did, you were doing the naked mambo with some other girl."

"The naked mambo?" Lizzie retorted incredulously. "What do you want me to do? Apologize for trying to move on with my life? You were with someone else. What did you think I would do?"

"What the hell are you talking about?" Jenny shouted as her arms flailed wildly.

"I saw the picture, Jenny," Lizzie said in cold detached voice. "If you had to find someone else, why did it have to be him?" she choked out as tears began to well up in her eyes.

Jenny swallowed her anger as she tried to understand what Lizzie was talking about. Something was wrong; she just knew it. "What picture?" she asked in a softer, more controlled voice.

"You and Robby kissing." Lizzie sniffed as she brushed the tears away. "Do you have any idea what that did to me to see you kissing that jerk? The one person who had always tried to come between us and treated me like dirt."

"Lizzie, I did date Robby but that wasn't until after I went to find you," Jenny tried to explain as her mind tried to fit the pieces together.

"Please," Lizzie scoffed. "I'm not stupid. When my mother came and bailed me out of Juvenile Hall, I told her that there was no way I was staying at that school and that you and I were going to be together. That's when she showed me the picture and told me that you were dating Robby and had forgotten all about me."

"Hold on," Jenny offered calmly as she took a shy step closer to Lizzie. "That isn't possible. When did this happen?"

"After I was arrested," Lizzie explained as she studied Jenny carefully. "November."

"Son of a . . . " Jenny muttered as she finally pieced it together. "The Halloween Dance."

"Jenny?" Lizzie asked carefully. "What is it?"

"I didn't kiss him," Jenny clarified. "He kissed me. Then I slapped his face and stormed out of the gym. I was so angry that I walked home. One of his friends took a picture. His mother and your mother worked together at a lot of church functions, didn't they?"

"Mrs. Ventnor was always a devoted Catholic," Lizzie moaned. "Not as devoted as my mother. Of course, I don't think the Pope is as devoted as my dear sweet mother. She sent me your prom picture too."

"That was later," Jenny explained with a heavy sigh. "I was so brokenhearted and I tried to convince myself that I wasn't gay. It didn't last long, and in the end I broke his heart."

"All these years," Lizzie said in regret. "You've got to hand it to my mother. She knew just what to do to convince me that you didn't love me. It was perfect."

"I did love you," Jenny said softly as she stepped closer to Lizzie. The blonde leaned into Jenny's body and hugged her tightly. Jenny instantly wrapped her arms around the smaller woman's body. Jenny swallowed the anger she felt towards Mrs. Carrington and what she had stolen from them as she simply enjoyed the warmth of Lizzie's body pressed against her own.

"I loved you too," Lizzie whispered against her chest. Jenny could feel the rapid beating of her heart as they pressed even closer together. "A part of me still . . . " Lizzie's words stopped as she suddenly stepped back and out of Jenny's embrace. "Okay," Lizzie said in a frustrated tone.

"Right," Jenny agreed with a shy smile. "The pesky reality of the here and now."

Jenny walked over and retrieved the book that Lizzie had hit her with. She handed it back to Lizzie carefully, not allowing their fingers to touch. "Can I walk you home, Sister Rachel?" Jenny offered, knowing that they still couldn't explore the underlying emotions they were both feeling.

"Thank you," Lizzie accepted. They began to walk down the street, each of them maintaining a proper distance from the other.

They didn't speak as they walked to Kate's apartment. Jenny shoved her hands deep inside the pockets of her coat so she wouldn't be tempted to touch her former lover. She was happy in one respect; the past hadn't been what she'd been led to believe it was. Still, that didn't change the present. Lizzie was still a nun and Jenny couldn't give in to the intense emotions that the small blonde had stirred up. Jenny couldn't allow herself to get her hopes up. For now she hoped that what she had learned might help her finally leave the past in the past. Of course, there was one major flaw in Jenny's theory. She couldn't stop her heart from racing every time she was near or thought about Lizzie.

CHAPTER THIRTEEN

As Jenny had predicted, Nuru gave her a very hard time about the hickey she was sporting. Jenny scowled at her partner and the other officers that participated in the teasing. Sometimes the fine men and women she served with behaved like a bunch of adolescents. The one notable exception was Kate of course. She simply glared at Jenny with an angry expression. Jenny didn't know if Kate was upset because she thought Lizzie might be involved or if her anger stemmed from the possibility that someone besides her sister had made the mark. Jenny really didn't care. She simply wanted to get through her shift without any further heckling from the boys at the station.

"You really enjoy doing that." Jenny snickered as her partner climbed back into the patrol car after issuing a speeding ticket.

"Yes, I do." Nuru smirked. "I just love hearing the lame excuses people come up with. Like I don't know they're lying. It just pleases me to burst their bubble."

"What was this one's excuse?" Jenny asked as they pulled out into the flow of traffic.

"Grandma needs a new kidney." Nuru laughed. "I pointed out that the hospital was in the other direction and that this road leads to the mall." She released a wicked cackle. "Speaking of lame excuses, you want to tell me about the vampire you ran into?"

"No," Jenny responded flatly, knowing that her friend wasn't going to simply drop the subject.

"Come on," Nuru urged her.

157

"Nothing to tell," Jenny dismissed her prodding, hoping to escape the conversation.

"Liar," Nuru grunted. "Come on, share or I'll just make up my own version."

"Brat," Jenny grumbled. "It was nothing. I met some girl at the club the other night and we went back to her place. We got a little hot and heavy and that's it."

"That's it?" Nuru responded in disbelief.

"That's it," Jenny asserted. "When things started to get interesting, I wasn't into it so I left."

"You what?" Nuru shouted.

"I left," Jenny answered her firmly. "I didn't want to sleep with her so I left."

"Why?" Nuru asked in bewilderment.

"Did you miss the part where I said I didn't want to sleep with her?" Jenny explained in exasperation.

"And?" Nuru sputtered, still not understanding what the problem was.

"You know you're the only person I know that can make me feel bad about being particular about who I go to bed with," Jenny sputtered out in frustration. "Having priorities and morals isn't a bad thing."

"If you say so," Nuru grumbled as the dispatch operator alerted them that they were needed. "Isn't that the Carrington's address?"

"Yes," Jenny responded with a weary sigh before responding to the call. "What did you do now?" she muttered under her breath, fearing that somehow Lizzie was involved with whatever was going on.

Mr. Donaldson, the building manager, met them as soon as they pulled up. He quickly explained that there had been a suspicious-looking man lurking around the building all morning. The strange man's interest seemed to be focused near or around Kate's apartment. They thanked him for being a good neighbor before heading up to the floor where Kate's apartment was located. Nuru went up the back stairs while Jenny went up the front.

Jenny and Nuru entered the long hallway from opposite ends at the same moment. It wasn't hard to find the man they were looking for since he was kneeling in front of Kate's front door trying to pick the lock. *'Good luck,'* Jenny thought with delight, knowing that Kate was smart enough to invest in the best locks available. By the way the man was grumbling she knew he wasn't having any success at gaining access to the apartment.

Jenny smiled, knowing that they had the intruder trapped between them. At almost six feet tall, Jenny knew that she was an imposing figure in her uniform. Her partner was even taller and even more frightening. The man glanced up at her with beady eyes and turned pale as he climbed to his feet. "Can I help you?" she asked sternly. He turned quickly in an effort to run and spotted Nuru approaching him. Jenny hoped he would be smart and just give himself up. He stood there for a moment, weighing his options.

As he bolted towards her, Jenny knew that he was as dumb as he looked. After all, the guy's attire screamed *'I'm a bad guy'*. He tried to knock her over in an effort to flee. Jenny easily gripped his waist and spun him around; Nuru joined in and they pushed the struggling man to the floor. As they wrestled with the man in black, Jenny caught a glimpse of a familiar figure approaching.

"Hi, ladies," Lizzie greeted them as Jenny was placing handcuffs on the man. Jenny cringed slightly at the sight of Lizzie dressed in her habit carrying two bags of groceries. "What brings you by?" Lizzie quipped as Nuru and Jenny forced the still struggling man up to his feet.

"Oh, we were just in the neighborhood, Sister," Jenny responded in a lighthearted tone. "I'm going to search you, weasel. Do you have anything in your pockets that might hurt me?"

"Fuck you," the man hissed.

"Watch your language," Nuru scolded him as she smacked him in the back of the head. "Sorry about that, Sister," Nuru apologized as Jenny chuckled. "What?"

"Nothing. It's just that I've heard you say worse," Jenny explained as she retrieved a .32 pistol from the man's waistband. "And as for the good Sister, I grew up with her and at times she could make a sailor blush."

"Flatterer," Lizzie jested, as she was about to place her key in the door.

"Don't go in there," Jenny instructed the nun in a harsh tone

159

while she continued to search the man.

"You're joking," Lizzie responded with a heavy sigh.

"I wish I was," Jenny informed her. "But he was trying to break in and I need to confirm that there's no one else inside."

"If he was trying to break in than he didn't get in, so it would stand to reason that there's no one else inside," Lizzie argued.

"Don't argue with me," Jenny groaned as she spun the man around and held the pistol up in front of him. "And you're under arrest. Here in the Commonwealth we have very strict gun laws. Even if you have a carry permit, which I doubt, it's very restrictive." She turned back to Lizzie who looked as if she was about to give Jenny a hard time. "You wait here," she instructed the upset little nun.

Jenny and Nuru informed the man of his rights as they led him down to the patrol car. Jenny bagged the gun in an evidence bag while Nuru called in what had happened. She left her partner to baby-sit the intruder while she returned upstairs. She was thankful to find Lizzie where she had left her. "Can we hurry this up?" Lizzie chastised her as Jenny took her keys away from her. "My ice cream is melting."

"What flavor?" Jenny asked as she unlocked the series of locks Kate had installed.

"Wouldn't you like to know?" Lizzie teased.

Jenny simply laughed in response, unable to look at Lizzie as she opened the door. There was something about seeing her in a habit that made the tall brunette very uncomfortable. "Stay here," Jenny instructed the smaller woman.

"Why?" Lizzie whined.

"Because I said so," Jenny spat back as she drew her gun and stepped into the apartment. She searched every nook and cranny to ensure that no one else was present. Confident that the apartment was empty, she returned to the living room and found Lizzie in the kitchen unpacking her groceries. "You have a real problem when it comes to authority, don't you?"

"So I've been told." Lizzie shrugged as she stepped out of the kitchen. Jenny winced slightly at the sight. "What? The outfit again?"

"Yes," Jenny admitted.

"Too bad since I think you look rather fetching in your work attire," Lizzie taunted her.

"Would you mind not doing that?" Jenny snapped.

"Do what?" Lizzie continued teasing her.

"Flirt with me," Jenny scolded her. "It's bad enough that you do it. But when you're dressed like that, I find it phenomenally disturbing."

"You're right," Lizzie conceded apologetically. "So do I want to know what's going on?"

"This is just a guess but I think your friend from South America is more interested in you than you think he is," Jenny explained. "I'd feel better if you didn't stay here." By the low growl Lizzie released, Jenny knew it would be a futile effort to get her to stay elsewhere. "Fine. Would you at least lock up and keep your eyes and ears open? I have a feeling Kate will be home early to keep an eye on you."

"Okay," Lizzie agreed.

"I'll stop back later to check on you," Jenny added as she made her way to the door.

"I don't need a babysitter," Lizzie fumed.

"Fine," Jenny grunted. "Just humor me for once."

"All right," Lizzie reluctantly agreed.

Later Jenny's suspicions were confirmed as a very frazzled Kate informed her that the man they'd arrested had confessed that Englewood had sent him. The drug lord was arrested once again. Kate still didn't relax since she couldn't leave early to check on her sister. She only calmed down when word from the DEA came that Englewood decided to make a deal. Jenny wasn't surprised that the man they'd arrested had turned in Englewood. It couldn't look good trying to bump off a nun and he probably doubted his safety when he discovered that the nun in question was the sister of a cop working in the very building he was being questioned in.

"Nuru and I are going on dinner break. Why don't we swing by your place and check on Lizzie?" Jenny offered. Kate smiled and thanked her. "It's all right; Englewood caved in. This is over," Jenny reassured her friend.

"So the only reason we're checking up on Sister Rachel is to make Sarge feel better?" Nuru teased her as they climbed back into the patrol car.

"Shut up and drive," Jenny snarled.

Once she was standing outside of Kate's apartment, the shrill screams she heard from inside sent a familiar panic through her. She started banging on the door, demanding entrance. Her body was trembling and the bile was rising in her throat. She knew who was on the other side of the door since she'd lived through this once before. Somewhere in her panic she recalled that she still had Lizzie's house keys. Her hands were shaking as she radioed down to her partner for help. She threw the door open once the lock was undone.

Jenny froze for a moment; she felt trapped in a horrible nightmare from the past. Her lover was curled up in a ball as her mother struck her in a wild frenzy. Jenny snapped back to the present as she rushed over and pulled Mrs. Carrington away from her daughter's prone body. "You bitch," Jenny hissed in the hysterical woman's ear as she snapped handcuffs on her wrists. "You have no idea how much I'm going to enjoy locking you up," Jenny added with another feral hiss in the wild woman's ear.

"What the hell is going on?" Nuru asked in a panic as Jenny shoved Mrs. Carrington over to her.

"Read Mrs. Carrington her rights and toss her in the car," Jenny shouted as she cradled Lizzie in her arms.

"Wait!" Nuru squeaked. "Mrs. Carrington? You want me to arrest Kate's mother?"

"Trust me; she'll thank you for it," Jenny reassured her hurriedly. She yanked her radio from her collar and called for an ambulance.

"Jenny," Lizzie whimpered against her body. "I don't need . . ."

"Ssh," Jenny hushed her protest. "You need to get checked out."

"Are you sure about this?" Nuru questioned her uncertainly.

"Get your filthy hands off me," Mrs. Carrington spat at Nuru in a disgusted tone.

"Well, that just made it easy," Nuru snapped. "Come on, lady," she growled as she began to cart Mrs. Carrington away.

"You're going to be sorry for this," Mrs. Carrington

threatened. "This is a family matter. Isn't that right, Mary Elizabeth?"

Jenny felt Lizzie stiffen against her as her mother's icy words reached her. "It doesn't matter," Nuru informed the awful woman. Jenny glared directly into the woman's icy gray eyes.

"Welcome to Massachusetts," Jenny coldly informed her. "She doesn't even need to press charges. We can remove violent *family* at our discretion."

"Come on," Nuru hissed with a sneer as she yanked the confused woman out of the apartment.

Never in Jenny's career had she been happier that they could arrest an abuser, even when the victim seemed resistant to press charges. Over the years it had proven to be useful in keeping many women safe from their *loved ones.* "I couldn't fight back," Lizzie sobbed against her body.

"It's okay," Jenny whispered softly. "I came back. This time I came back."

Later Jenny was sitting in a hard plastic chair in the emergency room waiting area, twirling her hat nervously as she waited for some news of Lizzie's condition. She kept a watchful eye on the door, knowing that Kate would come bursting through at any moment. Her heart sank as she saw a man approaching her. She noted how much older he seemed as she stood to greet him. She wondered if he hated her or blamed her for all the troubles that had befallen his once happy family. "Mr. Carrington, sir," she nervously greeted him as he gave her a cold stare.

Jenny held her breath as she watched his icy glare melt. He looked weary and defeated. "Jenny," he finally greeted her sadly. "Is she all right?"

"The doctors are still treating her," Jenny explained quickly as he studied her.

"Do I want to know what happened?" His voice creaked from the strain.

"My partner and I stopped by Kate's apartment to check on Lizzie," she began, fighting to act professionally. He gave her a curious glance. "There had been some trouble earlier."

"It does seem to follow her around," he said in an amused tone before his face fell.

"Yes, sir, it does," Jenny agreed with a shy smile. She hoped that her demeanor would help relax the man.

"Hmm." He smiled once again. "Like when she tried to give the neighbor's dog a bath." Jenny smiled at the memory of a very little Lizzie who tried to do a good deed and ended up turning the neighbor's prize collie purple.

"It was your wife," Jenny hesitantly informed him.

Mr. Carrington's facial expression quickly turned sullen once again. "My wife?" he began with a slight stammer as if the word was completely foreign to him. "Where is she?"

"Jail," Jenny muttered, wondering how he was going to accept the information.

Jenny stood nervously, twirling her hat as he rubbed his face. "Can I get you a cup of coffee, sir?" she finally offered, unable to endure the uneasy silence a moment longer. He nodded in acceptance. She moved quickly in an effort to get away from him.

"Jenny," he called out to her. The heavy timber of his voice halted her movement. Sheepishly she turned back to him. "I don't hate you," he tried to reassure her. "I don't blame you for any of this."

"Yes, you do," the brunette flatly informed him. "In a some small way, you do blame me." He opened his mouth to protest. "How could you not? I blame myself," she said, cutting him off before she turned away and left him alone.

As Jenny went in search of a vending machine or an open cafeteria, she knew in her heart that what she had said to Mr. Carrington was the truth. He was a parent, and even though he knew it wasn't true, he blamed Jenny for loving and probably seducing his little girl. She was the catalyst that had set everything in motion. And despite Jenny's own sense of reason, she agreed.

When Jenny returned to the sterile waiting room with the cup of mud dispensed by the vending machine, she found Kate and her father talking. Both of them looked terrible. "Here you are, sir," Jenny shyly offered the man the coffee. After he accepted it, she placed her hat back on her head, fully expecting both of them to send her on her way.

"She's fine," Kate wearily informed her. "The doctor was just here."

"Good," Jenny responded with a sigh of relief.

"She asked to see you," Kate continued as her father involuntarily flinched.

"Okay," Jenny responded slowly. "I'll just pop in and see her. Then I'll head back to the station to clock out. Are they keeping her overnight?"

"No," Kate informed her as Mr. Carrington stared at his shoes.

Jenny was more than a little troubled by this information. Although she was thrilled that Lizzie's injuries weren't severe enough to warrant hospitalization, she didn't like the idea of the small blonde being sent home when there was a very good chance her mother would be released that night. "I'll be taking her home," Kate asserted as her father sighed heavily.

"I still think that she would be safer with me," Mr. Carrington protested. "What if your mother gets out of jail?"

"Dad, she'll be safer with me," Kate continued to argue.

"You're both wrong," Jenny muttered, suddenly feeling like she had just finished running the Boston Marathon while carrying a ten pound sack on her shoulders.

Father and daughter looked at her as if she'd sprouted a third eye. "Mrs. Carrington will probably get out of jail very soon and she'll start looking for Lizzie. She will start at Kate's place first and then yours, sir," she softly explained. "I'm assuming that your wife has your address."

"Of course she does," he snapped as if the question was absurd.

"Forgive my intrusion, Mr. Carrington," she offered, using years of training in an effort to make the man a little more comfortable. Jenny wasn't thrilled with what she was about to suggest but it was a lot safer than what the two of them were suggesting. "Since Lizzie is comfortable with me and there's no way Mrs. Carrington can get my address, perhaps it would be prudent if she stayed with me? Just until Mrs. Carrington has a chance to calm down."

Jenny cringed slightly when Mr. Carrington scowled at her. "I'll just go and talk to Lizzie for a few moments while you discuss things," Jenny offered before bolting towards the treatment area. Sometimes being in uniform could be a very useful thing. The moment she stepped into the busy treatment area someone immediately stepped up to assist her.

"Hi," she offered shyly as she stepped behind the curtained area. Lizzie was lying on a small bed, staring up at the ceiling.

Lizzie gasped slightly as she sat up. "Easy there," Jenny cautioned her as she moved quickly to the small blonde's bedside. Gently she guided Lizzie back down onto the pillows. Lizzie placed a trembling hand on Jenny's forearm. The tall brunette left her hand resting on the blonde's shoulder, unwilling to break the warm connection they shared. She smiled when she felt Lizzie stroking her arm with her thumb. She knew that the smaller woman wasn't aware of what she was doing.

"Thank you," Lizzie whispered. Jenny knew that the blonde wasn't referring to being helped back to a comfortable position.

"You must think I'm a fool," Lizzie mumbled as she stared down at the sheet.

"What?" Jenny exclaimed.

"For not fighting back," Lizzie mumbled once again. "Everything inside of me screamed for me to defend myself; I just couldn't hit my own mother."

"I do understand," Jenny reassured her as she gave the smaller woman's shoulder a soft squeeze. "I don't agree, but I can understand it. Do you know that Kate and your dad are waiting to see you?" She was certain that Lizzie had only asked to see her because she was unaware that her family was there.

"They must be completely freaked out," Lizzie choked out.

"Hey, this isn't your fault," Jenny quickly reassured her. She had seen it before; victims could so easily assign guilt and blame to themselves.

"I know that," Lizzie responded grimly as she finally looked up at Jenny. The sadness clouding her normally brilliant eyes broke the brunette's heart. "In my mind I know what you're saying is true. I just wish I could convince the rest of me."

"Do you want to see your family?" Jenny asked quietly as she fought the need to wrap Lizzie up in her arms and never let her go.

"Yes," Lizzie quietly answered.

"I should warn you that they're very upset, and they're debating over where you should stay tonight," Jenny cautioned the smaller woman.

"Why?" Lizzie asked in confusion.

"Even though Nuru and I had every right to lock up your mother, chances are she's already free," Jenny explained carefully. She felt Lizzie's body stiffen as the little blonde's jaw clenched. "I suggested that you stay with me."

Lizzie looked up at her with a stunned expression. "There's no way your mother can find you there. And I'm afraid that she's probably even angrier than she was before."

"I could stay at a convent," Lizzie suggested as her eyes filled with tears.

"She can find you there," Jenny explained while her heart broke. She brushed Lizzie's tears from her cherubic features. Her heart warmed when Lizzie captured her hand with her own. They sat there frozen for a moment as they gazed into each other's eyes, searching for the right words to express what they were feeling at that moment.

Jenny could feel the tears welling up inside of her. She brought Lizzie's hand to her lips and placed a comforting kiss on the back of it before releasing it from her grasp. "I'm going to send your family in," she choked out before leaving Lizzie's bedside.

Somehow Jenny managed to compose herself by the time she returned to the waiting area to inform Kate and her father that Lizzie wanted to see them. She was planning on leaving as soon as they were inside, knowing that they wouldn't agree to send Lizzie home with her. But Kate asked her to stay. Once again Jenny was fidgeting in a hard plastic chair while she waited to find out what was going on. An agonizing twenty odd minutes later Kate reemerged.

"How are you doing?" the blonde asked in concern as she sat next Jenny. The tall brunette could only clear her throat in response since she no longer trusted herself to keep her fears hidden. "We've talked," Kate began gravely. "And everyone is in agreement that you're right, and Lizzie will be safer with you." Jenny blinked in surprise. She had been certain that Mr. Carrington and Lizzie wouldn't agree with her idea. "If it's all right with you, Dad will stay here and bring Lizzie to the station. I'll bring you back to the station now and you can get your things together." Jenny nodded as

167

she stood. "Thank you, Jenny."

"You don't . . . ," Jenny started to protest.

"Yes, I do," Kate asserted firmly as she stood beside the taller woman.

When they returned to the police station they discovered that Mrs. Carrington was still in custody, but not for long. Jenny took off with Lizzie the moment her father brought her to the station. Mr. Carrington drove them to Jenny's apartment building. During the entire drive no one spoke. Jenny was relieved that none of them felt a need to engage in the façade of trying to make small talk. The brunette watched the streets as they made their way across town to ensure that they weren't being followed.

Jenny kept a careful eye on the street traffic while Lizzie and her father exchanged their goodbyes. She was stunned when the older man touched her lightly on the arm and whispered a heartfelt 'thank you' before they made their way inside the building.

The first thing the tall brunette did once they were safely inside her apartment was to send Lizzie off for a long hot bath. She tossed some old sweats into the bathroom, careful to shield her eyes while she did so. Then she rechecked every lock and window. Then she paced until Lizzie finally emerged from the bathroom. She almost laughed at the sight of the tiny blonde swimming in her clothing. She apologized for the cramped quarters as Lizzie yawned. Then Jenny ducked into the bathroom and took a long hot shower.

When Jenny emerged from the shower she felt much better. She found Lizzie reclining on her bed, once again mesmerized by flicking the channels on the television. "You are way too fascinated by television," Jenny teased the blonde as she climbed up onto the bed.

"This coming from someone who used to eat paste," Lizzie grumbled as her eyes remained glued to the rapidly passing channels.

"Once!" Jenny squealed in protest. "And I only did it because you told to me to. 'Go on, Jenny, it tastes just like oatmeal'," Jenny mocked her.

"I can't believe you fell for that," Lizzie giggled as she put the remote down and looked at the scowling brunette.

"I was six," Jenny growled. "I should have known then that you were an evil little blonde."

Lizzie laughed once again and Jenny felt a strange sense of relief at seeing her friend smiling once again. "How are you doing?" Jenny asked carefully, not wanting to dampen her friend's mood.

"Okay," Lizzie sighed. She turned onto her side so they were facing one another. "The doctor said I'd be sore for a couple of weeks. I still can't believe she snapped again."

"I can," Jenny groaned. "What set her off? Or was she just being her evil old self?"

"I'm not up to talking about this now," Lizzie said shyly as her gaze drifted down to the bedspread.

"No worries," Jenny reassured her as the sounds of the television filled the dark room.

She hadn't been paying attention; the only thing she was aware of was how close they were to each other as their eyes met. Jenny could feel her heart beating a little faster as she felt her attraction for Lizzie creeping up on her once again. She almost laughed at herself, knowing that what she'd been feeling for Lizzie was beginning to blossom into something much deeper than a simple attraction. Her eyes drifted from Lizzie's gaze and with a will of their own began to roam up and down the smaller woman's body. Lizzie's body tempted her to reach out. She wasn't the girl Jenny had once known; Jenny just wasn't prepared for the woman she'd become.

Jenny looked back up at Lizzie who was once again staring at the television while she channel surfed. As Lizzie rapidly jumped from one channel to the next, Jenny was lost. She knew in her heart that the look of indifference Lizzie sported was nothing more than a smokescreen. She could feel the heat from her ex-lover's body burning her skin even though they weren't touching. Jenny knew that all she had to do was reach over and she could seduce the blonde with a simple touch. *'And then what?'* Jenny asked herself. She knew that if anything happened she would be taking away the one thing Lizzie needed in her life at that moment. She needed to have her own voice.

Knowing these things still didn't stop Jenny from admiring the body that was so close to her own. She simply rested her head on her pillow and stole glances at the woman who still seemed to possess a piece of her fragile heart. Jenny knew that her gaze was lingering longer and longer each time she looked over. She was sailing into dangerous waters, and it was time to turn back before one of them did something they would regret. Just as she was about to reach the shores of sanity, she heard it.

It was one of those things from her past that still haunted her and caused waves of passion to surge throughout her entire body. Jenny's pulse quickened as she felt herself being drawn into the music that was whispering from the television. The unlikely source of their passion was the theme song from Charlie's Angels. Jenny fought to calm her breathing as the corny music filtered through the air.

She looked over at the rapid rise and fall over Lizzie's chest. Apparently she wasn't the only one who still had a hard time explaining to people that the theme to Charlie's Angels was a complete turn on. It had all started when they were lovers. They were two teenaged girls in a small town and they used any excuse they could to spend time together. Jenny and Lizzie used the once-popular television show as an excuse to spend more time together. Every Wednesday night Lizzie would sleep over even though it was a school night. Jenny's parents couldn't understand their fascination with the television program. They also never understood why the girls chose to watch the show on the small television in Jenny's bedroom instead of the larger one in the family room. Her poor parents were blissfully unaware that they never made it past the opening credits before they were completely naked and exploring one another's bodies.

To this day Jenny still hadn't seen an entire episode of the show. When the movie came out just a few years ago, Wendy was delighted at the way Jenny took advantage of her in the tiny cinema. Jenny always felt guilty that she still thought about Lizzie that night. Jenny looked over to see that Lizzie's face had turned scarlet. Jenny caught the blonde's hand as she went to change the channel. Her fingers trembled as she held Lizzie's hand in her own. Lizzie's eyes fluttered shut as her breathing grew heavier. The temptation was proving to be too much for either of them. Jenny slid her hand up and caressed Lizzie's arm. Feeling the heat from Lizzie's body

170

caressing her fingers, Jenny understood that her touch was welcome.

Jenny watched as the remote slipped from Lizzie's grasp and fell onto the comforter with a heavy plop. Lizzie's arm lowered and invited Jenny in. Jenny slowly allowed her hand to drift down Lizzie's arm to the soft swell of her breasts. Lizzie's eyes remained shut as Jenny's hand continued its exploration down the curve of the blonde's body to her thigh. Lizzie opened her eyes and looked deep into Jenny's eyes while the brunette caressed her thigh. Jenny's excitement grew as Lizzie released a tiny groan. Jenny's hand seemed to have a will of its own as it slipped between Lizzie's thighs, creeping closer to her center.

"Jenny," Lizzie gasped. "Please . . . I . . ." Lizzie failed to continue and Jenny knew that the blonde was unable to say 'no' or to tell her to stop. It was what they both wanted. Jenny felt Lizzie's thighs opening, welcoming her touch. She watched as Lizzie's head fell back. Jenny lowered her head, eager to kiss Lizzie's neck, knowing that it would drive the smaller woman insane. She was close enough to Lizzie's body to hear the rapid beating of the blonde's heart.

Jenny could feel Lizzie's desire seeping through her sweatpants as the brunette's fingers inched dangerously close to her desire. Jenny leaned her body into Lizzie's with every intention of kissing the blonde senseless when Lizzie winced in pain. Jenny flew away from Lizzie in a blinding motion. Her eyes widened in horror as Lizzie sat up clutching her side.

"Are you all right?" Jenny asked in a panic.

"Fine," Lizzie stammered before blowing out a cleansing breath.

Jenny reached over, grabbed the remote, and quickly changed the channel as Lizzie nursed her bruised body. Lizzie finally relaxed and she turned back towards Jenny who watched every movement to reassure herself that the blonde was okay. "I'm fine," Lizzie offered gently. She smiled at Jenny before biting down on her bottom lip. "Give me strength," the blonde whispered as she rolled her eyes. Jenny could see Lizzie's eyes darkening once again with desire. The brunette jumped up off the bed.

"Would you say a prayer for me?" Jenny grumbled as she headed back towards her bathroom.

"No problem," Lizzie softly agreed. "Where are you going?"

"Shower!" Jenny snapped before she slammed the bathroom door.

Once in the safety of her bathroom, Jenny braced herself against the sink. "A long cold shower," she firmly instructed herself as she tried to calm her overheated body.

CHAPTER FOURTEEN

Hiding in the bathroom was probably not the best course of action, but for the moment it was all Jenny could think of. She'd taken a very long and very cold shower. *'How did we go from the emotional strain of her mother attacking her to almost groping each other?'* Jenny wondered as she questioned her own sanity. She was quickly realizing that some things about her former lover never changed. During their brief teenage romance Lizzie was able to move from zero to sixty without batting an eye. If Jenny was completely honest with herself, it was one of the things that drew her to the blonde. "Just like a moth to a flame," she grumbled.

Jenny finally stepped out of the bathroom wrapped in her favorite blue bathrobe. She could tell by the rise and fall of Lizzie's chest along with the earth shattering snores that the events of the day had finally overwhelmed the blonde and she was fast asleep. Quietly Jenny shuffled over to the kitchen that was divided by a tiny island from her living room and bedroom. She was careful not to make any noise as she put the teakettle on, selected her favorite tea, and grabbed her favorite oversized mug. Wendy had always given her a ration of crap about the large mug that sported an image of Dopey from Snow White on it. She smiled as she poured hot water into the mug; she wondered if Lizzie still had the other mug with Grumpy on it.

It had started as a joke between them. Jenny had always said that Grumpy matched Lizzie's personality before she had her first cup of coffee. The winter before they became lovers Jenny's family had gone to Disney World and she'd bought her best friend the biggest mug with Grumpy's face on it that she could find. Lizzie in turn paid her back the following spring by giving Jenny a huge mug with an image that she claimed reminded her of Jenny. The tall brunette had laughed herself silly when she saw Dopey's silly grin smiling up at her.

Jenny giggled as she sat on the stool in front of her breakfast bar and sipped her tea. She had to admit that they'd had a lot of good times together even before things became intimate between them. She looked over and her smile grew brighter as she watched Lizzie sleep. The memories once again crept in and this time she didn't fight them.

"What do you think?" Lizzie pleaded with her as they sat on the blonde's bed. Jenny didn't want to answer the question. She was terrified that her best friend would discover the feelings she had for her if she answered the question. She simply continued to brush Lizzie's long blonde hair.

"I think that you would look like a kid in braids," Jenny finally offered in an effort to avoid the real question Lizzie had just posed.

"Not about that!" Lizzie grumbled. "And I know I look like a twelve-year-old when I braid my hair, you goof. I was talking about Joel."

"Oh him," Jenny grunted as she allowed her fingers to enjoy the soft silky feeling of Lizzie's hair.

"Don't you like him?" Lizzie asked in concern.

"He's okay," Jenny responded noncommittally. She didn't want to tell Lizzie that she didn't like or trust Joel. She couldn't since she knew that her dislike stemmed from her unexplainable attachment to her best friend. Joel had been Lizzie's steady beau for the last couple of months and Jenny hated watching them together. She feared that Lizzie would start a sexual relationship with the lanky redhead, and then there would be no place for Jenny in the blonde's life.

"What's wrong?" Lizzie asked, pulling Jenny away from the miserable thoughts that had been plaguing her.

"Nothing," Jenny lied as she continued to brush Lizzie's hair. "So what do you think he got you for your birthday?" Lizzie's sweet

sixteen party was that night and Jenny had come over a little early to help her get ready.

"I have no idea," Lizzie huffed in frustration. "He said it was something special."

"I bet," Jenny groaned.

"What?" Lizzie pressed as she turned to Jenny.

Jenny's breath caught as she became lost in the emerald pools looking innocently up at her. "Nothing. It's just that...you know," Jenny stammered as she lowered her head to hide the blush that was creeping up her face.

"I'm not going to sleep with him," Lizzie reassured her as she removed the hairbrush from Jenny's grasp. The brunette's fingers tingled with excitement at Lizzie's touch. Then Lizzie cupped her face and turned Jenny's gaze back toward her own. "I'm not," Lizzie earnestly vowed.

"It's none of my business," Jenny confessed sadly. She pulled away from her friend's touch before she did something they'd both regret.

Jenny released a large gasp as she was knocked over and pinned to the bed. "Don't say that," Lizzie fumed as she held the larger girl's arms tightly. "You're my best friend and everything you say is important." Jenny grunted in response as she tried to free herself from Lizzie's grasp. She needed to distance herself from the compromising position; her body was enjoying it far too much. "Say it," Lizzie demanded.

"Everything I say is important," Jenny taunted her friend, knowing that she was dangerously close to being tickled to death.

"Not that," Lizzie growled fiercely as her nimble little digits dug into Jenny's sensitive side.

Jenny laughed hysterically as Lizzie assaulted her body with her fingers. She curled up in an effort to escape the tickling. Lizzie knew her and her body all too well and the attack escalated. "Say it," Lizzie demanded.

"Fine. I'm your best friend, you little freak." Jenny laughed as Lizzie's fingers stilled. Jenny's body was tingling as Lizzie hovered above her with a bright smile.

"And don't you forget it," Lizzie chastised her as she leaned closer to Jenny.

Jenny swallowed hard as she felt Lizzie's breath on her face. For a brief moment she was almost certain that Lizzie was going to kiss her, granting her the one thing her body and mind had been craving for ages. Suddenly Lizzie pulled away. "So who's your date tonight?" the blonde asked casually as if nothing had happened.

"Don't have one," Jenny responded as she sat up.

"Why not?" Lizzie squawked. "What happened to what's-his-name? You know - booger boy."

"Brian," Jenny corrected her. "I dumped him. So I guess I'll just be a wallflower tonight."

"Yeah, right," Lizzie snorted in amusement. "Every guy there will be flocking around you just like they always do. Thank God Robby isn't invited; I hate the way he hangs all over you."

"He doesn't mean anything by it," Jenny defended her neighbor.

"What? So you like him?" Lizzie spat out hostilely.

"No," Jenny quickly blurted out.

"Then why do you let him latch on to you like you're the last lifeboat on the Titanic?" Lizzie hissed.

"I do not," Jenny argued, still not understanding why Lizzie and Robby hated one another with such intensity.

"You do," Lizzie whined. "I can't stand him."

"Forget about him," Jenny said, trying to placate the pouting blonde as she reached for her purse and withdrew the tiny elegantly wrapped package she'd hidden inside. "It's your birthday; just relax and enjoy the party."

"Happy Birthday," Jenny stammered as her palms began to sweat. With trembling hands she gave Lizzie the present she'd saved up for months to buy.

"Thank you," Lizzie said with heartbreaking smile. Jenny held her breath as she watched Lizzie slowly unwrap the tiny box careful not to tear the paper. Lizzie's jaw dropped when she opened the velvet box that was unveiled.

"Do you like it?" Jenny nervously asked.

"I love it," Lizzie choked out as her eyes began to well up. "Put it on me?"

Jenny simply nodded as she removed the necklace with the

teardrop-shaped emerald. It was Lizzie's birthstone and she'd just had to buy the expensive necklace for her best friend. Her long fingers were shaking as she brushed Lizzie's hair aside and clasped the necklace. "Thank you," Lizzie repeated as she wrapped her arms around Jenny's waist. Jenny held her breath as her friend's breasts brushed against her own. Her heart was racing as she pulled her body away from her best friend's grasp.

That night Jenny lurked in the shadows as Lizzie entertained her guests while she hung on her boyfriend's arm. The sight was tearing Jenny apart. As she watched Lizzie dance with Joel in her backyard, it was like a knife through her heart. Then Lizzie did something that made everyone stop and stare. She abandoned Joel's side just as a slow song began and walked over to Jenny. The brunette was floored as Lizzie led her across the backyard and danced with her. It was the best moment of Jenny's life until the song ended and Lizzie gave her arm a gentle squeeze before she rejoined her boyfriend. A few days later Lizzie and Joel broke up. Jenny never asked why.

Jenny stared down at her now empty mug before her eyes drifted to Lizzie who had managed to cocoon herself in the blankets. "The old tuck and roll. I'll be lucky if I get a scrap of blanket." Jenny snorted slightly, amused by the situation, as the brunette simply accepted her fate. If she tried to crawl into her bed she would undoubtedly freeze since Lizzie had managed to trap the blankets beneath her. "Oh well," Jenny sighed as she turned the teakettle back on and grabbed a book from the shelf. She thumbed through it; she'd started to read it some time ago but had been forced to put it down when reality interrupted her quiet time.

She got caught up in the story as she prepared herself another cup of tea and took the steaming mug into the living room. She released a heavy sigh as she sat in her grandmother's rocking chair and wrapped her grandmother's afghan around herself. She sipped her tea before setting the mug down on the small table next to the rocker. Jenny opened the book again and found it impossible to focus on the words. Instead of reading the story that had once captivated her, she found her eyes constantly wandering back to Lizzie's slumbering form.

She couldn't keep the flood of memories at bay. She closed the book and set it down as she decided to stop fighting the tidal wave and simply allow the pleasant voices from the past to invade her mind. Jenny almost laughed out loud as she recalled the time she and Lizzie were just finishing junior high school.

"Come on, Jenny," Lizzie earnestly implored her. "This is going to be the coolest thing we've ever done."

"Lizzie, this is silly," Jenny whined as she wrapped her arm around her best friend's shoulders. "What if we get caught?"

"Please, Jenny, I really want to do this," Lizzie pleaded. Jenny took one look in the blonde's emerald eyes and agreed. Even then she couldn't refuse anything the blonde asked of her. So there she was on the last day of junior high willingly participating in yet another one of Lizzie's brilliant and insane ideas. Lizzie had wanted to make a statement. At least that was the way the exuberant blonde described her latest harebrained scheme. Each of them was wearing one roller skate as they clung to each other.

"We're going to fall." Jenny grumbled.

"Hold on to me; I won't let you fall, Jenny," Lizzie vowed as they nervously waited for the bell to ring announcing the end of the class period.

Soon the hallway would be flooded with students and teachers, each hurrying to reach their next class before the next bell rung. Jenny's heart was pounding with fear as the bell clanged and the hallway suddenly filled with hundreds of people. Lizzie gave them a push and they were sailing down the longest corridor in the school. They bounced and weaved as they rolled, clutching one another tightly in an effort to remain standing. They had almost reached their destination at the opposite end of the hall while the other students laughed at their antics. The journey came to an abrupt end when they slammed into Mr. Truman, the assistant vice principal; they almost sent the small man sailing through the air. Jenny could have sworn that the old man was trying to hide a smile as he ordered them to remove the skates and walk to their next class. It was the only reprimand the duo received.

"Oh, the things I let you talk me into," Jenny chuckled whimsically. The muffled sounds of sobbing broke through her happy memories. Horrified, she looked at Lizzie's shivering body as the blonde released a helpless whimper. Jenny bolted out of the rocker, tossing the afghan aside as she rushed to Lizzie's side.

"No! Please stop!" Lizzie screamed as her body curled up into a ball. Jenny climbed up onto the bed and wrapped her arms around Lizzie's trembling form.

"Ssh. I have you," Jenny whispered in Lizzie's ear as she rocked the smaller woman gently in her arms.

Lizzie struggled to free herself from Jenny's hold; the brunette continued to rock her gently as she whispered soft words in her ear. Lizzie's trembling finally faded and she relaxed into Jenny's warm embrace. Jenny rested her body against the headboard as she cradled Lizzie in her arms. A single teardrop slid down her cheek as she tightened her hold on the smaller woman. "I'm here, baby," Jenny reassured the sleeping woman. Jenny held Lizzie for what seemed like hours until she drifted off to sleep. While she slept, the past once again invaded her dreams.

"I guess hiking is out?" Jenny teased Lizzie as they sat across from one another in their usual booth at Dante's Diner.

"Cute," Lizzie retorted as her lips curled up into a snarl.

"Hey, I told you not to climb out my bedroom window," Jenny said softly. With an amused smirk she stared at Lizzie's foot that was still wrapped in a cast as a result of her escapade.

"Oh sure. I could have just strolled downstairs and said hi to your dad," Lizzie snorted. "And when he asked what I was doing there so late, I could just tell him I was ravishing . . ." Jenny leaned over and clamped her hand over Lizzie's lips before she could finished what she was saying.

Jenny blushed deeply as she recalled what she and Lizzie had been doing before they drifted off to sleep and her parents arrived home. She bit back a moan as Lizzie's tongue tickled the palm of her hand. "You're such a brat," Jenny scolded the giggling blonde as she removed her hand and wiped it on a napkin.

"What? Afraid you'll get cooties?" Lizzie teased her.

"I should spank you," Jenny threatened. Her blush grew

179

deeper as Lizzie simply wiggled her eyebrows in a suggestive manner. "What has gotten into you today?" Jenny laughed.

"You," Lizzie responded in a husky tone that sent a delightful shiver down Jenny's spine.

"Where can we go?" Jenny asked in a breathless whisper as she watched her lover's eyes darken with desire.

"Why? Are you planning on having your way with me?" Lizzie asked softly as she leaned over the table.

Jenny opened her mouth to respond when she felt a large mass plop down beside her. Jenny didn't need to look over to see that it was Robby. The disgusted scowl on Lizzie's face told her all that she needed to know.

"Hey, Jenny," Robby greeted her brightly as he placed his arm on the back of the booth.

"We were talking," Lizzie growled at him.

"Sorry, didn't see you, Lezzy," Robby offered in a condescending tone. Jenny hated it when he called Lizzie that. But what could she say? They both knew they had to keep their relationship a secret. "So, Jenny, do you want to go to the drive-in tonight?" he asked as he ignored the low threatening growl Lizzie directed at him.

"I'm busy," Jenny sighed in a dismissive manner, wondering why he just wouldn't take a hint. Her heart sank as she stared into her lover's eyes. She knew that Lizzie was silently pleading with her to tell Robby to go away. As much as she wanted him to leave them alone so they could go back to making plans for the night, she couldn't be rude to her neighbor.

"So change your plans," Robby persisted.

"No can do," Jenny offered as politely as she could. "Maybe some other time," she offered in hope that their uninvited guest would leave.

No sooner had the words left her mouth than Lizzie reacted by shoving her plate across the booth. Her half-eaten hamburger landed in Robby's lap. Lizzie crawled out of the booth, snatched up her crutches, and hobbled off. "Lizzie, wait!" Jenny called after her lover. She was unable to chase after the small blonde since Robby was blocking her exit.

"Let her go," Robby fumed as he tossed the remnants of

Lizzie's lunch onto the table.

"Robby, move," Jenny demanded.

"Seriously, she's a bitch. Let her go," Robby stressed as he tried to clean up his lap. "Jesus, what crawled up her ass today?" he asked, still not moving so Jenny could get out of the booth.

Jenny felt the anger explode from deep inside of her. She shoved Robby harshly, sending him flying out of the booth. The diner erupted in laughter when the other teenagers caught sight of the football player lying helpless on the floor as Jenny stepped over him. When she reached the parking lot Lizzie was nowhere to be seen. "Damn! For someone with a broken ankle she can move fast," Jenny muttered as she looked around for her lover. "I'm in such trouble."

It wasn't the first time Jenny and Lizzie had fought about Robby. It was the first time they'd had an argument since becoming lovers. It was also the first time Jenny bought a woman a present to say she was sorry. Then again it was also the first time she learned just how much fun making up could be. Jenny's eyes blinked open and she looked down at the blonde who was looking back up at her while she rested in Jenny's embrace.

"What are you in trouble for?" Lizzie asked her curiously.

"Just dreaming," Jenny said with soft smile. "Sorry, didn't mean to wake you."

"So what were you dreaming about?" Lizzie asked as she nestled against Jenny's shoulder.

Jenny rubbed the blonde's back in a soothing manner. "Oh, just some fight you and I had years ago. Robby ticked you off, and we ended up having a huge argument," Jenny explained.

"You'll have to be more specific," Lizzie informed her as she yawned and sat up.

Jenny's body instantly ached at the loss of contact. "We fought a lot because of him, didn't we?" Jenny asked as she thought about the run in she'd had with Robby the last time she'd seen him.

"Yeah," Lizzie grunted as she gave Jenny a challenging look. Although she hadn't seen the look in many years, Jenny was very familiar with it. "I can't say that I blame him though."

"Huh?" Jenny choked out, truly surprised by Lizzie's change

181

in attitude.

"Robby and I clashed because we were both in love with you," Lizzie explained calmly as she climbed off the bed and stretched her body. "How can I blame him for falling in love with you? How could he resist?" They found themselves locked in an intense gaze for a brief moment before Lizzie turned away. "Is it all right if I put some coffee on?"

"Go ahead," Jenny answered as she climbed off the bed and followed Lizzie into the kitchen. "I had a run in with Robby the other day," Jenny explained as Lizzie made herself at home in her kitchen.

"Really?" Lizzie responded blandly.

"You don't seem surprised," Jenny said as she grabbed the orange juice from the refrigerator.

"He didn't seem happy to see me," Lizzie explained with a shrug. "I'm certain that seeing the two of us together brought up some issues for him. And tell me that you're not going to drink that from the carton," Lizzie scolded the tall brunette who was about to raise the juice carton to her lips.

Jenny stopped moving, lowered the carton, and placed it on the counter. "Why would he have issues?" Jenny asked as she retrieved a glass from the cabinet and poured a glass of juice. "Do you want some?"

"Thank you," Lizzie said with a smile as she began to search the cabinets. "Robert has issues because he was in love with you," she explained. "Where are your coffee mugs?" the blonde asked in frustration.

"He knew about us? I was wondering about that the other day," Jenny said in bewilderment as she reached over Lizzie's head and grabbed a mug from the top shelf. "I have to wash the other one," she explained as she poured Lizzie a glass of juice before going back to the living room to collect the mug she'd used the night before.

"Of course he knew about us," Lizzie said with a hint of surprise. "You didn't know that?"

"No," Jenny answered honestly as she rinsed out her Dopey mug. "The first clue I had was when he said something the other day. I almost decked him."

Jenny almost laughed as Lizzie's eyes widened and she choked on her juice. "What did he say?" the blonde asked as she coughed.

"He accused you of turning me," Jenny grunted. She looked at her coffee maker to see if it had finished brewing their coffee. She grimaced when she noticed the machine was still chugging away.

"Into what?" Lizzie laughed.

"A lesbian," Jenny explained with a scowl.

"That is a shame." Lizzie sighed deeply.

"What?" Jenny asked in confusion.

"That he's still a clueless dork," Lizzie grumbled as she began to pour coffee for both of them. "Dopey?" the blonde exclaimed when she picked up the large mug.

Jenny blushed as she turned her attention to the floor. She finally looked up when Lizzie handed her mug filled with coffee. "Thanks," she shyly muttered. "So how did he know about us? More importantly, when did he find out?"

"I don't know," Lizzie answered her with a shrug. "It wasn't all that long after we became lovers. He and I had always vied for your attention. But that summer he started threatening me. By the things he said I assumed that he knew."

"He what?" Jenny blew out bitterly. "Why didn't you tell me?"

"I don't know really, other than I didn't want to upset you," Lizzie said calmly as she sipped her coffee.

"You didn't want to upset me?" Jenny hissed, not believing what she was hearing. "That rat bastard threatened my girlfriend. You should have told me. I'm going to ring his neck."

"Jenny, it was a long time ago," Lizzie tried to reason with her. "At the time I didn't care what he thought or said. I still don't. I was just happy knowing that we were together."

Jenny was still steaming as she dressed for work. "Can I trust you to stay here?" she asked as Lizzie ransacked her kitchen cabinets.

"If you promise to bring back something I can cook for dinner," Lizzie mumbled.

"You can cook?" Jenny exclaimed in surprise.

"Not really," Lizzie bashfully confessed. "But I thought I'd give it a shot."

"I don't think so," Jenny scoffed. "How about I bring home something I can cook for dinner?"

"Works for me," the nun readily agreed. "So by staying here you mean . . ."

"Here," Jenny barked. "As in you are not to leave the apartment."

"I need clothes," Lizzie protested.

"I'll get them," Jenny instructed the frowning blonde as she walked across the room and pulled her lock box out of a cabinet. "There's something else you can do for me," she continued as she pulled out the .38 she kept as a backup. She checked the pistol carefully as she stood and turned back towards Lizzie. "The safety is on," Jenny began to explain.

"No . . . no . . . no . . .no," Lizzie chastised her as she waved her hands in a dismissive manner. "Nuns and guns are a bad mix."

"I'd feel better if you had some protection," Jenny said, trying to reason with the aggravated woman.

"From my mother?" Lizzie countered. "Look, I know she's lost it, but I couldn't raise a hand to her. What makes you think I could use one of those? I'm a nun; we don't shoot people. That thing makes me nervous just looking at it."

"Fine," Jenny finally conceded, understanding Lizzie's point. Offering her gun to a civilian wasn't the smartest thing she'd ever done. "Look, it isn't just your mother who's hunting you down these days. So I'm just going to put it in my top dresser drawer."

"Good, then your bras will be well armed," Lizzie quipped. "So what am I suppose to do all day? I'm not used to being cooped up."

"Watch television," Jenny shrugged. "You seem to enjoy that."

As Jenny was about to leave, her breath caught at the sight of the smaller woman standing in her apartment clad in nothing but her bathrobe. Jenny released a heavy sigh before going out the door. As she walked to the station house, she wondered how long it would take Lizzie's short attention span to run out before she stole some of her clothes and made a break for it.

When Jenny arrived at the station and received her assignment for the day, it was heart wrenching to see how exhausted Kate looked. The tall blonde pulled her aside just as she was about to follow Nuru out to their patrol car. "A moment?" Kate requested wearily. Jenny simply nodded as she followed the sergeant back into the station house.

"How are you holding up?" Jenny carefully inquired.

"Just peachy," Kate sighed. "I've brought some clothes and stuff for Lizzie. Thank you for looking out for her."

"For the last time, you don't have to thank me," Jenny reassured her.

"My mother is out, and she's not a happy woman," Kate explained as she rubbed her face. Jenny could see the dark circles under the blonde's eyes.

"I suspected as much," Jenny said. "Any chance she'll be charged?"

"No," Kate groaned.

"Look, Lizzie can stay with me as long as she needs to," Jenny offered.

"You know, I understand that every family has its own dysfunctions but this is ridiculous," Kate grumbled. "Do you think there's any chance you can convince my pig-headed baby sister to get a restraining order?"

"Are you kidding me?" Jenny almost laughed, knowing that Lizzie would never agree to such a harsh course of action.

Kate released an exasperated breath. "Fine. Just give her a hug from me," Kate said, her voice trembling slightly. "And Lizzie's superior, Mother Agnes, wants to meet with you."

"Me?" Jenny squeaked out fearfully. "Why me?"

"I have no idea," Kate answered her with a shrug. "I'll catch you at the end of your shift."

Later that night Jenny grumbled as she climbed up a fire escape. "I hate it when they run," she groused as she climbed up onto the roof of an apartment building, searching the darkness for the scrawny little bugger they'd caught climbing out a window in the building. He'd dropped the DVD player he was carrying and bolted up the fire escape. While Nuru was bringing the squad car around the opposite side of the building, Jenny was forced to scale the fire escape.

Jenny heard the distinct sound of someone wheezing while

they tried to catch their breath. "Smokers just make this so easy," she whispered as she smirked. She quietly snuck around the air vent and found the man with his back to her, puffing like a steam engine. She grinned wickedly as she leaned down. "Boo," she whispered in his ear. His eyes were dilated as he stared up at her. "Great," she groaned, knowing that the boy was high and wouldn't be thinking clearly. The smell that assaulted her informed her that he had lost control of his bladder. She reached out to grab the teenager. Just as she had feared, he tried to scramble away from her. She grabbed him by the back of his shirt and forced him down to the ground.

"Get off me, you bitch," he spat at her as she placed the cuffs tightly around his wrists.

"You know I just can't hear that." She laughed as she pulled him to his feet. "You're under arrest."

Jenny radioed down to Nuru and informed her partner that she had the little weasel. She scanned the darkness for an exit since she had no intention of carrying the boy back down the fire escape. Bringing the ranting teenager back to the station house was no picnic; his stench filled the car as he released a stream of highly unflattering words.

After they had booked the boy, Jenny was relieved that the shift was finally over. She just wanted to go home and take a long hot shower. "You stink," Kate informed her as she approached her carrying a bag.

"The last one peed himself," Jenny explained in disgust.

"Things like that make me so happy I'm behind a desk." Kate laughed. "Here are Lizzie's things," she explained as she handed Jenny the bag. "And here's Mother Agnes' address," she continued as she shoved a slip of paper into Jenny's hand.

"I have to do this tonight?" Jenny whined.

"Please," Kate pleaded.

Jenny released a sigh as she nodded in agreement. "Good." Kate smirked. "But take a shower first. You reek."

"Thanks a lot," Jenny growled.

Jenny took Kate's advice and showered before taking a taxi over to the small house in Allston where Mother Agnes lived. She waited nervously in the sparse living room, looking around at the plain furnishing. "They need some plants or something," the brunette mumbled, thinking that her tiny little apartment wasn't so bad after all.

"It might help." She jumped at the sound of Mother Agnes' voice. Inexplicably the brunette stood up and waited for the older woman to greet her. She didn't understand why this frail woman instilled such fear in her.

"Please have a seat, Officer," Mother Agnes politely offered.

Jenny sat back down on the sofa as Mother Agnes joined her. "Thank you for meeting with me," the older woman said in a gentle tone that did nothing to relieve the anxiety that was surging through the brunette's body.

"I'm more than a little curious as to why you wanted to speak with me," Jenny finally blurted out as she tried to will herself to calm down. "Is this about the incident at the school?"

"Goodness no," Mother Agnes offered. "I think you know why I wanted to speak with you."

"No, I don't," Jenny stressed.

"Sister Rachel," Mother Agnes flatly offered.

"I didn't touch her," Jenny gasped in a sudden panic as the theme song from Charlie's Angels played in her head.

Mother Agnes' laughter broke through her thoughts. "My, you are a tense one, aren't you?" The nun laughed. "I spoke with Sister Rachel this afternoon," the woman continued as Jenny's crystal blue eyes widened in fear. Suddenly the panic was replaced with anger.

"Wait! She came here?" Jenny fumed. "I told her to stay put."

"You seem surprised." Mother Agnes laughed. "Yes, she came here to explain the difficulties with her family."

"Difficulties?" Jenny choked out is disbelief. "My, you gals certainly know how to whitewash things."

"Be that as it may," Mother Agnes addressed her sternly. "Sister Rachel needed to talk to someone. She asked if she could start her leave of absence sooner. I agreed and she is now on leave."

"Great; it will give her the time she needs to think," Jenny answered. "That still doesn't explain why I'm here."

"She has spoken about you a great deal over the years," Mother Agnes continued, completely unfazed by Jenny's outburst.

"She has?" Jenny practically gushed before she could rein in her emotions.

187

"Yes," Mother Agnes confirmed. "Your *friendship* has always meant a great deal to her."

"Friendship?" Jenny mumbled. She wondered if that was the way Lizzie had chosen to describe what they had shared.

"Whitewashing," Mother Agnes reassured her in soft tone. "Sister Rachel and I also discussed recent events."

"Recent?" Jenny squeaked out fearfully. She wondered if nuns still carried around those big rulers so they could whack people. "How recent?"

"My, you're as nervous as a long-tailed cat in a room full of rocking chairs." Mother Agnes chuckled. "Relax, Officer . . . Jenny," she added as she patted the brunette's hand. "I just wanted to caution you about letting things get out of hand so to speak."

"You mean keep my hands to myself," Jenny grunted as her brow furrowed.

"It would be in her best interest and yours if the two of you kept a careful watch on your emotions," Mother Agnes calmly explained.

"I know that," Jenny fumed. "I know that she needs to make her choice without *any* outside influences."

Jenny was furious, feeling that this woman was telling her to back off so Lizzie would remain a nun. "As do I," Mother Agnes agreed and Jenny felt her anger fading. "I'm just worried since the two of you are experiencing such intense emotions. Trust me, Jenny; I'm not judging or condemning either of you. I just want her to find her way. Even if her path leads her away from the church."

"Really?" Jenny asked suspiciously.

"Yes, really," Mother Agnes confirmed.

"That's all I want," Jenny agreed.

"Then we're in agreement?" Mother Agnes stressed.

"Yes, I'll keep my grubby hands off of her." Jenny almost laughed at the situation as she stood.

"Not to worry, my child," Mother Agnes reassured her as she led her to the door. "I feel that she already knows where she belongs; she's just afraid of taking the final step."

"She's leaving?" Jenny inquired eagerly.

"Possibly," Mother Agnes hedged.

"She's staying?" Jenny asked in a defeated tone.

"Possibly," Mother Agnes hedged once again.

"That is so annoying," Jenny grumbled as she stepped out into the cool night air.

"I know," Mother Agnes responded with a smile and a wink. "Stay safe, Jenny."

Jenny finally arrived back at her apartment after taking a bus and then enduring the crowded subway. She stopped for a pizza, no longer having any desire to do anything slightly domestic. She found Lizzie sitting on the bed, reading the paperback she'd abandoned the night before. She quickly brushed aside the thought of how adorable the blonde looked in the jeans and flannel blouse that were far too large for her tiny frame.

"I hope you like pizza," Jenny announced as she set the box on the breakfast bar.

"Sounds good," Lizzie responded as she bounced off the bed.

Lizzie opened the box and inhaled the delightful aroma. "Long day?" she asked as she continued to stare at the pizza.

"You could say that," Jenny groaned. "Kate sent over a bag of clothes for you," she explained as she grabbed a couple of plates and napkins. "I had to chase a junkie across a rooftop."

"Are you all right?" Lizzie asked in a panic.

"I'm fine," Jenny reassured her as she grabbed a slice of pizza, careful to gather up all of the dripping cheese. "Eat," Jenny instructed the blonde as she took a bite. "Oh, and I met with your boss after my shift."

"God?" Lizzie inquired curiously as she took a slice of pizza for herself.

"Not quite that far up the chain of command." Jenny chuckled. "Mother Agnes."

"Why?" Lizzie asked just as she was about to take a bite of the gooey cheese pizza.

"First tell me why you snuck out," Jenny demanded as she cast an icy glare at the blonde. The amused smirk Lizzie flashed her informed the brunette that the little nun wasn't buying her tough cop act for a minute.

"I needed to talk to her," Lizzie dryly explained.

"And you forgot how to use the telephone?" Jenny grunted in displeasure.

"I needed to do it in person," Lizzie tried to explain.

"So for the time being you're not a nun?" Jenny asked as they continued to eat.

"This is so good," Lizzie hummed. "I can't remember the last time I had pizza."

"I'm glad you like it," Jenny said with shrug, not missing the fact that Lizzie avoided her question.

Lizzie sighed as she put her plate down and then wiped her hands and face with the paper napkin. "No, I'm not a nun. For now," Lizzie stressed. "But if I break my vows, I can't go back."

"I understand," Jenny reassured her as she put down her own plate. They stood there for a moment in an uncomfortable silence. "Nothing has changed except for the time being you won't be freaking me out with your choice of wardrobe." Jenny paused as she patted Lizzie's hand. "I really do understand."

"I wish I did," Lizzie sadly confessed.

CHAPTER FIFTEEN

"I swear you're cheating," Jenny grumbled as she stared at the cards she held. She'd lost three games of gin rummy to her pesky new roommate.

"I'm a nun. We don't cheat at cards," Lizzie gloated.

"So you say," Jenny muttered as she finally discarded. She groaned as Lizzie snatched up the card she'd just put down.

"Gin," Lizzie exclaimed before sticking her tongue out at Jenny.

"You suck," Jenny grunted as she began to count up all the points she still held.

"You're such a poor loser," Lizzie shushed her.

"This coming from someone who tried to give me a wedgie every time I beat her at hoops." Jenny laughed as she totaled the score. "You win again." She looked across the bed and found Lizzie blushing. "What?"

"That wasn't why I tried to give you a wedgie," the blonde shyly confessed.

Jenny folded her arms across her chest and glared over at the smaller woman. "You little pervert," she chastised the blushing blonde. "So when did you get to be such a card shark?" she inquired as she started to clean up the cards that were strewn across her bed. They'd been sitting on the bed for a few hours since it was the only space big enough in Jenny's tiny apartment where they could play cards comfortably.

191

"The entertainment was limited to say the least in most of the places I've been living. I always took a deck of cards with me whenever I traveled," Lizzie explained as she stretched out on the bed. "I learned some really fun drinking games too."

"I bet you did." Jenny laughed as she placed the cards on the nightstand. "How's the studying going?"

"Good," Lizzie responded brightly. "The computer course I'm taking is the only one giving me trouble. I don't get it. I've seen first graders who can work on those things and I'm completely lost most of the time. Thanks for letting me use yours."

"No problem." Jenny yawned. "Don't worry; you'll get the hang of it. We need to set up an email account for you."

"Email - another thing I don't understand," Lizzie groaned. "Sister Agnes is almost eighty and she can send an email without batting an eye. I tried it the other day and I think I nuked Iowa."

"You'll get the hang of it." Jenny chuckled. "And once you do, no matter where you travel to you'll be able to keep in touch with everyone you know." Jenny's smile faded as she realized that Lizzie might be leaving the country at some time in the near future. Lizzie had been staying with her for just shy of a month and Jenny found that she was growing fond of living with her. This despite the cramped living quarters, the nightly battle for the blankets, and the cold showers she was forced to endure. In fact, she was becoming increasingly aware that she was a little too fond of Lizzie living with her.

Lizzie rolled over onto her side and rested her face against her hand. "I should think about moving back in with my sister," the blonde offered seeming to pick up on what Jenny was thinking.

"I know," Jenny grumbled as she began to pick at imaginary lint on the blanket. "You don't have to. You could stay here." Jenny continued to pick at the blanket. She could feel Lizzie watching her.

The silence was choking Jenny and she suddenly felt foolish. "I want to," Lizzie finally confessed in a voice just above a whisper. "And that's the problem," the blonde muttered. "It's getting harder and harder being so close to you."

"And you need space to think about things," Jenny responded with a heavy sigh. "I know," she added as she finally lifted her gaze. She tried to smile as Lizzie met her gaze.

"I don't understand why just being around you is such a temptation," Lizzie tried to explain. "I know that I wasn't very good at following my vocation, yet being with you is incredibly difficult. I've broken my vows six times and each time I hoped that I would get caught. Now if I do it again, I won't have accomplished what I set out to do."

"I really do understand," Jenny reassured her. "Wait! Six times? Do you mean that you've dated six women or do you mean you've only had sex six times since you've become a nun?"

"I've only had sex six times," Lizzie confirmed dryly.

"I can't believe it," Jenny choked out.

"What?" Lizzie asked in a bewildered tone. "Once is too many times."

"It's just that we used to do it six times a week," Jenny blurted out.

The blush covered the brunette's body once she realized what she had said. "True," Lizzie stammered uncomfortably. "But I'm not supposed to be intimate with anyone, including myself, ever."

"You can't touch yourself?" Jenny blurted out in horror. "What kind of deal is that?"

"Masturbation is against the rules," Lizzie grumbled. "Can we change the subject?"

Jenny pondered what Lizzie had just told her. She wasn't happy that there had been other women in the blonde's life, but now she understood why nuns always looked so serious. She shook her head to clear her thoughts and tried to focus on being a supportive friend and not a would be suitor.

"When are you thinking of calling Kate?" Jenny inquired, trying to sound positive. She had mulled over what Lizzie had said and it made sense. The nun's words weren't a revelation, but knowing that Lizzie wasn't a nun at the moment gave her inner self a sense of false hope.

"In a hurry to get rid of me?" Lizzie teased her with a slight shove.

"Yeah, you little card shark," Jenny quipped as she pulled Lizzie down and began to tickle the smaller woman. "Admit it! You were cheating!"

"You're just a sore loser," Lizzie squealed as she squirmed beneath the brunette. "What's the matter? Can't the big tough cop admit she got her butt kicked by a little nun?"

"I'll show you a butt kicking," Jenny asserted with a mock growl as her tickling increased. The brunette's heart began to race as her fingers glided up along the blonde's sensitive body. Jenny bit down on her bottom lip in an effort to stifle the moan that wanted out as Lizzie wrapped her legs around the brunette's waist. Jenny knew that Lizzie was simply trying to free herself but the feel of the blonde's body wiggling against her felt far too good. Jenny could feel her long neglected desires ignite as their bodies became entangled. The familiar pain of the past emerged as they began to roll around on the bed, each fighting for control.

It had been the same when she was a young woman and the two of them would become lost in a moment of physical closeness. Jenny's body was craving something she couldn't have, and if she didn't pull away soon she would do something both of them would regret. The difference between the innocent actions they shared before they became lovers and now was that Jenny fully understood what it was she wanted and needed. Distracted by her thoughts, Jenny lost control and Lizzie pinned her to the bed. "Uh huh!" Lizzie barked out triumphantly as she pinned Jenny's hands above her head and straddled her body.

Lizzie opened her mouth to speak but the words never came and her emerald eyes darkened. Jenny was lying helplessly beneath the blonde, captured by her fiery gaze. The brunette's breathing became ragged as she returned her former lover's gaze. The only sounds Jenny could hear were the pounding of her heart and Lizzie's labored breathing. The air in the tiny apartment sizzled with the intensity that was flowing between them.

The knock on the door did nothing to curb the force pulling them closer; Lizzie lowered her body until Jenny could feel the smaller woman's breath on her face. The brunette parted her lips in an effort to protest but the words failed to form as the persistent knocking continued. Jenny could feel her body trembling as Lizzie's body melted against her own. "Open up! It's the police," Kate shouted from the other side of the door.

Jenny and Lizzie erupted in a fit of laughter as they pulled away from one another. "If she only knew," Lizzie offered halfheartedly as she climbed off of Jenny.

"She'd be thrilled," Jenny tossed out as she climbed off the bed and stumbled towards the front door.

"Figures," Lizzie muttered as she shuffled over to the kitchen.

"Yes?" Jenny droned once she opened the door.

"I thought I was going to have to call the fire department," Kate exclaimed as she pushed her way into Jenny's apartment. "Yup, I was just about to call them and have them bring the Jaws of Life up here."

"You're sick; you know that, don't you?" Jenny said with scowl as she closed the door behind the blonde. "Come in and make yourself at home," she offered to the woman who had already removed her coat and took a seat in Jenny's rocking chair.

"Thanks," Kate beamed. "Squirt, bring me something to drink," she called to Lizzie who was sucking down a bottle of water.

"What am I running here? A hotel?" Jenny complained as she folded her arms across her chest. "Don't give her anything, Lizzie; she'll only keep coming back."

Lizzie snorted in amusement as she brought Kate a glass of apple juice. "When did I lose control?" Jenny said in exasperation. "So what brings you here other than my generosity?"

"I wanted to see Lizzie," Kate casually responded.

"Did you know she cheats at cards?" Jenny inquired seriously.

"I knew it!" Kate squawked. "You know, she conned me out of my paycheck right after she hit town."

"No, I won your paycheck," Lizzie boasted with a cocky grin. "Not my fault you can't bluff."

"Wait! You cleaned your sister out?" Jenny gasped. "What happened to all of that vow of poverty horse puckey?"

"I am poor," Lizzie argued. "They don't pay you cops enough. So, Kate, I was just going to call you."

"Of course you were. That would explain all of the laughing I heard out in the hallway," Kate responded coyly. "We need to talk about Mom."

"I know," Lizzie concurred. "When was the last time she came looking for me at your place?"

"Two nights after she was arrested," Kate hesitantly answered.

"Long enough," Lizzie continued. "I'm coming back to your place or moving in with Dad." Kate opened her mouth to protest but Lizzie silenced her with a wave of her hand. "I can't hide from her forever. And I know why you want me to stay here and that's out of the question."

"She's right, Kate," Jenny agreed.

"You're kicking her out?" Kate blurted out accusingly.

"No," Lizzie interjected. "She's not kicking me out, but this is Jenny's home and I need to go."

"Aren't the two of you getting along?" Kate pushed.

"Yes," Jenny answered as the tension grew inside of her. "That's the problem and you know it. Lizzie can't do what she needs to do while the two of us are living in such close quarters."

Kate sat there sipping her juice while Jenny and Lizzie stared at her. "I'm going for a walk," Jenny tossed out, no longer able to endure the eerie silence. She squeezed Lizzie's shoulder gently before heading out her front door. "When did my life get so complicated?" she sighed as she walked the streets and tried to enjoy the unexpected sunshine. "Maybe it always was," she continued, chatting to herself as she made her way towards the Charles River. The brunette weaved her way through the joggers and roller bladers until she found a comfortable place near the edge of the water to stretch out.

She listened to the sounds of the waves lapping against the shore as memories of tickling fests and wrestling matches filled her mind. "I'm obsessed," she reasoned as she absently tossed tiny pebbles she found into the water. "Even if she leaves the church there's no guarantee that I'll be what she wants. Is she what I want? Ugh! I hate being an adult," she announced as she cast another small stone into the water.

Frustrated and suddenly angry at her lot in life, Jenny buried her face in her hands as the memories and confusion once again consumed her. Lizzie had always been there with her sparkling green eyes. The small blonde had captivated her from the very beginning and Jenny was always helpless to resist. The years apart had done nothing to cool the flame that was Lizzie. Jenny knew that she needed to put some distance between them and she was shaking with fear at the thought of being separated from Lizzie. "What is wrong with me?" she sobbed into her hands.

"If Sally went to the market to buy five apples and three oranges, how much money did she have left?" Jenny muttered as she stared at the inane question in her textbook. "If Sally keeps eating like this, she's going to end up with rickets. And let's not forget all of those train and bus rides she takes. What kind of parents does this kid have?" Jenny peered over the top of her textbook to find Lizzie smiling back at her. "What?"

"You're insane; you know that, don't you?" Lizzie teased her in a light tone that did not match the darkness in the small blonde's emerald eyes. A shiver passed through Jenny's body as she fell into the smoldering gaze.

"Oh no you don't," Jenny cautioned her lover.

"What?" Lizzie innocently retorted. "I'm just sitting way over here on the bed, like you told me to do."

"I know that look," Jenny warned her. "That's why I'm sitting at my desk and you're way over there. We have to study."

"I'd rather study you," Lizzie responded in a breathy tone that left no doubt as to what her true intentions were.

"Study," Jenny barked. "Besides you're already very well acquainted with every inch of my body."

"Are you sure? I may have missed one or two places," Lizzie threw out eagerly as she began to climb off the bed.

A knock on the bedroom door halted Lizzie's movements. The blonde scowled as she threw herself back down on the bed. "Hey, Mom," Jenny greeted her mother as she stepped into the room with a tray of snacks.

"I thought you girls might be hungry," Mrs. Jacobs said as she placed the tray down on the desk.

"Thank you, Mrs. Jacobs," Lizzie said.

"Yeah, thanks, Mom," Jenny beamed since she was thankful that her mother had for the moment curbed her lover's insatiable desires.

Once her mother had left the tiny bedroom, Lizzie flew off the bed. "No you don't," Jenny cautioned her. "Time to get back to Sally and her poor shopping habits."

"I was just looking for something to nibble on," Lizzie

responded with a wide-eyed innocence as she pointed to the snack tray.

"Sorry," Jenny apologized as she turned her attention back to her math book.

Jenny gasped and her book fell from her hands as Lizzie's lips grazed the tender flesh of her neck. "I thought you wanted something to nibble on?" Jenny stammered as Lizzie's mouth feasted on her neck.

"I do," Lizzie offered hotly in her ear before she began to nibble on the brunette's sensitive earlobe. Jenny was struggling to breathe as she felt her lover's arms wrap around her. The brunette's resolve slipped away as she captured Lizzie in her arms and they fell to the floor.

Jenny's heart soared as she looked up at the one person who had always held it in the palm of her hands. "I love you, Jenny," Lizzie softly said before they found themselves kissing one another passionately. With wild abandonment they rolled around the floor, tugging at the other's clothing in a desperate need to free themselves of any barriers.

The look in Lizzie's eyes that day was filled with such love that it ensured that the blonde would always hold a piece of Jenny's heart. A shadow crept over her and Jenny turned to see Lizzie's emerald eyes staring back at her. For a brief moment she was certain that she could still see the same intense devotion she'd seen so many years ago reflected in those green pools. It faded quickly and was replaced by the overwhelming confusion that was strangling both of them. "I thought I'd find you here," Lizzie shyly offered before looking away.

Jenny exhaled deeply, wondering how long she'd been sitting there or why she hadn't noticed Lizzie. "Why is it so much harder this time?" Lizzie asked, echoing the thoughts that had plagued the brunette since her former lover reentered her life.

"Are you leaving with Kate?" Jenny asked in a slow careful tone as she looked out over the water.

"Yes."

"I'll wait until you're gone," Jenny continued in the same controlled tone. "Keep the key just in case."

"Jenny . . . ," Lizzie began in a strained voice.

"It's better this way," Jenny reasoned, still unable to look at the blonde. "You need to start living your life. And I need to start living mine. I'll always be here for you, but right now we need to be apart."

Silently Lizzie stood and complied with Jenny's wishes as she walked away. *'It's for the best,'* Jenny reassured herself repeatedly as she wondered why it felt like they had just broken up. And why did it hurt more than when she ended her relationship with Wendy?

Two weeks later Jenny was miserable; she found herself missing Lizzie more and more with each passing day. What troubled her most was that she was no longer missing the girl she had once loved but the woman she had grown into. So she did the only thing she could think of. The first Sunday she had off she took the train up to her parents. Running back to Mommy and Daddy wasn't the most mature course of action but it was the only thing that made the tall brunette feel a sense of comfort and safety.

"You're not getting tired, are you?" Jenny teased her father who was panting and sweating heavily after she made another basket. She had already beaten him in two straight games of hoops and was well on her way to her third victory.

"I'm just fine," he protested as he wiped the sweat from his brow.

"You sure?" Jenny quipped with a lighthearted laugh.

"Stop teasing your poor old father," her mother called out from the living room window.

"Who are you calling old?" Jerome Jacobs grumbled in response as he made a basket. It wasn't hard since his daughter was too busy laughing to block his advance. "So are you going to tell me why you decided to visit after this game?" he asked as he passed her the ball.

"Maybe I just missed you," Jenny teased in a thinly veiled attempt to hide her true feelings.

"Right," her father snorted in disbelief as he blocked her shot.

"Hey there, Jenny," an annoyingly familiar voice called out from behind them.

"Damn," Jenny sneered as she turned to see Robby strolling up the driveway.

"What's wrong?" her father asked quietly in concern.

"Nothing," Jenny lied as her lips curled up in disgust. "He said something to me the last time I was here that really got to me," she explained once she realized that her father had seen through her lie.

"Mind if I join you?" Robby inquired brightly.

"Actually I'm trying to spend some time with my parents," Jenny offered in an effort to get rid of Robby as quickly as possible. With everything else she'd been dealing with over the past few weeks, his narrow-minded ideas were the last thing she needed.

"Just a quick game?" Robby pressed.

"He was never a bright guy, was he?" Jerome muttered softly so only his daughter could hear his words.

Jenny realized something as he flashed his puppy dog eyes at her. He had been doing that to her for as long as they'd known one another. He had used her polite nature against her so he could spend time with her and drive a wedge between her and Lizzie. "Not this time," Jenny curtly said.

"What?" Robby responded in surprise.

"I said no."

"But it's just a game of hoops," Robby pleaded, oozing his boyish charm from every pore.

"No," Jenny repeated.

"Oh, I see," Robby pouted. Jenny was floored that a man of his age would actually resort to pouting in an effort to get his way.

Jenny twirled the basketball in her hands as her father sighed heavily beside her. Robby simply stood there looking at her with a forlorn expression. His jaw dropped slightly as he became aware that he wasn't going to win her over this time. "See ya around, Robby," Jenny casually tossed out as she turned her attention back to her father. "What was the score again?"

"Oh, I get it," Robby grunted from behind her, cutting off her father's words. "She's here."

"You arrogant little piss ant," Jenny growled as she spun around and shot the ball out onto the pavement. Her aim was dead on as the orange ball hit at just the right angle to come back up and strike Robby where it would hurt the most. His eyes bugged out as he clutched his manhood and dropped helplessly to his knees. His eyes were watering as he looked up at Mr. Jacobs for help.

"Don't look at me, kid. Who do you think taught her that move?" Jerome explained, his voice cracking at the sight of the younger man clutching himself.

Jenny could hear the front door slamming open and her mother's worried tone as she frantically asked about what was happening. Jenny was lost in a zone as all of the rage, anger, and pain caught up with her. She stormed over to the still-kneeling man, dropped down beside him, and locked his neck in her arm.

"Taught her that, too," her father boasted. Robby choked helplessly as she held him in a headlock.

"Jenny, the boy is turning blue. Let him go," her mother pleaded as the brunette tightened her hold.

"Tell me," she demanded. "When did you know?"

"What?" Robby choked out as he struggled to breathe.

"You knew that Lizzie was my lover. When did you find out?" Jenny hissed bitterly. "Come on, stud, you knew then. I just want to know how."

Robby was flailing helplessly in her grasp. His eyes drifted up to the window on the second floor of his home. Jenny followed his stare over to his house. Her eyes bulged out as they drifted back to her own home. "You were watching us!" she screamed as she realized for the first time that his childhood bedroom overlooked her own. "You freaking pervert! You were peeking into my bedroom!"

"Choke him harder," her father shouted out in disgust.

"Is that all you did?" Jenny demanded as she complied with her father's wish despite her mother's shouting. "Your mother and her mother were friends. Did you follow us around? You were the one, weren't you?"

"Yes," he barely managed to gasp out, his body trembling from the pain.

"Bastard," she spat out as the last piece fell into place. She was blinded by anger as she tightened her grip around his neck.

"Jenny?" a familiar voice called out to her. "Jenny," the voice repeated, somehow reaching the blind rage that was coursing through her body. "Let him go," the voice whispered softly as she felt her body being captured in a warm embrace. Jenny started to sob as she released Robby from her grasp. His face was red and he

201

continued to gasp for air as she turned into Lizzie's arms. "Ssh," the blonde whispered as she made comforting strokes along the sobbing brunette's back.

"It was him," Jenny cried as she held Lizzie tighter. "He was the one who told her."

"It's over," Lizzie reassured her. "Let it go."

Jenny looked up at the blonde, the tears still flooding her chiseled features. "He did this," she sobbed. "He conspired with her to keep us apart."

"It's over," Lizzie repeated as she brushed the tears from Jenny's face.

One look in Lizzie's eyes and Jenny could feel her tears drying. She swallowed hard as she tried to calm herself. "Time to let it go," Lizzie said with tenderness as she cupped Jenny's face in her hands. "Don't hate the man because of the rash choices a frightened boy made."

Jenny turned to see Robby still kneeling on the ground, the color slowly returning to his face. The guilt in his eyes spoke volumes. Out of the corner of her eye she could see her parents and Kate watching the scene; each of them was sporting a very frightened look. "Why?" Jenny sniffed as Robby looked away from her. "I want to know why you ruined my best friend's life?" she demanded as Lizzie's hands continued to rub her body in a vain attempt to soothe her.

"I loved you," Robby offered feebly.

"So you took her away from me?" Jenny spat out.

"No," Lizzie cautioned her as she pulled her back into a tender embrace. Jenny's head instinctively came to rest on the blonde's chest. "Forgive him and move on," Lizzie encouraged her as she ran her fingers through Jenny's hair and massaged her scalp. Lizzie's words swirled around her mind, mixing with the intense anger that was still threatening to consume her. She felt Lizzie's fingers caressing her face until they lifted her chin. Jenny stared deep into the blonde's electrifying eyes. "Please? For me?" Lizzie pleaded. "Forgive him."

Jenny's lips quivered, knowing that she could never refuse Lizzie. Her body ached as she turned her head slightly and looked over at Robby. He looked pitiful. "It's over," Jenny choked out. "I forgive you. Now just go," she offered in a heavy tone before she nestled her head against Lizzie's chest. She was only dimly aware of Robby and the others' departure as Lizzie held her tightly and rocked her in her arms.

Jenny was lost in the feel of Lizzie's tender embrace as her demons finally slipped away. She had no concept of how long they knelt on her parents' front lawn. She only pulled away from Lizzie's embrace when she felt the chill of the night air against her skin. "Feeling better?" Lizzie asked as she brushed errant strands of hair from Jenny's brow.

"I have a headache," Jenny confessed.

"No small wonder," Lizzie said with a gentle smile as she once again cupped Jenny's face in her hand.

"What are you doing here?" Jenny asked as she tried to understand just what had happened. She leaned into the blonde's touch and felt her body and soul finally calming.

"Kate and I drove up this morning," Lizzie began to explain. "We needed to try to convince our mother that she needs help."

"Did it work?" Jenny inquired before she released a contented sigh.

"No," Lizzie answered in a defeated tone.

"I guess we should go inside," Jenny reluctantly suggested, knowing that she would rather just stay on the lawn wrapped up in Lizzie's arms. The blonde nodded in agreement as they stood, brushing the dirt from their clothes. "Are the two of you heading back to town now?"

"Sort of," Lizzie responded hesitantly.

"What is it?" Jenny asked, a sudden sense of panic filling her.

"Kate is going back to town after she drops me off in Brighton," Lizzie carefully explained as her eyes drifted from Jenny's intense gaze.

"You're going back," Jenny stammered as her body reeled from the shock.

"Yes," Lizzie quietly confessed.

CHAPTER SIXTEEN

Jenny kept running until her lungs were ready to explode; she was in the woods just past Lizzie's childhood home. She released a horrific scream as she dropped to her knees. She had heard Lizzie's frantic pleas behind her as she ran. She couldn't make herself stop running, knowing that if she stopped she would be forced to face Lizzie. Before Lizzie had moved out of her apartment, the brunette had promised herself that no matter what Lizzie decided she would support her decision and do anything she could to keep their friendship. Now she realized that she'd been lying to herself. She honestly hadn't thought that Lizzie would go back.

"Jenny?" Lizzie choked out fearfully from behind her. Jenny still couldn't look at her. She wiped the tears from her eyes as her mind screamed at Lizzie to just go away and leave her alone with her pain.

"Go away," Jenny sobbed, her body aching.

"You don't understand," Lizzie pleaded. Jenny could feel Lizzie kneeling down behind her.

Her skin prickled as she felt how close Lizzie was. She jerked her shoulder violently when she felt the blonde's hand touch her. "Please just go," Jenny whimpered in a pitiful voice.

"Come with me," Lizzie pleaded.

"No." Jenny sniffed, her eyes remaining focused on the ground. "You've made your choice."

"Please?" Lizzie implored her weakly.

"Can't," Jenny managed to choke out as she felt her throat closing.

Jenny's body shook violently as she felt and heard Lizzie's footsteps growing dimmer. Her hands clawed at the dirt as she fought the pain. *'Just let her go; it's for the best,'* her mind screamed over and over again. Her heart refused to listen, no matter how hard she fought to reconcile herself with the reality of what had happened.

Jenny felt like a wounded animal as she curled up under a large oak tree. "I don't understand. How could she decide that going back is the right thing to do?" she whimpered as her mind replayed the time they'd spent together since Lizzie's mother had assaulted her. They had laughed, talked, flirted, snuggled, and gotten to know one another again. For Jenny the domestic situation had erased the years and miles that had separated them for so long.

"What does this song mean?" Lizzie asked as Jenny washed the dishes from the dinner they'd shared. The brunette quirked her head and listened to the song that was playing on the radio. She had to laugh when they realized each of them had decided to listen to an oldies station. 'When did all my favorite songs end up on the oldies station?' She wondered as she listened to the lyrics of Band of Gold *carefully as she tried to decipher what was bothering Lizzie. "The lyrics don't make sense," Lizzie explained. " 'Took me from a mother I had never known and on our honeymoon we slept in separate rooms.' Hello? What is she talking about?"*

"I don't know." Jenny laughed as she wiped her hands with the dishtowel. "But it has a nice beat and you can dance to it," Jenny reasoned, chuckling at the scowl Lizzie cast at her. "What was that other song?"

"What song?" Lizzie responded evasively.

"You know the one," Jenny teased her as she began to wrap the towel between her hands. 'The one you used to drive me completely insane about. What was it?"

"You were always insane," Lizzie teased.

"Only around you, short stuff," Jenny grunted. "Come on, what was it?" Jenny began to swing the towel in a threatening manner.

"I have no idea what you're talking about," Lizzie innocently retorted. Her eyes grew large as Jenny started flicking the towel at

her backside.

"Out with it!" Jenny demanded as she snapped the towel. "You were always whining about it until you drove me completely nuts."

"Okay!" Lizzie squealed. She darted across the living room as Jenny chased after her, snapping the towel against the blonde's backside. Lizzie attempted to make a dash for the front door when Jenny captured her in her arms. Jenny held the squirming woman tightly as she began to tickle her.

"Say it," Jenny demanded as her fingers showed no mercy as they continued to attack the smaller woman's rib cage.

"Copacabana!" Lizzie squealed out.

"Now see? That wasn't so hard," Jenny gloated as she reluctantly released Lizzie from her grasp. Much to her surprise and delight, Lizzie didn't move away; instead the blonde continued to lean into Jenny's body.

"I still want to know," Lizzie asserted as Jenny groaned.

"I'm sorry I started this," Jenny grumbled as she wrapped her arms around Lizzie, pausing for a moment to take in the sweet scent of her hair.

"But I want to know," Lizzie demanded as she released a throaty chuckle and relaxed further into Jenny's embrace.

"I want to know; I want to know," Jenny mimicked her.

"Come on, Jenny, aren't you the least bit curious?" Lizzie whined. "Think about it; we know what happened to Lola, but who shot who? Did Tony shoot Rico or did Rico shoot Tony?"

"Ugh," Jenny growled.

"Fine. What's for dessert?" Lizzie asked brightly as she leaned back and gazed into Jenny's eyes.

"You are impossible," Jenny said with a hard swallow. She wondered what would happen if she closed the small gap between them and kissed Lizzie. Instead Jenny released her hold on Lizzie's warm inviting body and stepped away from her. "I don't think you deserve dessert," she teased the blonde as she moved even further away from her.

"Oh, what are you going to do? Spank me?" Lizzie innocently tossed out.

A sudden rush coursed through Jenny's body as she stared at

Lizzie. Both of them turned beet red as the implication of what Lizzie had said hit them. Each of them struggled to breathe as they became locked in an intense gaze. They each muttered a lame excuse that would give them distance from the other and the moment passed.

"How do you go from that to staying in the church?" Jenny muttered miserably. She tried to understand how Lizzie had managed to forget how unhappy she was in her vocation. "It doesn't make sense."

Jenny was still thinking about Lizzie's sudden decision as she wearily made her way back to her parents' home. The stabbing pain in her heart increased when she was greeted by her parents' worried expressions. "I'm fine," she lied as she picked up the bible that was resting on the coffee table. She had returned it to her mother, still not understanding why she had given it to her.

"Kate said she didn't understand what was going on," her mother nervously informed her. "She said that Lizzie woke her up in the middle of the night and told her that they needed to see their mother and that she had to go to the convent. That's all she knows."

"Doesn't matter," Jenny mumbled out another lie as she clutched the bible to her chest. She was growing wearing of trying to convince herself that none of it matter, that Lizzie hadn't once again reached in and claimed her heart.

"Jenny?" he father nervously began.

"Can I stay here tonight?" Jenny pleaded like a small child.

"Of course," her mother quickly responded.

"Thank you," she muttered out the weak response as she began to climb the stairs.

"Do you want to talk? Do you need anything?" her mother asked worriedly.

"No," Jenny mumbled once again as she headed towards her childhood bedroom, feeling the need to hide away in one of the few places she felt safe.

She closed the door behind her and tossed the bible onto the bed. She glanced over at the bedroom window. Snarling as she approached it, she offered a single digit salute before she yanked the curtains shut. "Hope you saw that, you pervert," she hissed before climbing onto her bed and curling up into a ball.

She sobbed uncontrollably as she wrapped her arms around her knees. As her tears began to subside, she spied the bible resting next to her. "What is it that you were trying to tell me?" she questioned absently as she unfurled her aching body and picked up the bible. Jenny once again began to flip through the pages before deciding to give the reference section in the back a try. She sneered as she went through the women's names. In typical patriarchal fashion the women were only defined as 'wife of' or 'mother of' as if they did not possess any other historical significance.

Finally she came upon the name she was searching for - Rachel. Her crystal blue eyes widened with surprise as she read the short biography. *'Rachel, wife of Jacob.'* Her heart was pounding; she frantically wondered if what she was reading meant what she hoped it did. The tears overwhelmed her as she snapped the bible shut. *'Is it possible that Lizzie didn't forget me? In some small way did she take my name in an effort to keep me in her heart?'* Her head was pounding as she tried to understand if it was really true. And if it was true and Lizzie had defied her vows by still carrying her in her heart, then why would she go back?

The persistent pounding of her head and heart made sleep impossible. Jenny was physically and emotionally spent in the morning as her father drove her into the city. Both of her parents had pestered her with questions and concerns all morning. Jenny refused to answer since she was at a complete loss as to what was happening. Somehow she managed to gather herself together and make it to work on time. She avoided Kate and Nuru's constant inquires as to what was wrong. She was numb as she worked through her shift.

Finally it was time to call it a day; both she and her partner were grateful. All Jenny wanted was to go home and curl up into a ball until the pain went away. As she was changing in the locker room, Kate cornered her. "I don't want to talk about it," Jenny muttered bitterly. "I just want to be left alone."

"I don't understand what's happening either," Kate carefully began. "But I need you to come with me."

"No," Jenny uttered as her tired eyes fluttered shut.

"I know that I don't have any right to ask, but please come

with me?" Kate gently implored her.

"No," Jenny repeated as she leaned her head against her locker.

"Please? She's asked to see us," Kate pleaded helplessly.

Jenny just wanted all the pain to stop. "Fine," she conceded without understanding why she was giving in so easily. "It'll give me a chance to say goodbye. Your mother robbed me of that the last time," she added bitterly. Kate watched Jenny in concern as she began to change. The tall brunette changed her clothes and gathered her gear without a single thought. She followed Kate out of the station house, her body moving of its own accord.

Jenny stared blankly out the windshield of Kate's truck. She was lost in memories of Lizzie's body and stolen moments of their youth. At the time they'd been certain that their love would last forever. Time proved to be their enemy; in the present everything was teetering on a vulnerable edge. Jenny tried to center herself as Kate started the truck and drove out of the parking lot.

Jenny was only half listening to Kate as they drove along the city streets. "I tried to talk her into postponing this for at least one more day," Kate tried to explain. "She just thanked me and smiled. Then she asked if I could convince you to come up today. She said that she needed to talk to both of us." Jenny took a deep sobering breath as she wondered if perhaps the meeting might just be a good omen. She quickly dismissed the small glimmer of hope. Lizzie was gone and Sister Rachel had finally taken her place. She needed to support her friend's choice and begin to find her own way in life. Her heart had survived losing the blonde once; she silently vowed that she would once again endure.

Kate grew quiet as the trip continued. The journey to Saint Andrew's was short and uneventful. Jenny and Kate found themselves drowning in an uncomfortable silence as they neared the convent. As they pulled into the gravel parking lot, Jenny spied Lizzie waiting for them, dressed in her black habit and standing on the stone steps of the aging building. She could feel Lizzie's eyes on her as she stepped out of the truck. She was unable to return the blonde's gaze, knowing that the sight of Lizzie dressed in her habit had already proved to be far too painful.

'Where was the girl that I was so deeply in love with?

Where's the carefree woman who shared my home for the last few weeks? When did this stranger take her place?' a voice from deep inside of her searched for the reasoning behind Lizzie's actions. The voice that was speaking from her heart wanted to know what had happened to the new Lizzie, the woman who gloated after beating her at cards and snuggled with her at night. Where had she gone? Jenny's steps were deliberate as she approached the nun, wondering whom she would miss the most. Jenny was uncertain if it was the young teenager she had given herself to so freely or the older wiser woman who had stolen a place in her heart. Jenny felt that if she had given the woman a chance, both of them could have managed to get past the sins and mistakes from their past and started over again.

Mother Agnes stepped out of the ivy-covered building and took her place by Lizzie's side. "Thank you for coming," Lizzie calmly greeted them. Neither Jenny nor Kate could speak or look at the small nun. Jenny understood that like herself Kate also felt like a raw nerve.

"They're waiting for you, my child," Mother Agnes instructed Sister Rachel.

"Thank you, Reverend Mother," Sister Rachel answered respectfully. She motioned for Kate and Jenny to follow as Mother Agnes ushered the nun inside.

They entered a cold dark hallway; Mother Agnes instructed Jenny and Kate to wait in the wooden chairs that lined the dim corridor. Mother Agnes escorted Sister Rachel through a door adjacent to the chairs Jenny and Kate were sitting in. As the door was closing behind them, Jenny caught a glimpse of stern-looking nuns seated in chairs that formed a circle around the room.

"It looks like a firing squad in there," Kate said tensely. "This reminds me of when she took her vows. It was in this musty old church. The novices marched past us and the other families dressed in white. Then as they entered the chapel these really big nuns closed iron gates behind them. There we were all crammed together in this tiny alcove watching the ceremony from behind the gates. I felt helpless. I knew what a mistake Lizzie was making and there was nothing I could do to stop it. Later it was explained to me that the separation during the ceremony was symbolic of how the novices were leaving our family and entering God's. I haven't been back to church since."

"What do you think today is all about?" Jenny asked as she tried to understand why she and Kate were there.

"I have no idea," Kate grumbled. "All I know is that yesterday we had to see my mother and then Lizzie had to come here."

"What happened with your mother?" Jenny asked, eager to find something other than what was going on in the room across from them to focus on.

"I don't know," Kate tersely responded. "I only lasted about three seconds in my mother's company before I left her and Lizzie talking. I went to Dante's and had breakfast. When I got back, Lizzie was sitting on the sidewalk waiting for me. She said Mom wasn't going to seek help. That was it until we drove by your parents' house and found you strangling Robby."

As the hours passed, Jenny could feel the fear rising inside of her; she began to pace up and down the hallway in an effort to keep busy and warm. Finally the door opened. Jenny felt a new rush of panic sweep over her as she watched a row of nuns file out of the room. Each of the elderly women appeared to be exhausted as if they'd done battle with the devil himself. Jenny feared that Lizzie had been punished for the attraction they'd shared since her return to Boston. Lizzie had already explained to her that feeling desire for something wrong was just as much of a sin in the eyes of the church as acting on that desire.

"Sister Rachel would like to speak to both of you before you leave," Mother Agnes gently informed them as she stepped out of the room.

Jenny's heart sank as she stepped into the room. Lizzie was kneeling on the bare floor with her hands clasped in front of her. The blonde's eyes were shut and her head was lowered. *'Why, Lizzie?'* Jenny silently screamed in anger.

"Sister Rachel," Mother Agnes addressed the kneeling woman firmly. "You may speak to your guests before you join us in the chapel."

Lizzie opened her eyes and made the sign of the cross before she stood. "Thank you, Reverend Mother," she quietly addressed her superior.

"Don't be long," Mother Agnes cautioned her as she made her departure.

"Lizzie, how could you?" Kate blurted out as her anger took over. "Are you absolutely sure that this is what you want?"

Lizzie looked curiously at Kate and then Jenny as she took a cleansing breath. "Ladies," she began in a strong convincing tone before her face erupted in a mischievous smile. "I'm leaving."

"I know, for Zaire," Kate snapped.

"If either of you had just given me a chance to explain," Lizzie muttered with a hint of amusement. "I'm leaving," she repeated as they blankly stared at her. "The church. I'm leaving the church," she clarified. Jenny's heart leapt as her jaw dropped open.

"What?" Kate stammered.

Once the reality had sunk in Kate and Jenny moved to give Lizzie a hug. "Not yet," Lizzie cautioned them as she stepped shyly away.

"I don't understand," Jenny said in bewilderment. "If you're leaving then why are you here and why do you still have to dress like a penguin and go to chapel?"

"This isn't like quitting your job at Burger King," Lizzie scoffed with a sweet smile. "There's a process involved. You don't just say 'I quit' and walk out. I'll need to remain here for a few more days and it'll be difficult."

"Will they try to change your mind?" Jenny asked in concern.

"Some of my sisters will," Lizzie answered honestly. "The majority will not. They fail to understand why I'm not ashamed of my homosexuality. When I would go to confession, it took a great deal of courage to confess my desires for women. I would receive a stern lecture about the evils of being gay. Then I would have to perform a very harsh penance. I couldn't receive communion since I wasn't granted absolution. That certainly caused talk around the convent."

"Wait! You confessed so why couldn't you receive communion?" Kate blurted out.

"I couldn't," Lizzie dryly explained. "To be able to receive the body of Christ, I would need to be absolved for my sins. I can't be absolved if I fail to feel remorse. I never felt guilt or remorse for the way my heart feels and I can't lie about it either. This is not the vocation for someone like me. I don't blame any of them. The Catholic Church teaches us that being gay is a sin. I don't agree. And I'm not alone. For the most part these are very good women who do good work. They have a calling and that I do not share. I can't stay."

"So what happens now?" Jenny asked as she fought to keep the excitement out of her voice.

"In a few days time, I'll be an ex-nun on the loose and looking for a job," Lizzie explained brightly. "Which reminds me, Kate, would it be okay if I stayed with you until I get situated?"

"Of course," Kate exclaimed.

"I hate to break up this little party but I have to go," Lizzie reluctantly informed them.

A million questions buzzed around Jenny's mind as she watched Lizzie and Kate exchange their goodbyes. She lingered behind in hopes as spending just a few moments alone with Lizzie. "Are you certain that this is what you want to do?" Jenny asked, needing to confirm that it was true and Lizzie would be rejoining the world and possibly her life.

"Yes," Lizzie responded with a firm conviction.

Lizzie's emerald eyes held the taller woman captive as they stood there just looking at one another. "I think you should go before I get myself into any more trouble," Lizzie said in a quiet promising tone. Jenny wanted to reach out and pull Lizzie into her arms. She could feel the wave of energy passing between them. She stuffed her hands in her jacket pockets in an effort to keep her body at bay. "Just a few more days," Lizzie promised. "Then you and I will be free to talk."

Unable to trust her voice, Jenny simply nodded in response and walked out of the room. She felt like she was walking on air as she climbed into Kate's truck. "I can't believe it," Kate gleefully exclaimed as she started the truck. "So when are the two of you going to pick up where you left off?"

"You don't waste any time, do you?" Jenny laughed heartily. She felt truly alive for the first time in days. "Lizzie is just starting her life over again. There may not be a place in her heart for me," Jenny carefully explained in an effort to caution both of them against hoping for too much too soon.

Over the next few days Jenny was filled with an eager anticipation. She kept nagging Kate about when Lizzie would be returning to the real world. "I don't know," Kate shouted after the third day of Jenny's pestering. "Geez, get a grip, Jacobs. If you ask me again, I'm going to beat you senseless."

"I was just wondering if you've heard anything," Jenny lamely explained in an effort to defend her actions.

"Not since the last time you asked which was forty minutes ago. Now get away from my desk and get back to work," Kate scolded her.

Jenny was still running on nervous energy when she arrived at the station the following Friday morning. There was something about the way Kate smiled at her that sent her into overdrive. She bounced over to the tall blonde, wondering if she should risk her physical well being once again. She chewed on her bottom lip as she looked at her supervisor expectantly. "I picked her up last night," Kate casually tossed out.

"Why didn't you call me?" Jenny demanded. Her shoulders slumped as everyone in the police station stared at her. Kate laughed as Jenny blushed from her sudden outburst.

"I wanted some time alone with my sister," Kate explained. "I have a feeling that once the two of you start hanging out together, that I'll need an appointment to see her."

"Kate, that isn't true," Jenny argued in a much calmer tone. "Just because she left the church doesn't mean that anything is going to happen between the two of us."

"Right!" Kate barked out with a loud laugh. "Who are you trying to convince, me or you?"

Jenny's mouth opened and closed several times as she tried to think of a way to answer Kate's question without sounding like a lovesick teenager. "What are your plans this weekend?" Kate asked her with a sly smile.

"Nothing, just doing a little laundry and hanging around my place. Why?" Jenny responded eagerly, hoping that Kate was about to invite her over and she would be able to spend time with Lizzie.

"That doesn't sound very exciting," Kate teased her. "I, on the other hand, have a very full schedule."

"Really?" Jenny asked, wondering just where the conversation was heading.

"Yes, I have a date tonight," Kate informed her casually.

"Get out!" Jenny enthusiastically responded. "Who with?"

"Mitch Dunbar from the DEA," Kate answered as her face turned a light shade of pink. "And you don't have to sound so surprised," she growled.

"Sorry, but it has been awhile," Jenny apologized. "So you and that tall dark hunk who worked on the Englewood case, huh? Have a good time."

"Speaking of having a good time," Kate started slowly. "Since I'm going out tonight, Lizzie will be left home all alone. Perhaps she could use some company?"

"You push too hard," Jenny cautioned her as her mouth suddenly dried up.

"What can I say?" Kate smirked. "I happen to think that the two of you belong together." Jenny shouldn't have been stunned by Kate's bluntness, yet it still caught her off guard. "I've seen the way the two of you look at each other," Kate continued. "Jenny, I've never been blessed with having someone look at me the way you look at my little sister or the way she looks at you."

Jenny was unable to speak as the sudden reality hit home - Lizzie was free. She was afraid that if she just jumped in with both feet she could ruin what might be. She knew how she felt and what her heart was telling her. Discovering that Kate could also see just how deep her emotions ran frightened her. She could feel the blush creeping across her face. "I need to go," she finally blurted out. As she turned to leave, Kate grabbed her by the arm and guided her to the locker room away from prying eyes.

Kate pushed her down onto one of the wooden benches as she order the women who were using the room to take a hike. "Now hold on for just a moment," Kate began in a reassuring tone as she sat down next to Jenny. "I'm sorry if I put you on the spot or made you feel uncomfortable. You're right; I push to hard. What I don't understand is why you look like you're going to bolt now that all the obstacles are out of the way? Did I miss something? I could have sworn that you have feelings for my sister."

Jenny was fighting to control her erratic breathing as she tried to gather her thoughts. "What if it's too soon or it isn't meant to

216

be?" Jenny whimpered like a small child.

"I find it really hard to believe that you're getting a case of cold feet after everything the two of you went through for the past seventeen years?" Kate barked out.

Jenny was silent as she tried to understand why she was suddenly afraid to face Lizzie. "I do have cold feet," she confessed quietly. "Lizzie was everything to me. When I was ten she gave me my first kiss." Jenny laughed as Kate's eyes widened with surprise. "Relax. Like I said we were ten at the time. It wasn't a lover's kiss with a major tongue wrestling; it was sweet and innocent and after it happened we both pretended that it didn't. She was my first real crush. She was my first sexual experience. For the first half of my life Lizzie was my life. And then she was my first heartbreak."

"And now?" Kate encouraged.

"And now I have no idea what she means to me or what I mean to her," Jenny explained. "The only thing I've been certain of since Lizzie's reentered my life is that I never got over her. I'm afraid that what I'm feeling is just a memory. And if what I'm feeling today is real, what is she feeling?"

"I don't know what to tell you, Jenny," Kate gently offered. "Your fears and concerns are valid. Who knows what Lizzie's feeling now that she's changed her life? I do know one thing; you're not going to find the answers by avoiding her." Kate patted her knee before she stood and left her alone in the locker room.

Jenny remained seated on the cold wooden bench, lost in her thoughts until Nuru barged in and informed her that it was time for roll call. Jenny was still lost in her thoughts as Nuru drove them around the streets of Boston. "Want to talk about it?" her partner offered.

"No," Jenny answered her with a woeful sigh. Then something caught her eye. "Pull over."

"What is it?" Nuru asked hurriedly as she scanned the streets for trouble.

The patrol car hadn't come to a complete stop when Jenny threw open the door. "I'll be right back," she said quickly as she jumped from the squad car and darted towards the flower stand she'd spotted.

"I have a permit." The elderly Asian man scowled as Jenny

217

approached him.

"Cool," she said with a shrug. "I was just looking for some flowers."

"Oh?" he said with a toothy smile.

"Has someone been hassling you?" she asked as she looked over the buckets of flowers. The man simply grunted in response. "Tell you what. Why don't you help me pick out something nice, and while I'm looking, you can tell me all about it?"

The man spoke rapidly; mixing questions about the lady Jenny was shopping for and telling her about two of her brother officers who visited his stand every day. Jenny had to force the man to take her money once she'd selected her flowers. "For me?" Nuru gushed once Jenny climbed back into the squad car.

"What do you know about Dunne and Miller?" Jenny inquired as she processed what Mr. Akira had told her about the two patrolmen who visited him each day.

"Tell me you didn't buy flowers for one of those idiots," Nuru groused.

"Of course not." Jenny chuckled. "My love life might be confusing at the moment but I think that hopping the fence would be a drastic course of action. Drive me over to Carrington's apartment."

"Uh huh." Nuru beamed as she pulled out into traffic. "Plan on wooing a little blonde per chance?"

"Per chance." Jenny hummed as she inspected the bouquet of roses and irises.

"Hold on!" Nuru suddenly blurted out. "She's a nun."

"Not anymore," Jenny delightedly informed her partner. "She hung up the habit."

"Ah, how sweet," Nuru sighed. "You're trying to romance your high school sweetheart."

"Don't tell me that under that butch exterior of yours lies a hopeless romantic?" Jenny teased.

"Bite me," Nuru scoffed at the notion. "What does this have to do with Dunne and Miller?"

"Mr. Akira told me that they stop by every day and ask to see his permit then question him about his name and address. The guy was born here and they keep asking him for a green card," she summarized her conversation with the flower vendor.

"Sounds like them," Nuru grunted in response. "You should ask them how God made black people. It's one of their favorite jokes."

"Charming," Jenny sneered. "How is it that these guys are allowed to wear a badge?"

"Wake up, girl; some things just don't change," Nuru sadly responded. "Any chance that Mr. Akira will file a complaint?"

"No, he's worried that they'll try and get even with him," Jenny answered in defeat.

"He's right," Nuru concurred. "Okay, drop off your posies and then we'll head back to the station. I bet Carrington might have one or two ideas on how to help Mr. Akira out."

Jenny was nervous as she stood in front of Kate's apartment door. Her palms were sweating as she tucked the flowers behind her back and knocked on the door. The wait seemed to take an eternity; in reality it was a scant few moments before Lizzie opened the door. "Hi," the blonde greeted her with a brilliant smile.

Jenny felt as if she was falling as their eyes locked. "Uhm…here," she stammered as she pulled the flowers from behind her back and shyly handed them to the small blonde. Lizzie stared at them with a stunned expression. "They're a welcome home present," Jenny quickly recovered.

"Thank you." Lizzie smiled as she inhaled the delicate fragrance. "No one has ever given me flowers before," she absently confessed as her eyes drifted back up and once again captured Jenny's gaze.

"No one?" Jenny asked in disbelief.

"No." Lizzie shrugged.

"Well, then I'm proud to be the first," Jenny boasted as her knees trembled and her mouth dried up. "Uhm…I understand that Kate's going out for the evening?"

"Yes, she has a date. The hussy," Lizzie teased as her brow scrunched in confusion.

"I was wondering if you wanted to come over to my place for dinner or something?" Jenny managed to blurt out before she lost her nerve.

"Okay."

"Okay?"

"Yeah, okay." Lizzie laughed at Jenny's bumbling demeanor.

"Okay," Jenny repeated. "How about meeting me at my place about 8:30?"

"I'll see you then."

"Okay," Jenny repeated once again, only this time with a sense of confidence.

"Oh Jenny," Lizzie called out just as the brunette turned to leave.

Jenny watched as Lizzie shyly approached her. "Now that I can say this, I just want you to know that you look incredible hot in that uniform," Lizzie whispered as Jenny blushed. "I'll see you tonight."

"See you tonight." Jenny beamed as she bounced back down the stairs and rejoined her partner.

"I take it that things went well?" Nuru chuckled.

"I have a date." Jenny beamed before her smile vanished. "At least I hope it's a date. Oh brother, it's never easy with this girl."

"Relax." Nuru laughed. "At least with Sister Rachel, I mean Liz, you know what you're in for."

"What do you mean?"

"Remember what's-her-name? Tina or was it Tracy?" Nuru laughed.

"Trudy!" Jenny supplied as her eyes bulged at the memory. "Yes, another woman who's on my list of females that should come with a warning label."

"She wasn't that bad." Nuru laughed as she drove them back towards the station house. "How could you have known that she was a pyromaniac?"

"Trust me, her fondness for fire was one of her nicer quirks," Jenny groaned.

"Pity. That woman was drop dead gorgeous." Nuru sighed lustfully.

"Definitely, and really good in bed," Jenny agreed. "I had no idea she was a total fruitcake until we went to dinner that night and she set the table on fire."

Nuru was still laughing at Jenny's past plights when they stepped back into the station. Kate gave them a curious look when they asked to speak to her alone. They found an empty office and Jenny explained Mr. Akira's problem, carefully omitting that she'd stopped to buy flowers. Kate listened carefully before responding. "I've had problems with those two before. Without a complaint there isn't much I can do except inform I.A. again," Kate grumbled.

"And what happens to Mr. Akira?" Nuru griped.

"Let's just wait and see what I.A. has to say," Kate cautioned her. "They might want to talk to both of you."

"Fine. Just not here," Jenny agreed. "It is hard enough being out of the closet around this place without being seen talking to the rat squad."

"I'll work it out," Kate promised before she sent the two of them back out into the streets.

The rest of her shift was uneventful. Jenny felt a sudden panic when Kate explained that someone from Internal Affairs wanted to talk to her. She was already pressed for time since she had to rush home and make dinner for Lizzie. Jenny suddenly realized a way to make her timetable work without letting Kate know about her and Lizzie. She wasn't being petty; she just didn't want to deal with Kate's interference. All she wanted was for the night to be about Lizzie and her without any of the pressures that had been surrounding them. She instructed Kate to have the agent meet her at 84 Bennington Street, which was an Italian restaurant not far from her home. Kate looked confused as she agreed. "That'll teach you to meddle," Jenny gleefully muttered under her breath. She understood that Kate really did have their best interests at heart, but she didn't want any outside interference tonight. She called the restaurant and placed a large takeout order. She was not only killing two birds with one stone; she thought Lizzie might enjoy the evening more if Jenny didn't cook. She feared that she was so nervous that she would end up burning whatever she attempt to cook.

Jenny smiled when she saw a familiar face sitting at the bar awaiting her arrival. "Sam," she greeted her old friend from her days at the Academy.

"So, Jacobs how are you?" He smirked. "Are we doing dinner?" he added hopefully.

"Sorry, I'm picking up," she apologized.

"Bummer," he sighed. "So are you willing to have a drink with a member of the rat squad? Did you really refer to my department that way?"

"Of course I did," Jenny, quipped as she took a seat and ordered a club soda from the bartender.

"Let me guess; you and Wendy have something hot and heavy planned tonight?" he teased.

"Uhm…Wendy and I split up."

"Good, never liked her," Sam said in relief.

"Why didn't anyone tell me?" Jenny mumbled.

"Hey, if you're single now, I have a cousin . . ."

"No," she flatly refused as she sipped on her soda water.

"Just a thought," he eagerly offered as he gave her a playful nudge. "I guess I should get down to business. My department already has a file going on Dunne and Miller. I'm going to do everything I can to keep you and your partner out of this."

"I appreciate that."

"I know how hard it is to turn in a fellow officer," he reassured her. "Even harder when people find out. Even if they agree that these guys shouldn't be getting away with what they're doing, they'll still give you a hard time."

"Can you help Mr. Akira out?" she asked.

"I've already spoken to him and I'll be working with him at his stand for the next few weeks," Sam explained. "I'll be posing as his son."

"His son?" Jenny questioned. "Hold on, Seung," she said, addressing him by his given name. "How can you be his son since you're Korean and I'm pretty certain that Mr. Akira is Japanese?"

"He is." Sam chuckled. "Thankfully, when it comes to blockheads like Dunne and Miller, we all look alike."

"Well, good luck," Jenny, offered as her order arrived and she paid for it. "After this is over, why don't we get together for dinner? And don't bring your cousin."

"Have fun with whoever tonight." Sam laughed as she made her departure.

Jenny arrived at her apartment and began to get dinner ready. She thought about Sam's words and decide that she would have fun tonight. She had no intention of making this night about seduction;

all she really hoped for was an enjoyable evening with someone who was once again becoming her best friend. Whatever else did or did not happen that evening was up to the fates.

Jenny had just finished changing into a pair of black jeans and a cream-colored blouse when there was a knock on the door. Jenny quickly checked her appearance. "Okay, a little dressy but still casual," she blew out before she went to answer the door. She peeked quickly through the peephole and found Lizzie's distorted image awaiting her. She opened the door, completely stunned by the sight that greeted her.

The small blonde looked nervously up at her. Jenny was far too overwhelmed at the way she was dressed to notice Lizzie's uneasiness. The blonde was clad in a tight pair of jeans and an emerald silk vest that made her eyes sparkle. "Wow," Jenny finally blurted out as she continued to gape at the blonde.

"Can I come in?" Lizzie nervously asked.

"Of course," Jenny stammered as she stepped aside. She couldn't help but watch the sway of Lizzie's hips as she moved past her. She also couldn't help noticing the way the smaller woman's jeans clung nicely to her backside.

Jenny's eyes remained focused on Lizzie's body as she kicked the door shut. Lizzie jumped slightly at the sound of the resulting bang. "Here." Lizzie's voice trembled as she handed Jenny a bottle wrapped in a brown paper bag. Jenny reluctantly tore her gaze from Lizzie to inspect the bottle of champagne the blonde had offered her.

"Spirits!" she exclaimed. "Are you trying to get me drunk?"

"Maybe," Lizzie answered with a nervous chuckle.

The bottle slipped from Jenny's fingers as their eyes met. She placed it down on the table as she held Lizzie's gaze. Suddenly she had all the answers to every question that had plagued her for almost two decades. She could no longer contain her emotions. "I love you," she confessed, surprising both herself and her guest. Jenny hadn't meant to just blurt it out like that, but she did. She had finally said it and it felt good. Except that Lizzie stood there simply looking into her eyes. Everything was out in the open and Jenny stood there in the quiet stillness, feeling exposed while she awaited Lizzie's response.

With a gentle smile Lizzie quietly whispered her answer, "I

love you too. I always have, Jenny." The brunette didn't waste a moment as she quickly closed the distance between them. She leaned down and kissed the lips that she'd been craving. The heat from their kiss melted Jenny's heart. Lizzie gasped, as they broke apart. "Well, that answers one question," Lizzie panted.

"What's that?" Jenny murmured.

"I was wondering if tonight was a date or not," Lizzie softly explained.

"It is now," Jenny, asserted as she reached down and cupped Lizzie's face in her hands. Looking deep into Lizzie's eyes, Jenny became lost. She knew in her heart that this was truly forever. She guided Lizzie's face towards her and gently bushed her lips. The passion surged from deep inside of them. Jenny pulled Lizzie closer to her as she kissed her again and again while her heart pounded wildly. She felt Lizzie's lips part; knowing that it was an invitation, she brushed her tongue against the blonde's soft lips once again. Their tongues danced together as Jenny slid her hands down the nape of Lizzie's neck. Her hands explored further; her body was on fire as she slid one hand behind Lizzie's back. Her other hand glided down and cupped the blonde's breast.

The cool silk of Lizzie's vest under Jenny's touch electrified her fingers. A shock ran through her. They were panting heavily as they broke free from the fiery kiss. Jenny could barely catch her breath. As she drank in Lizzie's beauty she became intoxicated. Her hand was still caressing the blonde's breast. She could feel Lizzie's nipple becoming erect against her fingers. The combination of heat from Lizzie's body and the coolness of silk overpowered the brunette. No longer able to contain herself, she reached down and tore open Lizzie's vest. Somewhere in the back of her mind she heard the clicking of buttons as they scattered across the floor. Jenny's fingers drifted down to the clasp in the front of Lizzie's bra; she released it quickly, freeing the smaller woman's breasts.

She brushed the material aside so she could see her lover's body. Jenny ran her hands over Lizzie's firm breasts, teasing her nipples with the tips of her fingers. Jenny loved the feel of Lizzie's body responding to her touch. "Yes," Lizzie moaned as her head fell back. Jenny kissed the blonde's exposed neck. Her kisses grew in intensity as she worked her way down Lizzie's supple neck to her strong shoulders. Her tongue traced its way to Lizzie's breasts. Jenny felt Lizzie's arms wrapping around her body.

Jenny lifted her head and was captured in a smoky emerald gaze. They began kissing once again as they stumbled towards the bed. They fell onto it and Jenny covered her lover's body with her own. Her lips retraced their way down the blonde's neck to the supple valley of her cleavage. She ran her tongue along the swell of Lizzie's breasts and the blonde wrapped her arms and legs tightly around her.

As her body covered Lizzie's, Jenny's mouth began to tease her nipple. She felt Lizzie's hips arch against her body. It had been far too long since either of them had felt such an uncontrollable passion. Lizzie moaned with desire, driving Jenny to the edge. An inner voice was warning the brunette to slow down. Jenny ignored it as her body and heart took control. Her mouth tasted Lizzie's breast hungrily. Jenny murmured in delight as she feasted upon her lover's breast. She could feel Lizzie's body moving beneath her own. Soon she began to kiss her way down Lizzie's body. As she kissed Lizzie's stomach she could feel her shudder. Lizzie gasped as Jenny began to unbutton her jeans. Slowly Jenny lowered the blonde's jeans and underwear down her body as she kissed every inch of newly exposed flesh.

Jenny tossed her lover's clothing aside. She paused to admire Lizzie's body and slowly ran her hands over the beautiful naked form lying before her. Overcome with emotion, Jenny felt a single tear fall from her eye. As she wiped the teardrop from her cheek, Lizzie reached up and captured her hand.

"Jenny, are you all right?" Lizzie asked lovingly.

"Yes," Jenny said with a smile. "It's just that you're so beautiful," she spoke softly as she continued to run her fingers across Lizzie's soft skin. She had dreamt of touching Lizzie this way for such a very long time, perhaps longer than she ever realized. "I've spent my whole life looking for you," she confessed as the realization struck her.

Jenny leaned down and kissed Lizzie, hoping her kiss would speak for her. As their bodies became one, Jenny knew that Lizzie understood not only the passion she felt but the promise she was offering as well. Jenny felt Lizzie pulling her blouse from her jeans.

225

Her lips left Lizzie's as she raised her body from her lover's, still straddling the blonde's naked body. Lizzie reached up and gently caressed Jenny's breast. Jenny felt her body responding to her lover's touch. She watched as Lizzie's strong fingers unbuttoned each button on her shirt carefully, just as she had done so many years ago.

Jenny bit her lower lip, as the blouse was slipped off her body. Old passions merged with new desires. She was shaking as she stood and slowly removed the remainder of her clothing. "I did like the what you wearing very much, but I have to confess that you look so much better in nothing at all," Lizzie said softly as she watched the tall brunette undress.

Jenny couldn't wait any longer as she lowered her naked body to Lizzie's. She was driven by the desire to feel Lizzie's wetness embracing her own. As their bodies touched, they shivered as each of them gently placed a thigh between the other's legs. Their hips began to circle in rhythm. Their excitement built into a frenzy of passion. Jenny's hand caressed Lizzie's body, feeling its way across the blonde's hips. She moved her own body so that she could touch Lizzie's wetness.

Lizzie opened herself to Jenny as she called for the brunette to touch her. Jenny slid gently into Lizzie's wetness. Lizzie raised her hips against Jenny's hand with a frightening urgency. "Oh, Jenny! Yes, more," Lizzie cried out. Jenny responded to Lizzie's pleas by stroking her deeper and faster. She could feel Lizzie's body shudder beneath her. She wanted the blonde completely. She knew that she had never desired any woman as much as she desired the woman she was making love to. Jenny needed to taste Lizzie's sweetness and drown in her passion. She kissed her lover hungrily before her mouth began to worship its way down Lizzie's body. Jenny heard Lizzie gasp as her tongue slid along the swell of the blonde's breasts before tasting the valley between them.

The feel of Lizzie's desire brushing against her skin as the blonde released needy whimpers encouraged Jenny to continue her exploration. Her mouth teased and tasted her lover's quivering flesh as she blazed a determined path down her lover's body. She heard Lizzie release another gasp as Jenny's tongue trailed across the inside of the blonde's thigh. Jenny was savoring each drop of

Lizzie's desire as the blonde opened herself even further. Lizzie gently pressed against the back of Jenny's head, silently telling her what she wanted. Jenny took her into her mouth, her tongue teasing and tasting Lizzie's nectar with a fierce desire. She could hear Lizzie calling out her name as the blonde's body shook in ecstasy. Lizzie cried out again and again as her body arched even higher. With one final scream, Lizzie collapsed against the bed.

Jenny held her lover as the last waves of passion slipped from her body. As Lizzie's body stilled, she slipped her touch from her lover's warm wetness. Jenny could hear Lizzie moan softly as her touch left her. Jenny rested her head against Lizzie's thigh, her long dark tresses tickling the blonde's skin as she kissed her trembling flesh. *'I could stay this way forever,'* Jenny thought. She sighed with pleasure as her fingers traced the inside of Lizzie's thigh. Jenny knew that this was meant to be.

"I had forgotten," Lizzie whispered, still not in control of her voice.

"Forgotten what?" Jenny asked as she raised herself up so she could look into her lover's eyes.

"I had forgotten," Lizzie repeated, "what it's like to be with someone that you're in love with."

"I know," Jenny responded as she smiled down at Lizzie.

Jenny curled up next to Lizzie and took the smaller woman in her arms. As they rested in one another's embrace, Jenny listened to the sound of Lizzie's heart beating. After a moment she sat up again and looked down at her lover. "Do you think we would have stayed together?" she asked seriously. "I mean, if Robby hadn't done what he did, do you think we would stayed together back then?"

"I don't know, Jenny," Lizzie sighed as she caressed Jenny's arm. "Please don't misunderstand what I'm trying to say; it's just that teenage love has such a short shelf life."

"I know," Jenny agreed with a smile. "We probably would have drifted apart. We were so young."

"I do know one thing," Lizzie said as she gazed deeply into Jenny's eyes. "I loved you then and I love you now. But you're not the same person you were. The woman you are now truly holds my heart."

"I feel the same way," Jenny agreed as her hands began to

227

trace the supple curves of Lizzie's body. "I loved the girl you were, yet the feelings I have now are for the woman you've become."

"You are so beautiful, Jenny," Lizzie whispered as her emerald eyes drifted down Jenny's body. "Hey, where's that champagne?"

"I have no idea." Jenny chuckled as she looked around in bewilderment. Her quest inevitably led her back to Lizzie's body. Lizzie reached up and kissed her deeply. Jenny's lips parted and Lizzie eagerly accepted the invitation. Jenny had forgotten the magical way that Lizzie could please her with just one kiss.

Jenny felt Lizzie's hand cupping her breast. She moaned as her body moved against Lizzie's. The brunette's body was on fire as Lizzie's hand slipped from her breast and gently ran down her body. She shivered as Lizzie touched her and Jenny opened herself to her touch. "Yes," she moaned as she felt Lizzie inside of her. This is what she wanted. This is what she needed. Feeling Lizzie inside of her touched a part of her soul. Her hips began to thrust demandingly against Lizzie's hand. Her head was swimming as their passion grew. "Oh, Lizzie, please don't stop," she begged. There was a faint ringing in her ears as flashes of crimson filled her mind. *'This can't be happening! Not so soon!'* her mind screamed before all thought left her and she was no longer capable of thinking. A cry escaped from deep inside of her as her body tensed and arched against her lover. She could feel herself falling into Lizzie's arms.

Jenny trembled in her lover's embrace, unable to believe that she'd climaxed so quickly. Jenny cleared her dry throat as she lifted her body. "I was supposed to looking for something, wasn't I?" she mumbled. "Champagne, right?"

"I do like the way you search for things," Lizzie teased her.

"Table," Jenny choked out as she finally spied the missing bottle.

"We could misplace it again," Lizzie teased. Jenny laughed as Lizzie rolled her over and climbed off the bed. "Wait here," Lizzie said as she stood on shaky legs.

"Are you kidding?" Jenny laughed again. "I don't think I can walk."

Jenny watched Lizzie's body in the darkness until the blonde disappeared into the kitchen area. She listened to the shuffling and clanging coming from her kitchen as Lizzie continued her desperate search. "Here we are," Lizzie said triumphantly as she returned. She smiled as she clinked the two champagne glasses together. The ringing of crystal echoed through the darkness. Lizzie picked up the bottle of champagne before returning to the bed. Jenny watched as Lizzie placed her cargo on the nightstand. Then Lizzie pulled back the covers and guided Jenny up to the pillows.

Jenny sighed in contentment as Lizzie climbed in next to her and began to unwrap the foil and wire from the cork. Lizzie popped open the champagne bottle, catching the cork in her hand. Jenny squealed when the cold bubbles splashed over her naked body. "Oops. I'm sorry." Lizzie laughed as she placed the bottle on the floor. "Here, let me help clean that up," she whispered seductively. Jenny swallowed hard as she caught the fiery look in her lover's eyes. Using her tongue, Lizzie cleansed Jenny's body as she licked away each and every tiny bubble.

Jenny couldn't believe that once again she was ready or how quickly her body had reached the pinnacle of ecstasy. Lizzie's tongue worked its magic down her body. Jenny could hear herself moaning in pleasure as she once again parted herself for her lover's touch. Lizzie took her gently and slowly as Jenny's hips rocked with ecstasy. Lizzie took her time, murmuring with delight as she enjoyed the gift that Jenny was offering. Jenny felt her thighs shaking uncontrollably as she called out Lizzie's name. Her body rose against Lizzie's teasing. The waves of passion overtook her as she gripped the bed linen. She clenched the sheets so tightly that she tore them from the mattress. Sweat rolled down her body as she fell against the now-bare mattress. Soft pleasurable groans escaped her lips as she tried to catch her breath.

"Come here," Jenny called to her lover. Lizzie slowly made her way up Jenny's body, placing soft kisses along the way. Jenny took the blonde into her arms and held her tightly against her body. She never wanted to let the smaller woman go again. Electricity flowed between them from being so close. Jenny rolled Lizzie over so that they were facing one another as they began to kiss. Her fingers touched her lover gently. Without realizing what she was doing, her fingers drifted until they instinctively found their way to Lizzie's wetness. Jenny's desire grew as her lover's body responded to her touch. Lizzie softly called out Jenny's name as the brunette entered her. Jenny suckled her lover's neck as she felt Lizzie's touch mirroring her own. The brunette opened her body to Lizzie's touch. She felt Lizzie gently caressing her wetness as she dipped further into blonde's passion. They kissed as their hands and bodies moved in a passionate rhythm.

Much later they were cuddling in bed while they sipped champagne and talked quietly in the darkness. Despite the dark room, Jenny could still see her lover's emerald eyes watching her. "Can I ask you something?" Jenny asked as she ran her fingers through Lizzie's short blonde hair.

"Anything," Lizzie readily agreed.

"That first night, you know, the first time we made love." Jenny paused for a moment. "How did you know? I mean, how did you know what I wanted when I wasn't really sure myself?"

"I didn't," Lizzie sweetly answered as she placed a tender kiss on Jenny's cheek. "I mean, not at first anyway."

"You didn't?" Jenny responded in a puzzled tone. *'How can that be? Lizzie had been so confident that night,'* Jenny pondered.

"I didn't," Lizzie repeated with a light laugh. "I was so very afraid. Jenny, I had desired you for so very long. Remember my date at my sweet sixteen party?" Jenny nodded in response. "Did you ever wonder why I dumped him a few days later?" Jenny nodded once again. "I broke up with him because during my birthday party all I could think about was you."

"I never knew," Jenny responded. "I guess both of us were really good at hiding our feelings."

"The first night we were together I was terrified," Lizzie continued. "I thought if you knew how I felt, you wouldn't want to be near me ever again. I was so glad your bedroom was dark so I could hide my face. I couldn't wait for you to hand me that towel. All I wanted was to bury my face in it so I could hide my shame."

"I felt the same way," Jenny confessed. "It seems so silly now, how we felt so long ago. If that was the way you felt, then why did you kiss me? Other than that quick peck we shared when we were little kids, nothing had happened before that. So why that night?"

"I caught a brief glimpse of your face in the darkness," Lizzie responded with a sweet sincerity. "There was an all too familiar glimmer in your eyes. They were a reflection of my own. That's when I knew. Still, I couldn't be positive. I decided then and there to take a very big risk. When I finally touched you for the first time, I knew that it was right."

"You have no idea how happy I was and still am that you decided to take that risk," Jenny purred.

"I am too," Lizzie said. "After that night I knew that there was no turning back."

"I'm still amazed that neither of us knew anything about sex, not really anyway, and somehow our bodies just knew what to do." Jenny noted with a shy smile.

"They still do," Lizzie, offered in a husky tone as she drew Jenny closer to her.

Jenny leaned in and was just about to capture her lover's lips with her own when a familiar pitter-pat outside of the window stopped her movements. It was a familiar comforting sound. "Listen," she said as she listened to the steady rhythm. "Lizzie, it's raining." She held the blonde tighter as they listened to the rain brushing against the window. "I think that's a very good omen," she offered with a brilliant smile. "So tell me, Miss Carrington, does the rain still have the same effect on you?" Lizzie looked up at Jenny with a smoldering gaze. The blonde answered Jenny with a fiery kiss that stole the brunette's breath away.

They became lost in the feel of the other's touch as they began a long delayed journey together. Neither of them was certain as to what the future would offer, but they were confident in the knowledge that they had finally found what each of them had been seeking.

The End

About the Author

Mavis Applewater was born in Massachusetts in 1962.As a child she was an avid reader and honed her creative side to major in Theatre at Salem State College. While supporting herself waiting for her big break, she became a "resident" and well known bartender at a nightclub in Cambridge, MA.

Mavis has done several commercials and lots of extra work but her creative juices were still flowing so she turned to another one of her hidden talents, writing. This jump started her writing career and culminated with several manuscripts one of them being "The Brass Ring".

Currently Mavis lives with her partner of 11 years; they reside in the North Shore area of Massachusetts.

Introducing...
Art By Joy

By JoyArgento

Hi, allow me to introduce myself. My name is Joy Argento and I am the artist on all of these pieces. I have been doing artwork since I was a small child. That gives me about 35 years of experience. I majored in art in high school and took a few college art courses. Most of my work is done in either pencil or airbrush mixed with color pencils. I have recently added designing and creating artwork on the computer. Some of the work featured on these pages were created and "painted" on the computer. I am self taught in this as well as in the use of the airbrush.

I have been selling my art for the last 15 years and have had my work featured on trading cards, prints and in magazines. I have sold in galleries and to private collectors from all around the world.

I live in Western New York with my three kids, four cats, one dog and the love of my life. It is definitely a full house. I appreciate you taking the time to check out my artwork. Please feel free to email me with your thoughts or questions. Custom orders are always welcomed too.

Contact me at ArtByJoy@aol.com . I look forward to hearing from you.

Making Love

Towel Cuddling

Motorcycle Women

Joy Argento

Check out her work at
LimitlessD2D or at her website.
Remember: ArtByJoy@aol.com !

Order These Great Books Directly From Limitless, Dare 2 Dream Publishing

The Amazon Queen by L M Townsend	20.00	
Define Destiny by J M Dragon	20.00	The one that started it all…
Desert Hawk, revised by Katherine E. Standelll	18.00	Many new scenes
Golden Gate by Erin Jennifer Mar	18.00	
The Brass Ring By Mavis Applewater	18.00	HOT
Haunting Shadows by J M Dragon	18.00	
Spirit Harvest by Trish Shields	15.00	
PWP: Plot? What Plot? by Mavis Applewater	18.00	HOT
Journeys By Anne Azel	18.00	NEW
Memories Kill By S. B. Zarben	20.00	
Up The River, revised By Sam Ruskin	18.00	Many new scenes
	Total	

South Carolina residents add 5% sales tax.
Domestic shipping is $3.50 per book

Visit our website at: http://limitlessd2d.net

Please mail your orders with credit card info, check or money order to:

Limitless, Dare 2 Dream Publishing
100 Pin Oak Ct.
Lexington, SC 29073-7911

Please make checks or money orders payable to: Limitless.

I

Order More Great Books Directly From Limitless, Dare 2 Dream Publishing

Daughters of Artemis by L M Townsend	18.00	
Connecting Hearts By Val Brown and MJ Walker	18.00	
Mysti: Mistress of Dreams By Sam Ruskin	18.00	HOT
Family Connections By Val Brown & MJ Walker	18.00	Sequel to Connecting Hearts
A Thousand Shades of Feeling by Carolyn McBride	18.00	
The Amazon Nation By Carla Osborne	18.00	Great for research
Poetry from the Featherbed By pinfeather	18.00	If you think you hate poetry you haven't read this
None So Blind, 3rd Edition By LJ Maas	16.00	NEW
A Saving Solace By DS Bauden	18.00	NEW
Return of the Warrior By Katherine E. Standell	20.00	Sequel to Desert Hawk
Journey's End By LJ Maas	18.00	NEW
	Total	

South Carolina residents add 5% sales tax.
Domestic shipping is $3.50 per book
Please mail your orders with credit card info, check or money order to:
Limitless, Dare 2 Dream Publishing
100 Pin Oak Ct.
Lexington, SC 29073-7911
Please make checks or money orders payable to: Limitless.

II

Printed in the United States
17084LVS00004B/145